THE PRINCE AND THE PUPPET THIEF

JUSTIN ARNOLD

Copyright (c) 2021 by Justin Arnold

All rights reserved.

No part of this book may be reproduced, distributed or transmitted in any form, without prior written permission from the author, with exception of brief quotations in a book review.

Publisher's Note: This is a work of fiction. Any resemblances to actual people, living or deceased, or to companies, businesses, or locales is completely coincidental.

Published by Midnight Tide Publishing

www.midnighttidepublishing.com

Cover art designed by Gabriella Regina / GRbookcovers

Interior Formatting by Book Savvy Services

The Prince & The Puppet Thief / Justin Arnold. 1st ed.

ISBN 978-1953238-39-9 (print)

ISBN 9798201306212 (ebook)

For the ones like me.

1. SIMON THE SQUIRM LEARNS TO FLY

*O*nce, in a kingdom neither here nor there, lived a young thief whose only weapon was a book. The book, so he had heard, would tell him everything he needed to know in order to live a long and happy life. It promised to reveal to him the meaning of a mysterious thing called "ever after."

Except, the book rarely did anything for thieves like him, except stab him in the heart if he bent over too far.

"Ow!" He adjusted the book, tucked inside the pocket of his green leather doublet. Right where a dagger or other more useful weapon might be kept.

"Quiet!" Bloody Fingers boomed unseen. "Cannon balls don't say 'ow'."

"There isn't any room in here," said Simon. "I'm all pushed into myself."

Bloody Fingers' face appeared at the mouth of the cannon, twirling his fine black mustache. Simon looked with half-open eyes at his father, thinking that mustache must be his greatest source of pride, not his son. Why else would he have shoved him in this cannon with the intention of shooting him out?

"Just a few more minutes," Bloody Fingers said. "Are you ready?"

"Can one ever be ready for such glory?" Simon deadpanned.

Bloody Fingers raised an eyebrow. "Nervous, eh? Here, allow me to make you feel better. 'Once upon a time, there lived a young man named Simon The Squirm. He was an amazing chap for all of his seventeen years. He pulled off any theft without a problem. Never *ever* did he make a stupid mistake. Eventually, he made his old man proud. The end.'"

"Ahem?" Simon recognized the gruff voice of The Vizier, a tall and burly man whom Bloody Fingers referred to as his right-hand man, out in the alley. Simon saw the Vizier nudge Bloody Fingers with his elbow. He couldn't nudge him with his right hand nor his left, because he had no hands at all—just sharp hooks where hands ought to be.

"What?" spat Bloody Fingers.

"You have to end it right," said The Vizier. "And . . . "

"Oh," Bloody Fingers said. "'And Simon definitely did not get blown to dust when his old man shot him out of a cannon."

"*And* . . . " nudged The Vizier.

Bloody Fingers twisted his mouth downward. "Don't make me vomit."

"*And!*"

"*And* they lived *happily-ever-af-ter*." Bloody Fingers gagged as though the words tasted like rotten egg on his tongue. He looked down the cannon well to Simon. "Feel better, son?"

"You know," blinked Simon, "strangely enough I don't."

Blood Fingers shrugged and stood upright, smoothing a hair in his thick mustache down with a dab of spit. "Well, I tried. Personally, I thought the tale to be quite whimsical, charming, and poignant."

"And warm and fuzzy!" added The Vizier.

"Same thing," said Bloody Fingers.

Shoving his arms out from their place between his bent knees, Simon crawled to the mouth of the cannon and peeked out at the bandits.

There was The Vizier, of course. After him stood The Fop, who only joined the bandits to look stylish in his forest greens and a pointy cap with a red feather in it. Next to him stood Humphrey, who refused to have a nickname and took great pleasure in torturing victims. The fifth bandit was The Jester, who had no real name.

There's none who will save me, thought Simon, the sixth bandit for having no choice in the matter.

They'd called him Squirm all his life, because, as Bloody Fingers said, he wasn't a worm, but he could get squirmy, especially when it came to breaking laws and seeing blood. When counting him and his father, there were six bandits in total, and today they all had the most important job ever laid out for them. One to gain them the most valued treasure in all the land.

"I want those slippers!" Bloody Fingers jumped up and down, clapping his gloved hands. "I want them *now*, and I want to have a big laugh when we all try them on. And then . . . "

"We'll sell them and be rich!" said The Vizier.

"Yes, but that doesn't sound as funny as trying them on." Blood Fingers turned to The Jester. "See how it looks out there, Jesty."

The Jester merrily shook his rattle and left the alley without a word. He never said anything, but Simon didn't know if it was because he could not or would not. But his pleasing, if vague, smile kept the mood light.

"Father," Simon dared to say, "is it necessary for me to do this?"

"Necessarily necessary!" Bloody Fingers snapped his eyes to him. "Why do you ask?"

"It just seems to me that perhaps someone more, um," *better at thieving and not a bumbling bookworm,* "More skilled might do a better job?"

Bloody Fingers spat on the cobblestone. "We've been over this, Squirm. You're the youngest and therefore the smallest—"

"Humphrey is a head shorter than I am—"

"And the smallest should pop out of the cannon because when you're smaller you weigh less, and are more likely to fly up to the tower where the lost princess's slippers are kept."

The damned slippers, Simon sighed. It was all Bloody Fingers had cared about in the two months since Princess Isobel and one of the castle servants were kidnapped in the night, shortly after her engagement to some prince was announced. The slippers were fashioned of jewels from the prince's kingdom as a wedding present and were said to cost more than the castle of Incantus. He was tired of hearing about it.

"I don't weigh much less than you, Father," said Simon, trying every direction to be reprieved from this death mission.

"You certainly do!" Bloody Fingers patted his stomach. "I got too rowdy with the treats last holiday. You are a slip of a thing. A lanky, awkward, slip of a thing. So you will get in that cannon—"

"I already am . . ."

"And when we shoot you out, you'll fly up to the tower, you'll retrieve those slippers, and you'll say, 'Yes, Father'!"

"Yes *Father*," grumbled Simon. "Anything else?"

"Beef up." Bloody Fingers shoved Simon back down the cannon well. "You look like an urchin."

I am *an urchin*. Simon huffed as loudly as he could.

"Do you want to be a hero?" Bloody Fingers asked. "Or do would you rather be the blank line between the words of those silly stories you're always poring over?"

The book's corner pushed into Simon's heart as he resettled into place. He widened his eyes at his father and felt the heat flush his cheeks. He knew his father was mocking him, but he was right. Simon didn't want to be a blank line. He wanted to be the story.

Pursing his lips, Simon dropped his eyes to the dark metal of the cannon. The sound of jingling echoed its way back into the alley. Bloody Fingers giggled and looked away from Simon.

"There's Jesty! Jesty, what did you see?" The Jester shook his rattle.

"Clear enough? Where are the guards?"

Rattle rattle.

"Two at the drawbridge?"

Rattle.

"One in the watchtower?"

Rattle rattle rattle.

"And three have the day off!"

The Jester thrust out one of his pointy-toed shoes and bowed.

Bloody Fingers rubbed his hands together and grinned. "Well, there we are! A perfect time for a siege. We've only to get past the two at the drawbridge, really."

"And how shall we choreograph the getting past them?" it was The Fop who spoke now. Simon saw beyond the mouth of the cannon that he appeared more concerned with his fingernails when he spoke. "It might be threatening to approach them with a cannon."

"Don't you think I've thought of that?" Bloody Fingers demanded. "Vizy, show them what you crocheted with your hooks."

Simon peeked out of the cannon once more to see The Vizier pull a bundle from his satchel and unrolled a large, white piece of crochet.

"I do think it to be my best work," The Vizier said proudly, showing off his creation.

A large white cloud of yarn, with two pieces shaped like long ears, pink at their centers.

"Who could feel threatened by a cute bunny rabbit?" Bloody Fingers asked proudly. "We shall trick them by telling them it is a gift to His Royal Highness, the princess's betrothed. A token of grief for the lost princess, and a beacon of hope for her safe return and a happy marriage. Surely it shall put a smile on the prince's face."

"Does he like bunny rabbits?" Simon couldn't help but ask. "It isn't the manliest of creatures."

The Vizier shook his right hook at Simon. "I like bunny rabbits!"

Bloody Fingers pushed on Simon's head. "Get in your cannon!"

Simon sighed and slid back down into the cannon well. Immediately his thighs cramped. Too tall to curl up properly, his knees threatened to poke him in the eyes, if the book didn't slice through his flesh first. The bandits pulled the crocheted rabbit over the cannon mouth, sweeping the light out.

"It's like a tea cozy!" Simon heard The Fop muse.

"I do like tea," said Humphrey, "especially as I listen to the castrati-timbred screams of my victims."

"And that's why you're one of my favorites," Bloody Fingers said proudly.

Simon rolled his eyes so hard they threatened to fall out of his skull. Though Bloody Fingers' son, he knew he was far from a favorite. Oftentimes, Simon wondered who Bloody Fingers would choose if given the choice between Simon and his bandits. He had that answered today when he shoved him in this cannon just to steal some girl's shoes.

The wheels of the cannon spun, jostling Simon and sending one of his knees into the bridge of his nose. His heartbeat became loud booms. No going back now. They were doing this. All Simon could do was succeed and hope that the cannon wouldn't blow him to dust first.

The sounds of villagers made their muffled way into the dark cannon as the bandits rounded the corner out of the alley and out into the village square. *Ooh's* and *ahh's* reached Simon, and he could hear children call out with delight at the sight of the large rabbit.

He heard the faint sound of The Jester's rattle, as though he were out there leading a parade and not a siege.

Wooden planks creaked beneath him and the cannon came to a halt. They must be on the drawbridge now. His heart threatened to explode immediately. *Almost time.* A drop of sweat fell from a wave in his hair and dripped to his knee.

"State your business," a guard thundered outside the cannon.

"A present for the king's guest," said Bloody Fingers.

"Name?"

"His royal highness Prince Marco of Lands Upper—"

"No, *your* name!"

"Giacomo DuPonte," lied Bloody Fingers.

"Identification?"

Simon heard the nerves in his father's laugh as he said, "We are a ragtag band of artists and bohemians, sir. We do not carry identification."

Clearly, his father hadn't thought this completely through, too excited by the flash and theatrics of the big idea. This usually happened. Simon let out a quiet grumble.

"Wait a minute," a second guard said. "Don't I know you?"

"Me?" Bloody Fingers asked with mock surprise. "Of

course not! You've never met anyone named Giacomo in your life, I promise you that."

"He does look familiar," the other guard said. "They all do."

Simon's shoulders tensed.

"Sirs, I must insist that I am Giac—"

"Hold it!" one of the guards shouted. "I'd know that mustache anywhere!"

"You would?"

Simon twisted his lips in frustration. His father sounded *flattered*. Great! Now he wouldn't be able to resist the publicity, and they'd all hang for it. Simon banged his head against his kneecaps, unable to wriggle his arm free for a facepalm.

"I recognize the whole lot," the guard continued. "Didn't even bother to disguise yourselves. How stupid you are."

Among other things, thought Simon. *Idiotic, dramatic, fame mongering—just to name a few.*

He banged his head on his knee three more times.

The other guard gasped. "Oh! I see it now! He's—"

"Bloody Fingers!" outside the cannon, Simon could practically see the theatrical bow his father must be making. "Thief of hearts and gold, brute of the forest, the most feared villain in the kingdom of Incantus!" "Second most," the second guard said.

"Do what now?" Bloody Fingers asked.

"You're the second most feared villain in the kingdom. It says so on your wanted poster."

"Does not!"

"Does so," The Vizier muttered. "I've seen it many

times. Right below your name, in a comparably smaller print."

"Why're you called Bloody Fingers, anyhow?" asked the second guard.

"Don't you know?" the first guard asked. "He has six fingers."

"Six on one hand, like an extra finger? Or just six in total?"

"How should I know that? I've never seen his hands and look, he is wearing gloves now."

"See now," the second guard demanded. "Take off your gloves! I wish to count your fingers."

Simon's nerves shook him hard and he felt like he'd explode if they didn't get going soon. The book's corner stuck into his flesh so deeply that in any moment it would draw blood.

"Holy crowns!" Simon shouted, "Just light this candle, I can't take any more suspense! Am I going to blow up or not?"

"You are!" screamed Bloody Fingers. "I mean—you—oh, you know what I mean!"

"Hey now," a guard said, "that wonderfully crocheted rabbit is talking!"

The Vizier blushed. "It's not *that* wonderful."

The Jester wagged his rattle as Humphrey and the Fop pulled off the bunny rabbit cover to reveal the cannon underneath.

"Halt!" the guards chanted in unison.

"In the name of the king!" one shouted.

"You are all under arrest!" shouted the other.

Bloody Fingers sounded unimpressed as he threw a leg

THE PRINCE AND THE PUPPET THIEF

over the cannon and sat down as though he were riding a horse. "For what, pray tell?"

"For whatever it is you're about to do," a guard said.

"Well heavens, if I'm to be wanted for a crime, you should at least let me commit it first. Humphrey! You heard the boy, light this candle!"

Simon jolted as the cannon heaved forward, and Bloody Fingers rode forth on the cannon, causing the guards to scream and jump out of their way for fear that they would be blown up.

Inside the cannon, Simon took a deep breath and tried to settle on a thought. But knowing that it might be his last chance to think, he was unable to come up with anything important enough.

A view of the drawbridge became a view of the highest tower of the castle as the neck of the cannon pulled upwards. Behind them, villagers had crowded around to gawk and scream at the sight. Mostly they screamed at the cannon pointing at the castle, but others also screamed at the sight of the cute bunny rabbit, which lay deflated and sickly in a crotched pile on the cobblestone.

"Fire in the hole!" cried out Bloody Fingers as Humphrey struck a match and lit the fuse of the cannon. "Be ready, Squirm!"

Simon sucked in his breath and decided that thinking about what he had for dinner last night also was not important enough at this moment.

The flame grew lower on the cannon wick.

"Three . . . " Called out Blood Fingers. It grew shorter.

"Two..."

Simon didn't know what happened. One moment he was staring out the mouth of the cannon, and the next his eyes were filled with black smoke, and in that same second, he saw the castle.

Below him.

2. THE PRINCE IN THE TOWER

*S*imon had five seconds, if that, between being shot from the cannon and hitting the tower. Where we join him now, he had about two seconds left.

Someplace between kicking and clawing in the air, Simon found the tower growing larger and larger, the wide window leading out to a balcony, opening before him like the mouth of a terrible dragon.

Please swallow me whole! Simon begged silently.

In another half-second, he thrust his arms out, and in the final fractal of time, he rolled onto the balcony, breaking his fall with his elbows. The impact forced a pained shout from his throat, but luckily, it was short-lived. A thin plume of black smoke rose from his shoulder and he patted himself out.

He shook, barely able to catch his breath. But he was alive. He pushed himself to his feet and looked up at the roof of the tower looming above him. A moment ago, it had been a small, faraway point in the sky.

"I did it!" he shouted and let out the biggest laugh he'd

had in years. "Well, then! Eventually, maybe I'll make you proud, eh, Father?"

He spun around and nearly tripped over his own feet. He caught himself on the balcony rail, and found himself looking down at the kingdom of Incantus. His view blurred for a moment, and his stomach flipped over, seeing the tiny village below and the scurry of ant-like people on the drawbridge.

"Get the slippers," Simon told himself, spinning to face the entrance. He reached inside his doublet for his dagger, but his hand found only the book. *Oh no.*

He'd forgotten it again. The most important theft of his father's career, and he'd forgotten to acquire a real weapon. How could he make it out of the castle without anything to fend off a guard?

His knuckles whitened as he gripped the spine of the book even harder. He pulled it from his doublet and looked down at the worn cover, bent leather from years of use. A book of tales, fairy stories really, that he couldn't seem to let go of.

No matter. He'd bludgeon someone if he had to.

With a step as soft as he could manage in his too-big secondhand boots, he crept through the archway into the tower, craning his neck to take in the room. It was empty, thankfully.

The walls were covered in ornately framed portraits and gold threaded tapestries of the princess, posed at various ages, little girl to young woman. Simon had never seen her before, or knew much about her, for that matter. It's difficult to keep up with celebrity gossip when you're always running for your life.

"Yeah, definitely a princess," Simon gestured to the paintings with his book, as though he held an official diagnosis. He noted she always wore a shade of pink, with strings of pearls against her dark skin, a silver crown stuck smartly into her black curls.

Simon shuddered as he came deeper into the room, feeling the fifty pairs of oil painted eyes following his each step. He bowed, and forced himself to chuckle away his nerves.

"Your Highness," he whispered.

He slid his gaze to the center of the room and sighed. A stone pedestal, wrapped in marble vines and tiny pixies waving wands, stood waiting. Atop it, what he had come for. A pair of dancing slippers, glistening in the light of the chandelier above. The color of the shoes flickered in and out in the movement of the candle flames, from teal to rose, to emerald, sapphire and silver. The jeweled shoes would pay for an entirely new life. Perhaps he could convince his father to retire to the southern islands, and he to a castle in Lands Upper. Opposite ends of the earth.

Surely, something must be guarding them. Perhaps spikes would shoot up from the pedestal and impale his hands when he reached for the slippers? Or a giant ball of stone could fall from the ceiling and crush him?

With a deep breath, he thrust his book above the slippers and winced.

Nothing happened.

Slowly, he patted the slippers. The jewels hit the book with a short, sharp *clink*.

Yet nothing happened.

"Whew," Simon let out the air from his lungs and put

the book back in his doublet. He swept his arms out and snatched the slippers with his free hand.

A sharp click echoed within the pedestal, and the platform raised slightly, no longer held by the weight of the slippers, releasing a golden string that had been hidden among the vines and pixies. Simon reached to stop the string, but a second too late. The string grew taut, and somewhere behind a tapestry depicting the princess on a unicorn, sounded a clatter.

And a yelp of surprise.

Simon stumbled backward, shoving the heels of the slippers into the back of his pants.

Get-out-get-out-get-out—

Simon rushed out to the balcony and looked over the edge, searching for his father below. For The Vizier, for Humphrey. Even The Fop would be a welcome sight. But the drawbridge was vacant.

They've been captured! Simon thought, *I'm next!*

He had to run, to escape someway. But how? He couldn't see any doors for they must be hidden somewhere behind the portraits and tapestries. And he couldn't very well jump off the balcony. He'd have to fight whoever it was behind the tapestry and stop them from ruining his escape. He ran back into the tower.

"Good god," a deep yet still immature voice groaned.

A tapestry swept aside and in staggered a young man around Simon's age. He'd clearly been asleep. He rubbed his eyes, wide with bewilderment, with the back of his hand. Behind him, Simon saw a toppled chair, tied to the golden string, and an overturned pint, a pool of amber liquid soaking the floor.

This young man looked strikingly different from Simon. While Simon's hair grew in unruly waves running different directions, this young man's dark hair had seen a barber every other day, and Simon wondered how anyone could get such a princely-perfect head of hair. A gold crown wrapped around his forehead. He was dressed royally in a blue jacket brocaded with gold. He wore white breeches and black boots that had probably never been introduced to dirt.

Perfect prince. Simon rolled his eyes and forced himself to stop staring. He ran at him with a shriek and pummeled the prince to the floor.

"Woah!" the prince shouted. "Get off me!"

"Not another word!" Simon frantically tried to think of things he'd heard his father say to hostages. "Or I shall have Humphrey cut out your tongue and string me a new necklace!"

The prince stopped fighting for a moment and looked up at Simon. "That's disgusting."

"Ew, right?" Simon replied, but remembered himself and tightened his grip on the prince's collar. "*Which* is why you should be silent."

The prince gulped. Simon smirked despite himself and yanked the crown from the prince's head.

"I'll be taking this." He put it on. "And you will lead me to the castle door, or I'll cut ye navel to eyeball."

The prince squinted at him. "Have you a sword?"

"Well . . . " Simon pursed his lips. He couldn't wrestle the prince to door, and no guards would be intimidated by a book. "I have a dagger. A very sharp one, and it'll gut and fillet you if you don't do exactly as I say."

"Where?"

"What do you mean 'where'?"

"I don't see a dagger."

"That doesn't matter, I have it!" Simon patted his doublet, hoping the prince wouldn't notice that his weapon was book-shaped. "It's right here. I think it's still bloody from the last victim. Want to see it?"

"Yes."

Simon blinked, and his cheeks flushed at the sight of the prince smirking. "No! You were supposed to be grossed out by that."

The prince narrowed his eyes, his smirk only getting broader. "Why would blood gross me out?"

"You were grossed out by the tongue thing!" Simon's voice cracked. "I thought surely you'd be squeamish at a bloody dagger!"

The prince laughed at this and when he did, Simon caught the trace of alcohol on his breath. "You aren't very good at this whole plundering thing, are you?"

Simon's eyes widened and he sat up a bit, at a loss. This prince was half-drunk and it wasn't even noon. He balled his fist and swung it down into the prince's stomach.

"How was that?" he asked.

"Much better, actually," the prince coughed out. "Are you trying to prove something here?"

Simon refused to say yes, so he said nothing at all. Instead, he focused on standing and dragging the amused prince by the feet to the balcony, where he would find a way to get back down and get lost before he could be caught and end up like everyone else foolish enough to attempt this theft. Then he ran about the room, ripping the tapestries from the ceiling. The large oak door was revealed, but it was far too late for that.

He tied one end of a curtain to another and pulled it tight. It would have to do.

"What are you doing now?" the prince asked. He smirked, folding his arms and crossing his ankles, as though he were lazing about on a picnic instead of falling hostage to a bandit. "Trying to scale the tower?"

"Do you have a better idea for getting out of here?"

"I'm not *trying* to get out of here," responded the prince.

Boom. Boom. Boom.

Someone pounded on the door. Simon frantically climbed onto the balcony rail and looked down, which made him nearly fall from passing out at the sight. They really were high up, the lower towers of the castle a mile away. He'd never reach the bottom with these curtains.

"Your highness! An intruder is in the tower!" the voice of a guard called through the door.

The prince rolled his eyes. "I know."

The door swung open and in marched two guards, their swords drawn. Behind them stood a large man with long gray curls. Two curlers remained in his hair, bobbing as he ran, flourishing his long robe. Simon had seen him in portraits enough to know who this was. The King.

Just excellent.

"Marco!" the king cried out, running to the prince. "Are you hurt?"

"No, just entertained," said Prince Marco. "This has to be the worst bandit I have ever met."

"A shame the others weren't as bad," a guard said. "Ran way the moment we drew our swords. The cowards."

Simon's stomach dropped when he heard this. Ran away! He didn't doubt it. Bloody Fingers tended to run scared most of the time, but he had never left Simon behind. Until now.

I made a mistake alright, thought Simon, *a mistake in trusting you, Father.*

"Seize him!" the king pointed at Simon, who had stood on the balcony rails.

"Another step and I'll jump," Simon threatened.

The king shrugged. "That's fine, too. We'll leave you impaled on the lowest tower."

Simon flushed. Slowly, he stepped down from the balcony rail. "Would it help if I said that I was forced into this and had no choice?"

"No," replied the king.

"I didn't think so." Simon came a few steps into the room. The chandelier flickered above. *What would Bloody Fingers do,* was all he could think. "Stand back!" he loudly proclaimed, "All of you!"

"Or what," the king said, unimpressed.

"Or, you shall get an eye full of wax and glass," said Simon and he bolted toward the center of the room. He leapt onto the pedestal and jumped for the chandelier, holding on for dear life as he swung above the room.

"Guards—" began King Anders.

"Hold on," the prince put a hand on the king's shoulder. "I've *got* to see how this ends."

Simon swung back and forth, making and attempt to

backflip down and run from the room. But on the sixth swing, the rope that held the chandelier aloft frayed and it came crashing down, knocking Simon against the pedestal and rolling him to the floor. The jeweled slippers fell from the back of his pants and slid across the stones with horrible clinks.

The chandelier shattered around him and he groaned loudly, shielding himself from glass and metal, a few sprays of candle wax hitting his wrists.

With a chuckle, the prince folded his arms and stepped back. "Okay. I'm done now."

"Seize him!" the king wailed.

Simon cringed through the pain in his back and willingly put his arms up. The guards came forward and chained them immediately. Prince Marco stepped forward and bent down, picking up the slippers.

"Guards," the king said, "take this young ruffian away. Throw him in the dungeon, and ensure there are at least a couple of rats in the cell."

"You can keep the crown!" Prince Marco called to Simon as the guards dragged him away. "I have two more!"

Way to rub it in, thought Simon.

3. RATS

Simon pulled his feet from the dungeon floor and hugged his knees to his chest. The guards had been eager to please King Anders, and they'd gone above and beyond with the rats. The cell they'd tossed him into came equipped with not two, not three, but *six* of them, each fatter than the last. The sixth one looked large enough to eat Simon's toes for breakfast, if not a midnight snack.

It was dim, lit only by two rows of torches leading down the block of cells, and the moonlight barely made it through the tiny, barred window that loomed above him. Designed, no doubt, to taunt him with a sliver of the free world.

He held the opened book a bit higher and attempted to catch the light. He knew this book of tales wouldn't have any answers on how to escape without help. He'd read it enough times to know that a thief like him didn't have a story. He squinted, trying to scan the tiny pages no bigger than his palm. It was meant for children.

A rattling sound pulled him from focus. Could it be The Jester? He looked at the cold, straw sprinkled floor to see one of the rats dragging a dusty metal cup along the bars with its tail. He sighed.

"I'll call you Jester," Simon mumbled. He slid his eyes to a broken tailed rat. "You're Humphrey."

He went on to two more rats and named them Fop and Vizier, respectfully. He looked to the fattest rat, who turned itself around and wagged its rear-end at Simon as though it were actively trying to annoy him.

"Oh, you're definitely Father," he said. He swiveled on the hard bench and put his feet on the floor, leaned forward and gave a dramatic bow. "Bloody Fingers."

"No! No! No!" his cellmate, a raggedy crook, said between his missing teeth. "I done told you his name's Ignatius."

The old man hadn't seemed much interested in Simon all night other than to introduce him to the rats. A time or two he'd twisted his long gray beard into a rope and pretended to hang himself and laugh at Simon, sending sprays of spit down onto the rodents. When Simon had noted the smell of the dungeon and asked if mold was rampant, he had responded with, "Delicious, ain't it?" and so Simon had made a point not to notice him.

But when you're suffering for company, even a half-crazed man in the dungeon will do.

"I suppose you've been here longer than the rats," he offered.

"No, boy, I've been here 'cause of 'em."

"Because of them?"

"S'what I said."

Simon raised an eyebrow. "How did rats drag you into a life of crime?"

"Life of crime?" The old man scoffed. "I'm no prisoner! I'm the rat shepherd. Where they go, I go."

Failing to keep his nose from wrinkling, Simon asked, "You take care of rats? As in, for a living? And you go into dungeons for it?"

"Mhm," grunted the old man. "Way's I see's it, yer the only one stupid enough to be a prisoner."

This, Simon couldn't deny. Only the two of them were around, and it looked as though the dungeon cells must go on for quite a bit. And he was the one who got in the cannon and went through with the idiotic idea, after all. No one else to blame, though he really wished there were.

He looked down at the book. Was he really that desperate to *be* someone? Even if it meant he was a stupid someone, a dead man just waiting?

He thought of the prince and cringed. How stupid he must have looked, bumbling around, dragging him this way and that. The prince had been *entertained* by him! Not afraid or threatened, even when he punched him. He laughed at him.

"Everyone deserves a story for themselves, I think," Simon defended his stupidity. He rolled his eyes at himself and shoved the book back in his doublet. He shrugged, at least grateful that he'd never have to look at the prince again after such an embarrassing fiasco.

"Er," the old man huffed. "You want me ter scrawl that on yer grave later?"

Simon opened his mouth to respond, but the sound of a key turning in a lock sounded above and he snapped his mouth shut. The hiss of bolts opening and the steps of something, someone, coming down into the dungeon. Simon leaned back against the wall of the cell, his heart bouncing so high that it knocked against the roof of his mouth and dropped through his feet.

It can't be morning yet!

A chill shook his spine as a cloaked figure came around the corner and approached the cell, stepping into a small pool of torchlight. Simon felt his insides crumble as the blue cloak swept back, and a pale, never-worked hand lowered the hood.

Oh, no.

He gaped at Prince Marco of Lands Upper, and he wished his face would just catch fire if it was going to get so hot.

"You," Simon said.

"Me," said Marco. Simon shut his eyes before rolling them at the sight of that teasing smirk. "I wasn't going to visit, considering your ill-mannered greeting earlier today. You left quite a mark on my otherwise flawless abdomen, after all."

He rubbed the spot where Simon had punched him.

"Intrigue! Scandal!" The old man whistled and laughed.

The prince shot the old man a look. "Do you mind?"

The old man pulled his lips inside his mouth and blushed, stifling his giggles.

"Sorry that I punched you." Simon kept his eyes on his knees. "I hope your abdomen is once again flawless someday. But what do you want?" He gestured to his forehead, where the crown still sat askew. "I suppose you want this back."

Marco waved his hand. "I said you can keep it. I have two more, remember?"

"Oh. Gee. Thanks."

Marco shrugged. "Just do me a favor and let me have it back tomorrow afternoon.

Simon balled his fists. Just what did this boy want from him? In a few hours, he'd be dead, and this guy would be running around fighting dragons, being rich, and having portraits painted and ballads sung in his honor. Why did he feel the need to come rub it in?

"I'm so glad you aren't squeamish of blood, then."

"I might not have to worry about it." Marco shrugged again.

If he shrugs one more time—

"You mean a pardon?"

"I mean a bloodless death." He shrugged.

He did it again!

Simon stood up and came towards the bars. "You really like your morbid humor, don't you?" The prince shrugged.

"Stop that."

"Stop what?"

Simon reenacted his shrug, and gave an exaggerated smirk. He made a goofy noise, doing the most offensive imitation he could of the prince. "That! I'm a little too stressed out to be your entertainment right now. Don't you have people paid to do that?"

"They're asleep," said Marco. "Sorry. I'm being insensitive. But actually, I didn't come here to mess with you, though now I'm seeing and noting you're a pretty easy target."

"I am not—"

"I think I can help you."

Simon shut his mouth and inhaled. He considered the prince's expression, and found it to look sincere. He tilted his head. "I'm listening."

"It's a rather private matter . . . "

Prince Marco slid his eyes to the old man, who had scooped Ignatius the rat into his arms and sat rocking it like a baby and making kissing faces. After a moment, he noticed the prince staring at him with concern and he stood.

"I see," the old man said. "Can't be chums, can we? Well, I don't stay's where's I'm not wanted. Ignatius and ma'self'll do jes' fine elsewhere."

With a dramatic show of it, he stood and fished in his pocket, produced a key, unlocked the cell, and once Marco jumped back, he exited, being sure to slam the door behind him. He went two cells down, let himself in, locked it, and sat.

"You had a key?!" Simon shouted.

Marco looked to Simon. "What kind of kingdom is this?"

"*Right*?!" Simon agreed. "Did you notice that King Anders still had curlers in his hair?"

"To think I shall marry into this." Marco let out a singular laugh and tightened his lips, but a few still escaped. "Sorry, not trying to offend. Alright, maybe a little. I mean, come on, who *is* that?"

He gestured to the old man, who had struck up a game of peekaboo with the rat.

"How do you think you can help?"

Marco stepped nearer to the bars. He cocked his head. "Come here."

Simon took a step closer and wrapped his hands around the bars. The sleeve of the prince's jacket brushed against his knuckles as he raised a cupped hand to his mouth, but Simon tried not to notice the contact, or the silent shiver it created.

"I know where Isobel is," whispered the prince, and Simon noted that this time he didn't have alcohol on his breath.

"Who?"

"The lost princess. The one whose slippers you tried to steal?"

"Oh, *that* lost princess."

Marco raised his eyes to the ceiling. "Yes."

"Alright, well why haven't you said so?"

Shaking his head, Marco sighed. "It's . . . it's a difficult situation. But, I've had word from her."

He reached into his cloak and rifled through an inner pocket. When his hand reemerged it held a folded piece of parchment. "I don't know how she managed to get it to me, but when I awakened this morning, there it sat on my balcony, atop a purple pillow. That's why I volunteered to stand watch in the tower. I had to think it all through."

"You were asleep," Simon couldn't help but point out.

The prince smirked. "Thinking makes me sleepy."

"Thinking, or grog?" Simon asked, remembering the overturned pint.

Marco's expression tightened and for a second, making Simon feel bad for mentioning it. "That, too."

"Do you think it could really be her?" Simon asked for a subject change.

"Well, yes," Marco said. "I've only known her a short while, but I think it sounds like her. But . . . "

He looked to the ceiling again, and for the first time Simon saw something in his eyes that wasn't amusement.

Shame, perhaps? Concern? He couldn't be sure.

"But?"

"I barely know her!" Marco ejected. "I mean, do I want to risk my life for someone I don't love?"

Simon narrowed his eyes. "You don't love her, but you're marrying her?"

The prince's smirk appeared again, tight again. "That's the way of the crown. My older brother got the kingdom. I get a wife."

"What a compromise."

A moment of silence fell between them. Simon had assumed the prince had it all together. That everything must be *perfect* for him. Get the damsel, have the happiness. Wasn't that how it was supposed to work? But he felt sorry for the prince. He knew all too well what it was like to live a life you didn't choose. To be born into something that just isn't what you want.

"So," began Simon slowly, "what does this have to do with me?"

"Do you know anything about mines?" asked Marco.

"I know what they are, and I don't think it's fair to make dwarfs work in them just because they're small."

Marco chuckled. "Mines go miles below the earth.

Sometimes they get so low that they lose air. Or gases appear that could kill the miners if they breathe them in."

"Again with the morbid."

"So!" Marco raised his voice a bit and gripped the bars of the cell, just above Simon's hands. That shut him up. "They send a bird ahead to test it. If the canary dies, then they know it's not safe and they need to get out."

Simon gasped. "That's cruel! I'll be writing the dwarf council about this."

"Don't be ridiculous," said the prince. "If you had to choose, would you rather one bird die, or an entire group of dwarfs?"

"Neither!"

"No, you have to choose one. That's the game."

"I don't like this game."

With a frustrated sigh, Marco gritted his teeth. "Obviously, one canary is just one canary. Whereas you would lose more lives if it were a pack of dwarfs. You'd choose for them to be safe."

Simon took pleasure in being the one to give the smirk now. "Oh, that's right. You're from a mining kingdom."

"That's beside the point!" Marco grunted. "Are you usually this distracting?"

"No," Simon said honestly. "You just pull it out of me."

"Alright," Marco took a step back. "Forget I mentioned it."

"Hold on." Simon lifted his palm in surrender. "Fine. Continue."

"That was it," said Marco. "That was my whole piece."

Simon cocked his head to one side. "You want me to be a canary?"

"I don't know what's waiting out there where Isobel is concerned," the prince confessed. "It could be a trap, for all I know."

Simon scanned the prince up and down. "Who'd want to trap *you*?"

"You're right. What on earth would someone want with a royal prince's ransom? You ought to know, *bandit*."

Simon's cheeks flushed at the way he said the word. Or rather *spat* the word. Humiliating.

"Well, I thought it was your *job* to go after her, *lover boy*."

Marco took a deep breath and tapped his foot, but Simon noticed that a grin had broken across his face.

"You really are annoying."

"You're the one who called me an easy target."

"Fair." Marco nodded. He held up the parchment. "So?"

Simon had no idea how to rescue a princess. He couldn't even steal a pair of shoes, and he constantly forgot to bring a real weapon. How could he possibly succeed here? But it was that or wait to die and be forgotten.

And if I do somehow manage to pull it off…well, that would be pretty great.

"If I do this," began Simon, "I can go free?"

"Yes." Marco nodded. "Not only that, but I can promise you riches worth far more than those slippers. You'd never have to steal again. You can go where you please."

Lands Upper. And I can ship Father to the Southern Islands. Freedom.

Marco slipped a hand between the bars and offered the note. Simon took the parchment, his finger sliding against the prince's palms. It had no callouses. "Deal."

Marco bowed his head. "A pleasure. Just read the parchment and wait."

Simon unfolded the message and held it close to his eyes to read. "By the way, tell your father-in-law-to-be to light the dungeon better, I can't read this. What does it say?"

He looked up, but the prince had gone.

"Might not be brave," shouted the old man, bouncing Ignatius on his knee, "be he sure can run fast!"

Simon didn't know how much time he had to figure all this out, or what to do.

Out of someone else's crazy scheme and into another, he thought. *Storybook of my life.*

He squinted harder at the parchment, trying to make out the words scrawled in a slanted hand.

Marco,
I hope this message has found you at all. And if it has, I hope you're ready, because I have found a way that I can be found. I cannot tell my location, because I don't actually know where it is, but I've worked around that after much convincing.

They'll find you tonight. Closer to dawn, so I think really that would be tomorrow? No need to go looking, they will find you. Just try to keep still.

Love,
Princess Isobel

"They?" Simon asked out loud. "Who's they?"

Through the dark, a wooden pair of fists reached through the bars and slammed against Simon's face, knocking him out cold.

4. THE LOST PRINCESS

When one is knocked unconscious, it isn't often that they remember what happened between then and waking up, unless of course they had a dream. Simon the Squirm did not have a dream while he was unconscious, and he hadn't felt himself being carried, either. But whomever the wooden hands belonged to must have carried him, because as he blinked his eyelids open, he didn't see the ceiling of the dungeon.

What he saw were the night stars.

We're off to a great start, he thought. *Not even five minutes into the quest and I've already been injured.*

He grunted, a sharp pulse in his temples making him close his eyes immediately.

"No sudden moves." He heard a feminine voice call in the dark. "Or they'll just have to knock you out again."

Simon rested his cheek against the ground and forced his eyes to reopen, trying to gain his bearings. The sky only lasted for the space of a short circle, for he found himself inside some sort of tent, striped in purple and blue, with an open roof. Beams and pulleys hung above, strung with unlit paper lanterns. He couldn't see the owner of the voice, or any other living thing for that matter.

Finally, he stopped looking about. The left side of his face throbbed. He'd have quite a bruise there soon if he didn't already. Maybe some blood too, if the wooden hands had punched hard enough.

That's insane, he thought. *Hands aren't made of wood, whether those hands are punching someone or not.*

Simon slowly lifted his head. "Um, where am I?"

"Don't you worry about that," the voice said harshly. "Just explain why you are here."

"The message . . . " Simon fumbled around himself for the parchment, but he only felt soft earth.

"Looking for this?" The parchment fluttered into the beam of moonlight and landed on Simon's stomach.

"Who are you?" Simon squinted into the darkness, looking for anyone, a shadowy figure at least. "Are you Princess Isobel?"

The voice ignored Simon. "You are not Prince Marco."

Simon pushed himself up. "Of course I'm not—"

Something behind Simon reached out and pushed him back down. When he turned to identify who, or what, it was, they had retreated into the darkness.

"Yet you wear his crown," said the voice.

"What? I—Oh." Simon reached up and felt his head, where the prince's crown still rested. No wonder Marco had wanted Simon to keep it. It would identify him to his kidnapper. "I can explain that easily enough."

She didn't respond, and for a moment Simon thought that she had left.

He heard a soft footfall and a slow stirring moved from a far corner of the tent. Simon slid his eyes to a pool of moonlight on the dirt floor. A pink-slippered foot stepped into the light, followed by the figure of a young woman. But not quite so. For, as the light illuminated her fully, Simon widened his eyes to see that the girl was not even human.

She was made entirely out of wood.

A handful of thin silver strings wrapped around her like a boa, leading to a wooden cross that dragged out behind her.

Simon felt the air leave his lungs. "You're a-a-a—"

"Princess," said Princess Isobel.

"I was going to say a marion—"

"Princess Isobel." She cut him off again, unblinking.

"Marionette!" Simon spat out. "Holy crowns, you're a puppet!"

Something pushed him from behind again, and now they all came from the shadows. Two marionettes, then three. Yet they were people. People with expressions, and eye colors of green and blue, with hair so human you could cut it and expect it to grow back within a month. Each wore a soldier's red uniform.

Yet they were all made of wood. An army of wooden soldiers.

"You're all puppets!" Simon looked back to the princess, and jumped to find she had come at him and stooped just inches from his face, looking at him with large, glassy, amber-colored eyes. When she spoke, no air left her lungs, as though she were solid. Like a tree.

"I am *not* a puppet," she said in a low growl. "You can control puppets."

"Oh," Simon felt his face flush, "of course! I would never try to control you-I- I just meant," he gestured to her strings, "You- you have, um——"

"The upper hand," Isobel finished for him.

Simon's eyes grew wide. "Yes. Yes, you do."

"So then, I'm going to need you to answer all of my questions." Isobel stood upright, folding her arms. "And if you don't answer them, or if you try to be cheeky, Lefty here will just have to knock you out again. Understand?"

She gestured behind Simon, and he craned his neck back to see a tall, looming soldier pounding his left fist into his right palm.

Simon snapped his attention back to the princess and nodded.

"Good," smiled the wooden princess. "Now, how did you get this message?"

"Prince Marco gave it to me."

"He gave it to you."

"Yes."

"Why?"

"So I could find you." Simon offered his hands as a sign of peace.

The princess's upper lip quivered and she took a deep breath. "Why didn't he just come for me himself?"

Simon cocked an eyebrow. "He had a hair appointment."

Isobel snapped her eyes to the soldier behind him. "Lefty?"

A hard wooden fist smacked into Simon's right shoulder.

"Ow!"

"Why didn't he come for me?!" Isobel pressed.

Simon wasn't sure how to answer this. How do you explain to a lady why her future husband doesn't want to personally check on her? But then he recalled something Marco had said.

"He didn't know if it was a trap or not," explained Simon.

"So he sent you to be the canary." Isobel rolled her eyes.

"Oh, you know about mining?"

"Of course I know about mining, my future husband is the prince of a mining land," Isobel snapped. She softened and looked at her wooden hands. "So he didn't want to risk having to fight for me."

"What? No, that isn't it, I don't think-"

"So what? He was just going to stick a crown on you and hope I wouldn't notice?"

Simon looked around himself, frantic to get the princess and get going. Anything could be lurking around here. The princess needed to stop worrying and just come with him.

He titled his head at her. "I don't know why you're taking it so personally. Marco said you don't really know each other well, so it's not worth getting upset over that I'm here instead of him."

A small smiled painted itself onto Isobel's carved lips. "I take it you aren't well versed in the curses of royals."

Simon found his eyes scanning the wooden princess up and down. "Clearly I know nothing of curses at all."

Princess Isobel's face twisted into a scowl. "Impertinent! *That's* how I knew you weren't my prince."

"I was impertinent in my sleep?"

"*And* you're far too lean. Underfed. And no muscle, so clearly you have no tutors or coaches to ensure you become strong."

"Don't worry, no offense taken."

"Who *are* you?" Isobel asked, her voice raising. The soldiers whispered among themselves, as though this were some sort of theatrical play they were watching and it was time for a scene change and some discussion.

I'm Simon the Squirm, thought Simon. *The world's worst thief, who was forced into this whole thing due to another plan I was forced into. I really only want to go back to Prince Marco and tell him you're here and waiting, and a bit sassy if you don't mind my saying so, so that I can go free, not die, and go get my own life.*

But none of that felt like the right thing to say. This princess wasn't playing around, especially now that she was upset that he was even there. He needed to be impressive. He needed to look like he knew what he was doing.

"I'll tell you if you'll call off your pupp—your pals here," Simon stared the princess down.

The princess stared hard at him, and Simon hoped she wouldn't notice his hands were shaking. Finally, she slid her eyes to the puppets and nodded. They backed away, allowing him to stand.

Simon fumbled for words while he took his time to

brush himself off. He needed the princess to trust him and to come with him, and fast. He'd already had enough of this. Magic talking puppets and emotional princesses. He needed to be more than Simon. He needed to be someone else. Actually, he'd need to be *someone* at all.

Sweeping a low, dramatic bow, he said, "Well, milady. You'll be interested to know that your, um, *subjects*, have captured none other than the one and only Bloody Fingers."

It was a theatrical gesture he'd seen his father do a hundred times, and he hoped that the princess had never seen a wanted poster.

The soldiers gasped, but Isobel's mouth tightened into a small bow.

"You?" she raised an eyebrow.

"Indeed." Simon forced as big a confident smile as he could muster. "The most feared villain in the kingdom of Incantus."

"Second."

"Say what now?"

"Second most feared," said Isobel. "I've heard my father, *the king*, speak of you. I think he's put a hefty price on your head."

"Shucks."

"Just a moment." Isobel narrowed her eyes. "I seem to remember hearing that Bloody Fingers has a thick black mustache."

"I heard that too," one of the soldiers said in a deep gruff voice. "He's terribly proud of it, I've heard."

Simon instinctively felt at the smooth skin above his lip.

"My 'stache? Oh, yes." He whimpered grandly. "My beautiful 'stache! Lost it in a sword fight, I did. The blackguard. The dastardly devil shaved it right off! I've kept it in a box, my 'stache, until I can find a proper surgeon to reattach it."

"Couldn't you let it grow back?" the soldier asked, perplexed.

"I want the one I already had!" shouted Simon, dabbing his eyes. "So luscious. So perfect."

Simon couldn't believe it. Where was all of this bravado coming from? Just this morning he'd barely been able to get a word in at all, and now he was annoying princes, lying to princesses, and convincing an entire room of magical wooden soldiers that he was a feared bandit to be respected? He would have to stay consistent with it from here on out.

"I am indeed a thief," Simon continued, "And now I shall thieve *you*."

Isobel put her hands on her hips. "Excuse me?!"

"You heard me. Please come quietly, I've had quite a long day and I just want to get it over with."

"You will do no such thing!" Isobel stamped her foot. "I wrote that letter for Prince Marco, and I'm going to wait right here for him! He can come get me if he wants me!"

She folded her arms and pouted.

Simon felt his blood rising. "Look here. Today alone I have been shot out of a cannon, roughed up by guards, pestered by a rat shepherd, and knocked out by a magical band of puppets." The soldiers began to protest, but

Simon raised his voice. "Now, I said I'm thieving you, and I shall, so *hold still!*"

Simon ran forward and grabbed the wooden cross dangling at the princess's side. He yanked it and she twirled, her own strings wrapping around her. He pulled her close as a hostage.

"Stand back! All of you!" he gestured to the wooden soldiers, "I've a dagger in my doublet, and if you come too close, I'll-I'll-I'll . . . cut your strings!"

The soldiers cried out.

"Unhand me!" Isobel struggled.

"Absolutely not," Simon said, "I'm taking you back to your kingdom and to Prince Marco."

Isobel's eyes widened and she tried to get loose of Simon's grip. "No! You can't take me back there! I can't be seen like this!"

Simon dragged her toward the tent flap. He'd get her out of here and then somehow calm her down so they could figure a way back together. He'd tell her he wasn't a fierce bandit, just a fool who got mixed up in this, and all would come to a happy end.

Right?

"You princesses," Simon said, still putting on his best Bloody Fingers impression, "always so hung up on your looks. No one cares, *doll face.*"

"Rude!" Isobel cried. "Let me go, you- you *rude boy.*"

"Ouch."

The soldiers were gathered around, merely watching, anxious to help their princess, but also fearful of getting their strings cut. Simon couldn't help but feel impressed

THE PRINCE AND THE PUPPET THIEF

with himself at this. Maybe he wasn't so bad at this after all.

Look at me, Father! He thought, *I've escaped death* and *stolen a princess! I think that tops your whole slippers idea.*

He neared the flap of the tent. Almost to freedom.

Unholy shrieks forced Simon to halt. He looked back to see the soldiers with their heads thrown back, arms stiffly held out, screaming. But whether they were cries of fear or a battle cry, Simon couldn't be certain.

He let go of the princess, his eyes drawn to the open ceiling of the tent as each lantern ignited, each flame a different color, casting the tent, and the soldiers, in hues of green, purple, and gold.

"You really shouldn't have tried that," Isobel said to Simon, her voice quivering.

Fog drifted in through the hole at the top of the tent, blocking out the sky.

"What is that?" Simon asked, trying with everything to keep his voice from shaking.

The fog began to take shape, slowly but surely gaining the outline of a large, shadowy figure.

"Not what," Princess Isobel's voice shook. "Who."

"*Who* is that?" Simon whispered.

Isobel's reply was so quiet that Simon could barely hear her whisper, "The Maestroa. *First* most feared villain in the kingdom of Incantus."

5. CURSES

"The *My-stro-ah?*" Simon phonetically punched the name.

"Who is in my kingdom?" The Maestroa's voice boomed, causing the sides of the tent to wave as though the wind would peel them away.

Simon's knees threatened to give out and he prayed they wouldn't. Next to him, Isobel swept a low curtsy and cast her eyes down.

When no one responded, the foggy silhouette of The Maestroa stepped forward. "You cannot fool me. I know someone is here who does not belong."

Simon knew it would be the polite thing to step forward and introduce himself, but he also knew that one shouldn't be polite with someone who most likely meant to harm him.

"Answer me," demanded The Maestroa, "Or I'll light every single one of you aflame."

There was the noise of fingers snapping and a great

ball of orange fire ignited in the center of the tent. The soldiers screamed.

Simon pushed himself forward. "It's me!"

The flame extinguished itself with a hiss. The Maestroa let out a quiet laugh and, stepping through the smoke left by the fire, revealed himself in the light of the lanterns.

Actually, The Maestroa revealed *her*self. For Simon could see now that the Maestroa was actually a woman. A rather tall woman in a man's ringleader jacket, purple and embroidered with chords of gold and fanning out around her waist like an umbrella, or the spiked collar of a fierce dragon.

Or, were they a woman? Simon had never seen someone like The Maestroa before, masculine features melting into feminine attributes, like a firework of all sexes. He tried not to gawk, and for a moment found himself in awe of their unbelievable beauty. The Maestroa, *they*, were clearly not to be trifled with, and he snapped his mouth shut.

The Maestroa grinned, baring large white teeth as their purple eyes seemed to glow.

"A boy!" They held their hands up excitedly. "We don't have one of those yet."

Simon leaned back as The Maestroa took another step forward. They caught sight of his crown and at once let out an enormous, thundering laugh that made the lanterns swing above.

"Oh my!" they cried. "What luck, what joy! Here, I've caught myself a prince!"

Isobel snorted, extinguishing the small seed of flattery that Simon felt.

The Maestroa slid their eyes to Isobel. "What is so funny, Isobel?"

"Nothing," murmured Isobel.

With a shake of their head, the Maestroa rolled their eyes. "You're so simple. Whatever can I do with you?" Isobel winced. The Maestroa took no heed and turned their gaze back to Simon, whose stomach did another flip. "So tell me, Your Highness, just what are you doing on my showgrounds?"

"Showgrounds?" questioned Simon. "I don't know."

"Don't tell me that you are a simpleton, too," said The Maestroa. "One dumb royal is bad enough. I really must check my acquisitions more thoroughly. Isn't that right, Isobel?"

Isobel gave a slight, forced nod.

Simon coughed to make himself speak up. "I was just passing these fine showgrounds you have here, and I wished to see what I could see . . . so . . . um . . . " The crown tilted on his head. He reached up to reposition it and stood up straighter. "I-I've seen many wondrous things, but I really ought to be on my way now, as my manservant is bound to be waiting. So I'll just show myself out, and I'll be sure to give a rave review to all of my courtiers and noble steeds!"

He turned to the tent flap.

"Stop!" The Maestroa shouted.

Simon halted. He heard the spiked heels of The Maestroa's boots impale the ground as they neared him.

"There is still much to see," they said in a voice so sweet it made Simon's insides curdle.

"Another day." Simon looked back at The Maestroa, trying his best to sound firm and noble.

The Maestroa swept a hand and the tent flaps closed securely behind Simon.

"The lights weren't on, and I don't think you'd have just wandered casually by. No one comes this far into the forest," The Maestroa said plainly. "We are miles away from Incantus or any other kingdom for that matter, so I don't believe you could have just gallivanted off in search of a fun time. Especially at this hour."

"I couldn't have?" Simon challenged.

"Oh, you princes are all alike." The Maestroa strutted around, wringing their hands. "Sitting around and pining or brooding, and then you casually catch wind of some princess in need and off you go, off to save her, with the hope of a kiss and happily ever after. Because you're all just so *handsome* and *strong* and all around *perfect*, aren't you?" They spat on the ground. "Makes me *sick*."

"If you think that's flattering, you ought to hear their honesty about princ*esses*." Isobel rolled her eyes.

"No cheek from you." The Maestroa wagged a long finger at the princess. Their eyes darted back to Simon. "Isn't that why you've come?"

Simon considered his words. Really, he had no claim in any of this, he wasn't even a prince, he was here on behalf of the man The Maestroa had just described.

I'm screwed.

"Maybe," was the only thing he could come up with.

Isobel shot him a disgusted glance. "Thief!" she mouthed.

The Maestroa laughed, a high-pitched giggle that hurt Simon's ears. They clapped their hands and bounced on their heels. "I knew it! I just knew it! Very well then, go on, Isobel. Kiss him."

"What?" Princess Isobel's eyes widened.

"He's come all this way just to rescue you. Now is the part of the story where you show your undying devotion and kiss him." The Maestroa clasped their hands over their heart and cooed. "I just *love* happy endings."

Simon stood planted, swaying slowly back and forth. This was getting awkward rather quickly.

"I don't want to." Isobel folded her arms.

The Maestroa grabbed her shoulders and brought her over to Simon. Then they took *his* shoulders and made them face each other.

"Foolish youths! This is the way it goes. Kiss, and then you can both go free."

The Maestroa took a step back and put their fists on their hips expectantly.

It seemed simple enough for Simon, but there must be a trick. He looked at Isobel and she at him. Her eyes were wide and so shiny that he thought she might cry. She was so close to him he could almost hear her thoughts. *You're Bloody Fingers. Do something.*

But that was a lie, and now he couldn't do much of anything except stand there waiting for his first kiss under the most uneasy circumstances, and think nothing except what an idiot he was for standing there at all.

"Well?" The Maestroa tapped their foot. "Is it true love or is it not?"

Isobel snapped her gaze to the Maestroa, her painted lips quivering. "You're so much crueler than you need to be."

She tore open the tent flap, which struggled with The Maestroa's magical grip, and ran out.

"That's awkward." The Maestroa chuckled.

"Can I go now?" Simon asked.

The Maestroa snapped their fingers and the soldiers came marching toward him.

He turned to the tent flap, attempting escape, but felt the pull of invisible strings as the Maestroa clapped their hands like thunder.

When Simon whirled around, he met the eyes of The Maestroa's staring back into his as their long hands reached for him.

"You won't be going anywhere."

6. GLORIOUS MORNING

Marco paced the balcony of his chambers. Dawn was approaching quickly, and he wished that he had slept at least a little. As it was, he had only gone so far as to change into his pajamas and leave the bed unturned. Below, the kingdom glittered with the morning lanterns of early risers, the bakers and the merchants preparing for the day. Marco envied those people, the ones whose biggest concern was whether there would be enough loaves of bread to last the day, or whether or not they could even sell those loaves. It sounded appealing, compared to worries of your future father-in-law finding out that you'd set free the prisoner that said father-in-law was planning to have killed that morning.

Marco hadn't any idea how long such a mission would take. He didn't even know if Simon would come back at all. He just wanted to help him, and also get out of doing it himself.

A familiar and numbing sense of shame wrapped through his chest.

Stop it. He shook his head. *You're no storybook hero. It isn't on you to save every damsel that calls for help.*

But this made him feel worse. Though Marco was fonder of parties and lazy days than going off on quests, he still had a moral compass, and the invisible arrow of that compass was spinning in a frenzy.

I need a drink, he thought.

Behind him, inside the bed chamber, he heard the soft whine of a turning door handle. He looked back and watched as a servant entered and began to stoke the fire. The man took little notice of Marco, though certainly he would have seen the prince hadn't been in bed. He made a point of not acknowledging it.

With a sigh, Marco came inside and went behind the changing screen to undress. He washed and changed, not allowing the servant to dress him. He might be lazy, but he wasn't useless.

"Your Highness," he heard the servant say beyond the screen, "did you sleep well?"

"Yes," lied Marco.

"Very good," the servant responded mechanically. "His majesty wishes you to join him in his chambers at your ready, sire."

Marco winced. Excellent, already summoned to King Anders, and no idea of how to tell him what happened. Somehow during his hours of pacing, of fretting and worrying, he hadn't been able to come up with the right way to phrase the news.

After donning one of his extra crowns, he allowed the

servant to escort him to the king's chambers. Marco had been placed in the east wing, whereas King Anders slept in the west, leaving a long walk for him to feel uncomfortable with the quiet servant.

"So," began Marco when the silence between them grew too loud, "what's your name anyways?"

The servant looked at the prince, surprised. "Hans, Your Highness."

"Ah."

"Why do you ask?" The servant's voice quivered. "Was the fire not stoked to your liking? I can do better."

"Not at all. Just making conversation."

"Oh."

"Do have other expressions besides that one? I've grown tired of it."

Hans the servant gasped and quickly changed his usual stiff expression. He raised his eyebrows and popped his eyes, stuck his lips out like a duck. "Is that better, Your Highness?"

Marco grunted. "Stop that."

The servant returned his expression to the usual stoic one. "Of course, Your Highness."

"I was only messing with you," said Marco. When Hans the servant merely blinked he added, "I was joking."

Hans blinked at the prince, and then broke into a loud, shrieking laugh. "Very good, Your Highness!"

Marco tried to keep his sigh to himself. He wished the subjects here would be more open to joking around. In the weeks he'd been here, the only one who'd entertained him at all was the thief, and he was long gone, if ever to return.

Marco had enjoyed his smile.

THE PRINCE AND THE PUPPET THIEF

They came at last to King Anders' chambers, and Hans the Servant pounded the gold lion-shaped door knocker. A tall, gangly courtier with a goatee answered.

"An inquiry from the king as to who is here," he said dully.

"A prince from away to see His Majesty," responded Hans, just as dully.

"A prince summoned by his Majesty on this glorious morning?" confirmed the gangly servant dully.

"A prince wary of this silliness, stepping through the door," Marco said dully and pushed past the two servants into the room.

King Anders sat at his dressing table, sipping some sort of red tea while yet another servant in a tall, powdered wig busied his hands with unrolling the king's curlers so that his long gray hair hung in perfectly symmetrical ringlets.

Marco thought he looked like a great big frog in a wig, but he knew better than to laugh and say so, for any king that made his servants speak in such a way wasn't prone to taking a good-natured jab.

"Marco, my boy!" King Anders smiled in the mirror reflection at the prince. "What a glorious morning it is, don't you think?"

Prince Marco glanced at the large window, where the sun rose behind heavy gray clouds that were threatening a storm.

"Indeed," he replied half-heartedly.

"*Yow!*" shouted the king. He slapped the servant's hand away from his curls. "Gently, Gustave! Gently! We aren't yanking a wishbone!"

"Yes, Your Majesty," said Gustave. His tongue hit the underside of his upper teeth when he spoke, so that his S's were nonexistent, and instead it came out, 'Yeth, Your Majethty.'

King Anders slid his eyes to Marco. "So difficult to get a good royal hairdresser these days, don't you think?"

Marco raised his hand to his own short dark hair. He hadn't even needed to brush it this morning. "Oh yes, certainly."

King Anders nodded approval and turned to powder his face. Marco felt unsure of this kingdom, where royals painted their faces with goo and lamented the lack of perfect long curls. It made him miss his own mining town, where everyone came as they were and there weren't these pretenses. His parents had warned him it would be more 'stylish'. By that they meant 'pretentious'.

But when you're the spare, not the heir, you don't get to be choosy.

King Anders stood and crossed to the window. He sucked in a deep breath as though the window were open and he were taking in the fresh air.

"How I just love a morning execution," he mused. "Makes me feel as though I've conquered the entire day."

Marco's chest tightened. Time to confess. He took in his own deep breath. "Yes, Your Majesty. Um, about that —"

King Anders let out a deep laugh from his belly. "None of that 'Your Majesty' stuff! Simply call me 'Papa'."

Marco stopped himself from cringing. He wasn't married into this family yet and barely knew any of them.

Calling him 'Papa' when he had his own perfectly good father seemed a bit much, but he was the guest, and also about to reveal to a man that enjoyed ordering executions that he set the prisoner free, so he thought best to play along.

"Yes, um, *Papa.*" The word felt sour on his tongue. "About that. Should we really start the day with death?"

"What?" King Anders turned to him. "What put that fool notion into your mind?"

"Oh, it's just, I don't know. It seems, um, the rest of the day might be a let down if you started with something so big. You might get bored."

"So I'll do some needlework," King Anders said. "I love needlework just as much."

"Oh? Oh. Well—"

But Marco stopped talking, taken aback by King Anders' sudden smile. His eyes seemed as though they would water and he sighed. "I'm so happy you're here."

"You are?"

"Of course! With you here, we are one step closer to my baby girl being wed." King Anders clasped his hands together. "One inch further to my little princess coming home."

"But that's just it, Your Maj—Papa. I—"

"And now that you're here, I can see plainly that I won't have to worry about ugly grandchildren." King Anders rose from his dressing table and sat on the edge of his bed. "That would really be unacceptable, you know."

"I could imagine. But you really ought to know something."

"Enough talk," King Anders said. "No need to thank

me! Together we shall find a way to bring Isobel back to her rightful home, but first things first. The matter of the ruffian in the dungeon. Gaspard—" he pointed to the gangly and dull servant, "—go tell the upper floor guards to tell the lower floor guards, to tell the lower-lower-floor guard, to convey it to the jailers, to whisper to the executioner to bring the ruffian out and I shall be there soon."

"Yes, sire." Gaspard swept a low bow and left the chambers.

"Come, my boy." King Anders slapped Marco's back. "Time to see justice done."

"Sir, I really need you to listen to me." Impatience strained Marco's voice. No sleep and the crowd of butterflies he'd borne in his stomach were getting the best of him.

"What could be so important?" snapped King Anders.

Gaspard came back into the room, his face pale.

"Your—Your Majesty?"

"What are you doing here?" asked the king. "You were supposed to tell the upper-floor guards to tell the lower floor guards to tell the—"

"I did, sire," Gaspard said. "But the executioner has whispered back to the jailers, who told the lower-lower floor guard, who in turn told the lower-floor guards—"

"Get to it, man!" King Anders shouted. "What did the upper-floor guards tell you?"

"The prisoner has escaped," spilled Gaspard.

"He what?"

"He escaped, sire. In the night. No one knows how, and all that's left in the dungeon is an old book of tales and some old man who is teaching the rats how to tap dance."

"Then bring *him*!"

"He isn't a prisoner, sire. Just a strange man of his own will."

King Anders' face grew red. "How did he
escape? As I recall, he was a feeble minded fool of a boy."

"That's what I wanted to tell you," groaned Marco, dropping onto the edge of the king's bed and throwing his face into his hands.

"I didn't need you to tell me that, I could see he was a fool on my own," the king huffed.

"No!" said Marco. "That he escaped."

When Marco dared to look between his fingers, he could see the king's face change into an expression of rage, and his heartbeat sped up.

"You knew? You knew and you did not alert me at once?"

"I helped him," Marco confessed as his stomach flipped.

"You what?!" King Anders screamed.

"I helped him escape!" Marco shouted back, lifting his face from his hands. "But you must understand—"

"Get him back!" King Anders bolted to Marco and shook him by the collar. "Get. Him. Back!"

"If you'll only listen to me!"

"I listened! I heard every word that I allowed you to utter, and now I am ordering you as King of Incantus to get back the thief!"

"But the princess—"

"He stole her slippers, and he must pay for his crimes! Now you go out there and you bring him back!"

"I just wanted him to—"

"You bring him back right now, or I'll have *your* head and I don't care how many wars I start over it!"

He dropped Marco to the ground and swayed back and forth, putting the back of his hand to his forehead. "Gustave . . . Gaspard . . . catch me, I shall fall!" He fell backward onto the bed. Gustave, Gaspard, and Hans all ran to the king immediately and fanned him with their handkerchiefs.

"Go now!" he declared to Marco, who found it rather hard to stand back up with his knees shaking so violently. "If you are not back by sundown, I shall come and fetch you myself!"

"Can I at least take a nap first?" pleaded Marco. "I didn't sleep last night, and—"

"OUT!"

7. LOOT

"Why, oh why?"

Simon the Squirm knew he shouldn't whine. He'd been alive enough years to know that whining not only gets you nowhere, but for him it also got a smack on the back of the head from Bloody Fingers, or the Vizier if Bloody Fingers couldn't be bothered. And if the Vizier couldn't be bothered, there was nothing more humiliating than being smacked by the Jester with that silly rattle. But when you've found yourself in some sort of cavern, without knowledge of how far below the earth you are, and an evil magician known only as the Maestroa, so close you can smell the bread and blueberry jam they had for dinner on their breath, it is difficult not to whine just a little bit. Especially when you didn't sleep the night before because you were awake worrying about your imminent death.

"Why, oh why?"

"Don't you know that whining gets you nowhere?" the Maestroa asked.

"Yes," sobbed Simon, "but there's not much else to do."

The Maestroa sighed and turned to the wooden soldiers, who were gathered around them at attention, gripping a very long rope. "Up he goes."

At once they pulled, and Simon went up in the air, for the rope was tied around his chest.

"Is this absolutely necessary?" he couldn't help but question once they had him up. He tried not to look down, as there were some twenty or so feet between him and the ground.

"Yes," said the Maestroa simply.

Simon kicked his legs a few times, but found it was no use and so he stopped, instead swaying above them like a human chandelier. Marco's crown slipped from his head and fell to the ground, where it bounced with a clatter.

Simon gasped. "Is it broken?!"

"No." The Maestroa inspected it. "Though it isn't yours, so I don't see why you care."

Simon coughed quietly and tried to sound more noble. "Why, of course it is mine."

The Maestroa rolled their purple eyes. "Oh, drop it. I know you aren't a royal. What prince would wear his crown with that outfit?"

Simon looked down at his plain brown trousers and dirty boots swinging below his torso. He noticed for the first time there were a couple of small tears in his doublet.

"You're obviously some sort of peasant. A thief maybe."

"Thanks." Simon smirked.

"Though a terrible one, if that's so."

"Thanks." Simon frowned.

"I didn't think Isobel would care, really. She can't afford to be too choosy, can she?" The Maestroa glanced at the wooden soldiers, who laughed on their cue. When The Maestroa had enough, they cut the soldiers off with a wave of their hand. "So why did you come here? *How* did you come here?"

Simon wasn't sure how to answer that. He couldn't tell the truth, not now. "I . . . um . . . ?"

He looked at the soldiers, but all of their eyes were wide and eyebrows raised. One discreetly shook his head. He couldn't say they brought him here either.

"I wished to pillage and steal all the treasures I could find," he settled on. "Your lair was simply in my path."

The Maestroa considered this and Simon couldn't tell if they believed him or not. Finally, they shrugged.

"Well, that wasn't a very good story."

Simon furrowed his eyebrows at The Maestroa. "I'm sorry . . . ?"

"I shall tell you a better one."

The Maestroa waved their hand and the walls of the cavern were washed in blue light. Shadows faded into view. A castle, a tower really. Through the cut-out window, the silhouette of a girl in a crown peered out.

"Once upon a time." The Maestroa looked up at Simon with a grin. "Don't you just love that line?"

"It's, uh, my favorite," said Simon.

The Maestroa nodded, turned back to the shadows. "Once upon a time, there lived a beautiful princess who lived in a magnificent castle in the happiest kingdom there ever was. She wanted for nothing but the promise that one day she would be loved and love in turn. But alas, the young princess was cursed."

The shadows shifted and the tower fell away to reveal the princess bound, her arms held out to the side by a pair of strings. Above her, a hand controlled those strings to make the princess dance.

"She was cursed by a puppeteer to dance and entertain night and day, never to see her happy kingdom again." The Maestroa looked up. "Thoughts thus far?"

"I could use a little back story on the puppeteer." Simon raised an eyebrow.

The Maestroa twisted their nose up. "Then, one day, a young man found the princess."

The shadow of a suitor in a crown walked across the cavern wall. He threw his head back to indicate his surprise as he saw the princess.

"He fell in love the moment he saw her, with her beauty, her charm, and her grace." The Maestroa's voice softened, becoming more interested in the story itself than anything around them.

Simon cursed silently to himself for forgetting his dagger. He could easily be cutting himself down now.

"And so the young man vowed, then and there, that he would save her," continued The Maestroa. "And they could live happily ever after."

The blue light faded, the shadow show over.

"The beginning and the end," they said. "But what about the middle?"

"I don't follow," said Simon.

"It wouldn't be so easy." The Maestroa's eyes gleamed. "There would be many trials in between, I'm sure."

"I don't see why there has to be conflict." Simon shrugged. "Some tales should just be happy."

The Maestroa shook their head and took a step back.

"I'm afraid this isn't one of those tales, young man." They turned to go.

"Wait, don't leave! Let me down!" Simon shouted.

"Oh, there's nothing to be afraid of! It's just a fairy story." The Maestroa cackled and vanished in a cloud of purple fog.

The wooden soldiers marched away.

"Hey! Stop! Halt!" Simon called.

But they were gone, somewhere in the black shadows of the cavern, until the sound of their marching faded away completely.

Simon was alone, swaying twenty feet above the ground with no way to set himself loose, short of cutting the rope with his teeth. But that would take a terribly long time, and he couldn't stand the thought of rope scraping in his mouth. So, he did the only thing he could do. He closed his eyes and fell asleep, exhaustion finally winning.

He wasn't sure how long he slept. Only for a few moments, for soon the sound of thunder roused him.

Boom. Short little bursts of thunder that lasted only seconds at a time. *Boom.* One after another. *Boom.*

Simon opened his eyes. The thunder grew closer, coming from behind. He kicked one leg, trying to spin himself. But before he could complete the circle, a breeze picked up and blew him side to side as he heard a mighty whisper.

"*Looooot.*"

Simon turned his head, catching a glimpse of a large wooden face peering at him.

"*Looty-Loot,*" it said.

Simon screamed as a large wooden hand swatted at him, then the other, back and forth as though Simon were a ball on a string, something you'd use to entertain cats or dogs.

Thrusting his head back, he managed to spin around and found himself staring directly into the eyes of a wooden giant, as tall as Simon was high.

The giant's face pulled into a grin. He heaved a quiet laugh at Simon.

"*Looooot!*" he shouted, and Simon screamed again, for the giant reached up and wrapped his wooden hand around Simon's body and yanked Simon back and forth, the rope pulling tighter and tighter on Simon's chest so that he couldn't breathe.

The giant grunted and raised Simon high above his head before slamming him downward. This sent Simon's stomach flipping up into his throat, and the rope above broke from above, and now he was inside the giant's grip with nothing to catch him if he fell.

"Stop!" Simon shouted. "No!"

The giant tossed Simon back and forth between his palms, and Simon struggled to get away. The giant cupped his palms and Simon tumbled onto his knees, shaking, as the giant raised him to eye level.

Seeing the large eyes so close made Simon's blood curdle, and he stood, arms out, throwing his body into those eyes as hard as he could and clawed them with his fingers.

The giant let out a wail and moved his hands to rub his eyes, sending Simon plummeting down to the earth, screaming all the way. He hit against the knee of the giant's leg, and slid down his shin the rest of the way. He shot off the giant's foot and landed on the ground with a much softer thud than he'd feared seconds before.

He pushed himself up and ran into the shadows of the cavern, untying the rope around his chest and dropping it to the floor. He rounded a boulder and crouched.

With a deep but uneven breath, he peeked around to see the giant struggling to see, wailing and sobbing.

If he was going to escape, Simon had to do so right now. He looked around the cavern, trying to figure out his path. The wooden soldiers had marched out *that* way, he pointed with his mind. But the giant stood between him and the exit.

He'd have to be fast.

Simon might not have been the most agile of boys, and maybe he wasn't a very good thief. But all those years escaping guards and angry shop owners with his father and the bandits had made him a fast runner at least.

He bolted, pushing off the rock for momentum. As he neared the legs of the giant, its feet moved inward to block his path.

Simon dropped one leg and slid through the dirt and mounds of giant footprints. The heels of the giant slammed together just as he hit the other side, almost crushing Simon between them.

He continued toward the darkness.

Wood knocked against him, pushing him to the ground instantly, and the giant's hand had him once more.

Simon let out a yell and struggled against the hand, nearly getting out.

Nearly. If only he hadn't felt something jagged stab the back of his thigh.

He screamed.

The hand left him, and the giant wailed as another voice shouted.

"Bad Loot!" the voice scolded.. "Bad, *bad* Loot!"

Simon rolled onto his back and pulled his knee to his chest, holding the back of his thigh as he panted and held back tears of pain. When he pulled his hand away, it was wet with blood.

The giant's wail softened to a whimper. Softer footsteps now, and soon Simon looked up to see Princess Isobel standing above him.

"Are you alive?" she asked.

Simon grunted through his pain. "What kind of question is that?"

"You're talking, so yes, you're fine," she said and went back to the giant.

Simon forced himself to sit up a bit, and he saw that the giant was now sitting on the ground, wringing his hands as he cried. Isobel slapped his foot.

"You *should* be sorry!" she said. "That wasn't nice, Loot!"

"*Looty-looty-loot-loot*," the giant said, as though to explain himself. Isobel rubbed his foot, scratching here and there, and the giant giggled.

"Oh, I know, you're just so happy to play, aren't you," Isobel said in a voice so baby-ish and sweet that it made Simon's teeth hurt.

Finally, she looked to Simon, one painted eyebrow raised. She walked to him, fists on her hips. "I suppose I'll help you."

"You suppose?"

Without waiting, Isobel flipped Simon over and inspected his wound.

"Woah! How about, 'Please may I manhandle you'?" Simon asked.

"No time for that," Isobel said. "Looks like you've got a nasty splinter."

"*Looty-Loot.*" The giant sounded as though he were in mourning.

"It's all right, Loot," Isobel coddled the giant. "He knows it was an accident."

"I do?" questioned Simon.

"Yes," said Isobel with a pointed air. The argument was final. "Now, we've got to get that attended to before it's infected. Follow me, please."

Simon flipped back over and put his non-bloodied hand out to her. Isobel looked at it with surprise, as though she expected a flower to grow from his fingertips.

"Um, wanna help me stand?" hinted Simon, trying to hide his frustration.

"Oh!" Isobel rolled her eyes. She took his hand with tight lips and pulled him to his feet. "Yes. Sorry. I'm not used to helping others."

Hazard of being rich? Simon let himself think, but not say aloud.

"Are you able to walk?" Isobel asked. "If not, I can have Loot carry you."

"No!" Simon protested too loudly. The giant whimpered, so he added, "I mean, no thank you."

Isobel nudged Simon. "Tell him you like him."

"Excuse me?"

"He's sorry. Tell him it's all right."

"I will not. He almost killed me!"

"So?"

Simon raised an eyebrow at the princess. She replanted her fists on her hips firmly and cocked her head at him expectantly, as though to signal that this was a royal decree. Simon sighed and forced himself to face the giant. He looked up some twenty or so feet at the looming figure, who pathetically fumbled his hands together.

"Um—"

"Bow to him," whispered Isobel. "Show some respect."

Simon rolled his eyes, but forced himself to bow. The giant stopped fretting above him and looked down. Simon squinted up at him. Was the giant hopeful?

"I forgive you," said Simon. "Hope we can be friends."

The giant giggled, delighted, and clapped his hands. "*Loot.*"

"Now, was that so difficult?" Isobel asked.

"I think it was fair for me to be afraid—"

"Follow me, please."

Isobel headed to the darkness of the cavern, kissing her palm and waving it at Loot as she went. Simon awkwardly raised his bloody hand and waved it at the giant as well, who gave him a respectful nod.

Simon limped behind the princess through the darkness. As they passed through shadows, the breaths he took became laced with faded smells of long-gone aromas. Roasted hazelnuts and burning caramel.

Ahead, the early morning sunlight grew visible from behind a thin, fabric-like screen. Princess Isobel neared the screen and parted it. Simon blinked, surprised that not only *was* it fabric, but a tent flap.

He followed her out into the morning, and halted. They were standing in an entire compound of circus tents, all with different colored stripes, standing beneath strings of unlit lanterns. The Maestroa's showgrounds. He looked back at the flap to get a look at the cavern, but stared only at an ordinary tent, with stripes the color of smoke and stone. "But that was a—"

"It was theatre, thief." Isobel didn't stop walking, nor did she look back, nearing another tent, this one striped in pink and sparkling gold. "Sets and scenery. Please come inside."

She disappeared between the tent flaps.

Simon looked around himself, noting the high, ornately wrought gates that loomed over the showgrounds to keep out unwanted visitors.

Or, Simon thought, t*o keep visitors in.*

8. MAGIC AND GLASS

Once he passed through the tent flaps, Simon felt a bit disappointed. After learning the cavern had been inside a tent and it was all scenes, he expected to find something more magical or grand. Instead, he found a bedroom. Granted, a bedroom fit for a princess, with a large four-post bed that had pink velvet curtains hanging on its golden frame, a white marble fireplace, and a terrace with the view of a forest painted on canvas beyond the high gilded window.

But a bedroom, nonetheless.

Isobel plopped onto a sofa, as though she were the one with the injured leg, while Simon awkwardly leaned against the wall.

How can a tent have solid walls?

"Flora!" Isobel called. "Where are you?" After a moment with no response, Isobel sat up. "Flora!"

In shuffled a servant, and Simon had to prevent himself from crying out in surprise. The servant that

THE PRINCE AND THE PUPPET THIEF

entered was a young woman, probably around his and Isobel's age.

Yet, she was made entirely of glass. White porcelain and painted, to be exact. Like the figurines that usually got smashed in the shops his father robbed.

"You called?" Flora asked without enthusiasm.

"We need your help," Isobel said. "It seems the thief is injured."

Simon shrank under Flora's glare as she cast her eyes to him and cocked a painted eyebrow.

"Should he be here?"

"Probably not, but I don't see any way around it," Isobel said. "I need you to mend his leg before it gets infected."

"Yes, because I'm a nursemaid." Flora rolled her painted blue eyes.

"No, you're my handmaid, and I'm asking you to mend his leg." Isobel stood up and shot Flora a dramatic look. "It's so hard to find good help these days!"

Flora's lip twitched and her voice fell to a mumble. "I'm the best help you could ever have."

Isobel laughed and took Flora's hand. "I'm just kidding you. But really, I don't know how to nurse an injury and Loot plays so roughly. Can you do your best?"

"I can try," sighed Flora. "But I need him to quit gawking at me as though I were a fire breathing dragon."

Simon felt his jaw snap shut. "I'm sorry. I've just never seen—"

"A strong, independent woman?" snapped Isobel.

"I can handle myself." Flora slid her glass feet toward Simon. "A strong, independent woman?" she repeated.

"A *glass* woman," Simon corrected. "Actually, I've never seen most of what I've seen in the past hour."

Flora had come right upon Simon, and he didn't bother to stop her when she slid her arm beneath his armpit and forced him to lean on her. She helped him over to the sofa and threw him down, a stark contrast to the care she seemed to emit just seconds before.

"And for the record, just because I breathe fire, does not make me a dragon." She hissed after she said this, and laughed at Simon's intimidated expression. "Some brave bandit, eh Isobel?"

"Be nice." Isobel sat on the floor, fanning her skirts out with hinged fingers. "We're all stuck here together."

Simon tried not to gawk at the sight of bending glass as Flora managed to kneel next to the sofa.

"Where does it hurt?"

"You don't have to talk to me like I'm a little boy," said Simon.

"All right, then take it like a big strong man." Flora flipped Simon onto his stomach, ignored his grunt, and grabbed the large splinter. "This will hurt."

She yanked it from the back of Simon's thigh and ignored his shouts of pain.

"You're a regular saint, Flora." Isobel tried not to laugh.

"He'll be fine.".

"Will I, though? Will I be fine?" argued Simon.

"Shush." Flora stood and left the room. When she returned, she held a glass bottle filled with a glowing blue liquid and strips of bandages.

"What is it?" Simon looked at the bottle.

"Something that'll sting a lot," Flora replied as she knelt again. "And you better hold still."

The wound seared more pain through his body as Flora poured the liquid over Simon's leg without regard to how much she was using or that it soaked the back of his trouser leg. Finally, she put the bottle down and pressed the bandage into the wound, soaking it all back up.

"Could you maybe, I don't know, try to be gentle?"

"I haven't the energy, nor the care of your opinion," said Flora.

Simon didn't understand why this girl was being so rude or going out of her way to give him pain. Or Isobel, for that matter, who wasn't even looking, and seemed more interested in playing with her skirt hem between her thumb and forefinger.

I have to get out of here, Simon thought. *Just figure it out, take the money, and run to Lands Upper as fast as you can.*

"What is all this?" he asked.

"Bandages." Flora tied the last one more tightly than she needed to. "To stop the bleeding and help the wound close."

"No, I mean what is all *this*?" He gestured to the room around him as Flora pulled him up and sat him upright on the sofa. "Magic tents that have theatrical sets, and wooden princesses, and glass—" Flora snarled. "*Human* girls, who serve them? It's like, it's like . . . "

"Like a fairy tale?" Isobel finished for him, placing her skirt hem delicately back on the ground.

"Yes."

"That's because it is." Isobel stood and crossed to the bed. She sat at the edge of it and cocked her head at

Simon. "It's a fairy tale. A made-up, cliched, totally forced fairy tale. We all play a role in it."

"But why?"

Isobel shrugged. "Because The Maestroa decided, and that's all we get to know. I'm the cursed princess, Flora is my faithful handmaid, and you're an idiot for taking that message meant for my future husband. Because now you're the rogue who gets to battle it out." She let out a groan.

"Well don't sound *too* happy to have me," said Simon.

"Shush," Flora said for the second time. "She's merely taking a dramatic pause."

"You were supposed to be Marco!" whined Isobe. "Not-not-Bloody Fingers! What is your real name, anyway?"

"Nicobar," Simon said, taking private glee that his father wasn't there to stop him from revealing his real name instead of Simon's own. "Nicobar Holt, if you please."

"Well, Mr. Holt, you ruined it all."

"How?"

"Because you're not Marco." Isobel couldn't help but laugh. "So much for the whole 'true love's kiss' angle."

"Ah, but it's some good old-fashioned spite," said Simon. "That would stick it to the old magician."

"Don't you get it?" Isobel stood. "They made it so that I have to fall for some man who comes along and finds me pretty and helpless-and—" she gagged, "in distress."

Flora went to Isobel and patted her hand gently.

Nice to see she can care if she tries, thought Simon.

"There's still hope," said Flora. "There's some sort of way."

"Have you ever considered escape?" Simon asked.

"Did Loot drop you on your head?" Isobel rolled her eyes to the ceiling. "Of course I have."

"I'm not an idiot," said Simon, more defensively than he wanted to. "You're making it really hard for me to feel sorry for you, you know."

"She doesn't need your pity," Flora snapped. "If you want to escape, go on, escape! We'll do just fine on our own!"

"I can't do that," said Simon. "I'm here on behalf of the prince. I can't leave without you."

"Why not?" asked Isobel.

Because then I don't have any hope of a pardon, and I refuse to die because you're a brat. Simon couldn't let himself say this out loud, so he chose to stay quiet.

When he didn't respond, Isobel answered for him. "Money, I suppose." Simon shrugged. "Well, we won't come. I can't be seen this way."

She threw herself down on the bed and cried. Flora leaned over and rubbed her shoulder.

"You look fine," she said.

"No I don't, I'm a lump of pine!" whined Isobel.

Simon stood. "All right, that's enough."

He sauntered towards the bed, ignoring how the wound stung.

"How dare you use that tone, peasant!" Flora snapped.

"Shush!" said.

"I don't shush, *you* shush," said Flora.

"I'm a mirror, reflect what I do." Simon pretended to zip his lips closed.

Flora gasped. "Is that a glass joke?"

"I have no stake in this whatsoever, I'm just trying to survive. So you're both going to sit and deal while I do what I need to in order to get out of this whole mess. You're going to get reunited with your corner-cutting prince, whether you want to be or not, and then I am going home, where I'm going to reflect on my mistakes and decide what vocation to try my hand at instead, so I can just be free and content, because that's what I want. Good? Good."

The princess and the glass girl protested, but they'd been so stunned by Simon's speech that they didn't realize he'd grabbed the bedsheets as he spoke, and they found themselves rolled up inside like a carpet before they could escape. After tying the end closed, Simon crossed his arms and looked proudly at the bundle, containing a now stolen puppet and her trusty, if rude, handmaid. Sadly, Flora would have to come along.

He grabbed the end of the bundle and pulled them from the bed.

"Careful, or I'll shatter!" screamed Flora.

"Oh, darn, what a pity that would be," Simon grumbled as he dragged them to the curtain flap.

"Unhand us! You rogue! You villain!" Isobel cried regally.

Simon began to protest but paused. Isobel's voice had changed, growing higher in pitch, and now he knew why she screamed when he tried to kidnap her earlier. It wasn't because she was afraid of him. It's because she was

THE PRINCE AND THE PUPPET THIEF

playing the part. Princess kidnapped by a bandit, of course she would scream.

But that was also a quick way to call The Maestroa down.

He knelt and whispered, "Do you want the magician to come?"

Isobel paused. "No."

"Then act like you're being saved or something. Or just be quiet. That would be an interesting part of the story."

Isobel groaned. "I don't like you."

"All right." Simon dragged them through the tent flap, ignoring the fountain of four-lettered words that Flora spouted from within the bundle.

But outside the tent, Simon halted, his heart picking up pace. The soldiers marched toward them, wooden swords pointed. He looked about, but everywhere there were only tents, more scenes, more trials to find himself in. He had to get out of whatever place this was. Out of The Maestroa's grip. They'd have to brave the forest.

He dragged the bundle around the back of the tent as quickly as he could, the muscles in his arms burning, and noted he would need to do more push-ups once he returned home.

The gate loomed behind the tent. He looked left, the gate continued on, wrapping around the tents like a jail cell. He looked right and still it continued on. Except for —*a ha!* Simon saw an opening in the gate. The exit, curtained in purple velvet. He resumed dragging the bundle as the wooden soldiers marched around the tent.

"Halt!" a soldier ordered. "You can't do that!"

Simon ignored him and kept on toward the curtain.

"No! Not there!" warned the soldier. "Don't!"

Simon was right at the curtain now.

"Men, prepare to spear!" ordered the soldier and they all held their swords high.

Simon had to be fast, or a splinter in his thigh was the least of injuries he'd need to worry about.

"This is almost too easy," he said as he dragged the wooden princess and her glass handmaid through the curtain just as the soldiers threw their swords.

9. FORTUNES

If Marco were given a choice of who to take on a quest with him, Hans the servant would not have been that choice. He hadn't even known his name until a few hours before, and so far he wasn't so impressed with Hans' personality, if indeed he even had one.

But he had to take *someone*, mainly because Marco couldn't carry everything himself, and especially because King Anders only allowed him to take one of the horses.

And so he rode across the drawbridge on Apollo, a white steed. Marco was already getting annoyed with this horse, because he kept swaying his long neck left to right, as though he were trying to hear every sound. Or maybe because he just couldn't walk straight.

Hans clung on, his gangly arms wrapped tight around Marco's waist, trying hard not to cry out in fear whenever Apollo swayed.

Whenever he did, Marco's satchel, carrying fruit, bread, and the jeweled engagement slippers, threatened to slip from his shoulder and into the moat.

"Will you be still?!" Marco shouted.

Hans yelped with fright. "I am sorry, sire! I have never ridden a horse before!"

"Never?"

"Too frightened, sire," explained Hans. "They always look at me as though I were an apple to gnaw on, and I very much wish never to be gnawed upon."

"Well, if you don't hold still I'll make certain that you get gnawed upon," Marco promised.

Hans gulped. "Very well, sire."

He squeezed Marco's waist even tighter, and now Marco could hardly breathe. But at least the servant held still, so he didn't say anything more about it.

Peasants cheered as they passed, and Marco smiled and waved with all the charm he could manage. He felt exhausted, having paced his balcony all night, and didn't much feel like putting on an image. Duty never takes a break when you're wearing a crown.

Once they had trotted down half the main cobblestone street of the kingdom, Hans loosened his grip and sat up tall.

"Oh, I believe I shall get used to this, sire!" he said. "The beast has gnawed upon nary a finger."

"Same."

"Truly, sire?"

"Yes, we're practically twins." Marco rolled his eyes.

He could feel the heat from Hans' face as he blushed.

"Oh, sire, really," he said. "So, what do we do now?"

"Have you kept an eye out for the fugitive?" asked Marco.

"Yes, sire, of course," Hans replied. "One eye to be

exact. I've had the other one closed out of fear, you see, but my other eye hasn't even blinked for fear of missing him. But now that eye is quite dry and I haven't seen anyone who appears to be a fugitive."

"He doesn't look much like a fugitive," said Marco, trying to make himself sound less impatient. "He's just a normal looking boy."

"Normal looking?"

"He doesn't look like he's capable of stealing anything," explained Marco. "Very innocent looking. About my age, I think."

"You think?"

"Well, I didn't stop to check any birth records while setting him free." Marco's impatience won over. "He's just a sweet looking guy."

Hans paused. "Sweet looking?"

Marco coughed and said, in a deeper tone, "As in mannerly."

"I wasn't insinuating—"

"Of course you weren't."

"My uncles give wonderful dinner parties."

"What?"

"They play the pianoforte and allow all of us to wear their fashionable hats once we've had too much grog."

Marco pulled the reins so that Apollo halted. He turned his head to look at Hans as well as he could. "You've been going to parties and not inviting me?"

Hans widened his eyes and blushed again. "Oh no, sire! I mean yes, sire! I mean— Oh!" He yelped and tried not to cry. "I never thought you might enjoy my uncles' dinner parties!"

"Hans, I'm just messing with you!"

Hans winced and cried out in emotional agony. "Well, if you continue to frighten me, then I shall mess *myself!*"

Marco narrowed his eyes. "Don't. You. Dare."

Hans winced, and re-closed his left eye while the other went back to watching the streets. Marco jiggled the reins and Apollo resumed his trot, swaying left and right. It was all beginning to make Marco feel dizzy.

"Sire," Hans began timidly after a long silence. "I've never been on a quest before. What do we do exactly?"

"What do we do?" Marco asked with offense. "We . . . well, we . . . you know. We, um . . . we quest!"

"We quest, sire?"

"Yes of course. Anyone knows that you quest on a quest."

"I suppose, sire, that I don't understand what questing is."

"It's when you go on a quest."

"To do what?"

"To quest!"

Marco urged the horse onward, feeling the shame creep inside his stomach. Really, he had no idea where to go or what to do. He'd never even been to the grocer, much less on a quest for a lost princess and an escaped prisoner. If he were going to a party, or off to the tavern to flirt and drink until dawn, he'd be right at home. This was new, and it filled him with the feeling of being very small. He knew that compared to other princes, he wasn't much of a leader in the making. He desperately wanted a drink right about now.

THE PRINCE AND THE PUPPET THIEF

He looked around for something, anything, to give him a sign.

"There!" He pointed. "That's where we go."

Hans peeked over Marco's shoulder and looked with one dry, red eye. "There, sire? Are you quite sure?"

"Yes!" Marco said and steered Apollo off the cobblestone street to a large circus tent that stood in the alleyway.

Outside hung a sign that read in looped scrawl:

FORTUNES, SECRETS, BITTER TRUTHS. YOUR JOURNEY BEGINS HERE.

Below that was the painting of a purple eye, under which was scrawled *MADAME CALUMNIA WAITS*.

"That's who we must speak with," declared Marco and he alighted from Apollo, tethering him to a discarded crate.

"Madame Cal-um-nee-ah?" Hans sounded it out. "Is that the fugitive?"

"No, the fugitive is a male." Marco rolled his eyes.

"Oh, right." Hans held tightly to Apollo, looking between the saddle beneath him and the ground. "Um, sire? Could you-um-possibly . . . "

Marco sighed and reached up to Hans, grabbed him under his noodle-like arms and pulled him from the horse. Hans yelped as he tumbled downward, but Marco caught him under his armpits and stood him upright.

"Thank you, sire." Hans let out a deep breath.

Marco approached the entrance to the tent. The faint smell of herbs and caramel pushed into his nose as he parted the flap. He crossed inside and fell over a round table covered in purple cloth. He caught himself on a dusty crystal ball. Frantically, he pushed himself from the table and his head knocked against the lantern, sending it swaying and washing the tent in the ghostly light of its green flame.

Can fire even be green? thought Marco, readjusting his crown.

"Hark, do I hear a stranger approach?" a low voice called in the shadows. From behind a long white sheet, Madame Calumnia entered. A long silk scarf wrapped around her head, containing her hair. She wore a series of necklaces and chains, with so many rings upon her fingers that Marco could hardly see the flesh beneath. But what kept drawing him in were her eyes, which seemed to glow purple in the dim light.

"Oh my." She cooed at the sight of Marco and swept a low curtsy. "And to what do I owe such a pleasure, Your Highness?"

Marco eyed the odd objects around the tent, the crystal ball and shelf of bottles filled with liquids of strange glowing colors.

"I need some information, Madame," Prince Marco said, turning on his 'royal' voice with ease.

Madame Calumnia grinned. "The prince needs my other-worldly services?"

"I can pay you, if you can do as you promise," responded Marco.

With a flourish of her wrist, Madame Calumnia swept the back of her hand to her forehead. "Yes, yes, I believe I can feel the spirits stirring even now. Please, gentlemen, sit down. Hurry, hurry, before the spirits have gone."

She came to the table and sat in a large throne-like

chair with a tall backrest, carved with the faces of wolves and ravens. Marco took a seat on a plain stool next to Hans, who simply sat on his knees, brushing the dirt from his kneecaps.

Madame Calumnia inspected the crystal ball. She eyed the hand print in the dust and looked at Marco with suspicion. But when he opened his mouth to explain, she waved his words away and blew the remainder of the dust away.

She swept her hands around the ball until a fog the color of green apples appeared within. Marco tensed. He'd never seen magic before. He half expected the ball to remain as it was. For this woman to be a crook. Yet there she was, conjuring fog and making the lantern flicker above her, the flame going in, and out, and in.

Finally, Marco yawned.

"My fortune telling is too boring for his royal highness?" Madame Calumnia asked with strained sweetness.

"I don't go much for magic," joked the prince. "To be honest I'm just really tired."

Reaching to the shelves behind her, Madame Calumnia rummaged until she came upon a round, long necked bottle filled with pale yellow liquid.

"Drink this." She handed it to Marco.

He swirled the bottle, watching the liquid sparkle. He wasn't sure if he ought to drink a potion from a strange fortune teller, but he also wasn't one to turn down a drink. Uncorking it with a pop, he guzzled it down.

His eyes blinked rapidly, and his muscles twitched and pulled. A chill erupted on his flesh, and he sat up straight.

"How do you feel?" asked Madame Calumnia.

"Like I slept for days," said Marco, wide-eyed.

"Rise and shine." Madame Calumnia nodded. "Shall we?"

She leaned to the ball, but when Marco joined, she gently pressed her fingers to his forehead and pushed him back. "Not too close, Your Highness. It may blind your royal blue eyes."

"What do you see?" he asked. "The thief?"

Madame Calumnia's eyebrow twitched, some faint recognition drawn as she gazed. "The thief? Yes, oh yes, the thief. He is in the forest."

"These forests of Incantus?" asked Marco.

"No, no, *the* forest. The forest of wishes, just beyond *these* forests," Madame Calumnia almost whispered. "The forest of tales and of dreams come true."

"I don't get it."

"That's because you're a stupid boy who can't believe what's right in front of you," snapped Madame Calumnia.

Marco began to stand. "Excuse me?"

"Oh, nothing! Nothing," Madame Calumnia explained, blinking quickly. "I cannot control what the spirits of truth say, Your Highness. They speak through me."

Marco was hesitant to be convinced, but he sat back down. "Continue."

"Sire, should we really be dabbling in magic?" Hans whispered, "One of my uncles dabbled in it once, and now his right hand cannot stop making shadow puppets. It's entertaining, but his hand is always cramped, and I couldn't bear eternal hand cramps."

"Shh." Marco didn't look over.

"But sire—"

"He said 'shh', you wart!" snapped Madame Calumnia. "I mean-I mean-Yes. I see, in your future, both of you-a journey's end. A happy end. Yes, all shall come to a happy end. Truth shall be revealed."

"What of the thief?"

"The thief shall be found, you shall see him plain."

"What of my betrothed?"

"Your betrothed?"

"The lost Princess Isobel, what of her?"

Madame Calumnia's eyes lit up at this. "Oh. Yes. Yes, she shall be found."

"How do I get them back?" Marco asked.

Madame Calumnia's eyes rolled back into her head and moaned, frantically wagging her tongue. She waved her arms above her head. The sight unnerved Marco, and caused Hans to cry like a child requesting his mommy.

Finally, Madame Calumnia spoke. "True love shall conquer all. And all shall come to a happy end."

The fog in the crystal ball made the shape of a valentine heart. After a short moment, it burst, returning to its cloudy form. The lights ceased flickering and Madame Calumnia stood. "I take cash only."

Marco reached into the inner pocket of his jacket and produced a few coins, dropping them into the fortune teller's open palm.

"Thank you, big spender." Madame Calumnia cringed at the paltry amount. She removed one of her necklaces, a plain string that carried a small sachet of what seemed to be herbs. She tossed it to Hans. "That will protect you."

Hans looked at the sachet curiously before putting it around his neck. "Thank you?"

"So, where exactly is this forest, Madame?" asked Marco asked.

Madame Columnia laughed. "Just outside, dears."

She reached for the white sheet and pulled it back to reveal a large hole in the tent. Beyond it, they could see trees and shrubs, so green and bright that both Hans and Marco couldn't help but say "*Ooooooh.*"

A white horse trotted past the hole.

"Apollo!" Prince Marco stood. "He's gotten loose. Come on, Hans."

"Right away, Sire."

"Take heed, and be careful, your highness!" Madame Calumnia called out.

Marco turned to ask the fortune teller to repeat herself, but the tent was gone. He rubbed his eyes and looked again. The entire kingdom had vanished, replaced by thick forest all around them. Somewhere ahead, he heard Apollo galloping.

"Oh, sire," said Hans, his voice trembling. "This can't be right. What fortune teller possesses such power?"

"Shh." Marco dropped his own voice to a whisper. "First rule of quests- always have your bearings." *Or so I assume*, he didn't add aloud.

He looked from tree to tree. Trunks of green, gray, and blue shrouded in milky fog. This wasn't like the forest surrounding Incantus, where the trees were all brown and you could see hundreds of feet ahead. This forest was more like one he'd seen in a storybook in his library at home. He didn't read as a rule, but he enjoyed the

THE PRINCE AND THE PUPPET THIEF

pictures, and he remembered that this wasn't the sort of forest you wanted to find yourself in.

"And to answer your question," whispered Marco, "I don't think that was any ordinary fortune teller."

Hans adjusted the sachet of herbs around his neck, which had become tangled with his fidgeting. "You don't reckon."

"What?"

"Nothing, sire," said Hans.

Ahead, Apollo neighed.

"Apollo?" called out Marco. "Come here, buddy!" He whistled, but the horse did not come.

"Apollo," Marco called again. "Apollo!"

He laid a hand to his belt, but the sword wasn't there. Of course he'd hitched it to the horse along with everything else. He wasn't even armed in this strange place.

"I really don't know what I'm doing," he admitted.

"Honesty is a virtue, sire," Hans offered, shuffling his feet.

Finally, Prince Marco straightened his back and began walking toward the sounds of his horse. "Well, come on then, we have to get Apollo sooner or later."

He walked through the trees, taking care to walk in a straight line should he need to backtrack. Hans stumbled along behind him, mumbling under his breath about mud and worms.

Through the fog, Marco made out the shape of the horse in the distance, and he quickened his step.

Almost there. He cupped his hand to call out once more, and—

He tripped over something large and fell to the

ground. Hans sounded a soprano's scream, and then he too tumbled down, landing on Marco.

"Get off!" Marco tried pushing Hans from him, but whatever they'd tripped over wrapped around his left ankle and pulled. Marco sat up the best he could to see that it was the root of a tree, moving and slithering like the body of a great snake.

A branch bent above them, the twigs tangled into something like a large hand, pulling both prince and servant into the air and swinging them around.

"Sire!" screamed Hans. "Oh, sire! Save me! Save me!"

"I have to save myself before I can do that!" Marco shouted. "Put me down-uh-tree!"

But the tree continued to swing them around, so that their stomachs flipped with each drop.

"I-I-Oh!" cried Hans. "I don't think these trees fall under the jurisdiction of your crown, sire!"

Prince Marco struggled against the tree's grip, but it was no use. It had him caught, digging into the brocade of his jacket. His crown fell to the ground and bounced with a sickening crack as it broke in half.

All the blood rushed to his head and he felt faint. Just as everything began to go black, he heard the rebel yell of some unseen assailant.

Something sliced at the tree branches and he cried out, afraid he would get stabbed by whatever, or whoever, had shown up. For a moment, he thought he could hear the boughs of the tree groan with pain. The grip of the branches loosened, and Marco shoved his arms upward and pulled himself free.

He went tumbling down, narrowly missing the points

of his own crown as he landed with a thud on the dirt below. Hans screamed, and then he too fell, landing in a shrub.

Marco stared dumbly at Hans, who stared dumbly ahead, unblinking, his hands and feet shaking violently.

Finally, Hans spoke, quietly. "I . . . hate . . . quests."

And then he fainted.

In front of Marco, a hand lowered, offering to help him stand. Marco reached out and took it, pulled himself to his feet against the lightly muscled arm.

"Thank you," said Marco breathlessly. "But if you're only going to turn around and rob or kill me now, at least give me warning so I can try to run."

"Robbing you didn't work out well the first time," said his rescuer.

Marco lifted his gaze and locked eyes on the thief.

"So I guess, since options are limited, I'll just kill you." Simon winked.

10. STOLEN HEARTS

Simon held the sword as steadily as he could, but his hands still shook. He'd never battled a fighting tree before, and he had never rescued a prince. Especially the same one who had released him from the dungeon only hours before.

Just be cool and collected, he thought. *Stay cool.*

For a second, he watched a smirk break across Marco's face, but as soon as it had appeared, it disappeared, replaced by a frown and raised eyebrows.

"All right. Easy now," said Marco. "We can work it out! I promised your freedom. What else do you want? More money? More jewels? I have a gold encrusted bed.

That alone could buy you a castle in the southern islands."

Simon wasn't sure if this was a joke, so he pushed the sword a little closer. When Marco winced, he let out at a laugh and lowered the sword.

So I can be intimidating.

"I'm joking with you."

Marco sighed. "Not funny."

"Good thing that horse ran amok too, or I wouldn't have been able to cut you down. And I'm glad to see you *can* come out of that castle." Simon impaled the sword in the dirt and leaned cavalierly on the handle, trying to seem at ease and confident. "I thought I'd have to drag the princess all the way to you myself."

"Wait, you mean you've found Isobel?"

Simon slipped from the sword and stumbled backwards. He hoped Marco didn't notice him blushing as he straightened his stance. "More like I was set upon by her."

Marco raised an eyebrow. "See. A bit of a pain, isn't she?"

Simon cocked his head. "Must be a royals thing."

Marco opened his mouth to retort when Hans jumped from the shrub behind Simon and wrapped his arms tightly around him.

"Citizens arrest! Citizens arrest!" Hans wailed. "You'd do best to hold still and give back His Highness' sword. I might be weak, but I can dish out quite a stinging slap when I've a mind!"

Simon looked to the prince for help.

"Hans, no." Marco put his hands out in protest. "Let him go!"

"But sire," said Hans said. "This delinquent attacked you!"

"Let him go."

"Ah, you wish to rough him up? Yes sire, that would be quite good. Really bloody up his nose so that he can't smell his porridge for a week. That'll show him."

Simon watched Marco snap his fingers and point to

the ground, as though commanding a yappy dog. "Down, Hans."

With a wince, Hans stepped back. Simon rubbed his arms, surprised to find that his circulation had been cut off. "That's quite a grip, sir."

"Why thank you, delinquent." Hans blushed. "I do ten push-ups every morning, luncheon, and eve."

"So where is she?" asked Marco.

With a cringe, Simon rubbed the back of his neck. "Ah, yes. About that. Well, like I said, she was very, shall we say, obstinate?"

Simon pulled the sword from the ground and pointed to the large white sheet tied into a sack, which squirmed and writhed on the ground.

Simon looked back at Marco to survey his reaction and found him laughing.

"Resourceful!"

Marco went to the sack and untied the top. The sheet cascaded down to reveal Isobel and Flora struggling inside. The glass girl was unable to stand and so Isobel helped her, pulling her up with her own string. She tossed the wooden cross over her shoulder like a scarf and stared Marco down.

"Princess," said Simon, adopting a noble voice. "May

I present His Royal Highness, Prince Marco."

Isobel narrowed her stare. Marco coughed, sizing the princess up with a look of both intrigue and what seemed to be nerves. He bowed. "Your Highness. You look so . . . what a lovely hairdo."

He was on the ground clutching his jaw two seconds

later. Isobel had wasted no time in giving him a hard punch.

"What was that for?!" Marco winced.

"For being an arrogant, lazy, no-good son of a—"

"Watch what you say about my mother," Marco cut her off. "Or do you mean my father, because if that's the case—"

"How could you just leave me to rot?!"

"I think you broke my jaw." Marco pushed himself up to stare her down, still rubbing his face. "What are you made of, anyways? Oak? Cherrywood?"

Isobel shrieked and balled her hands into fists again. Flora came forward and rammed her head against Marco's chest, sending him to the ground once more.

"Yow!" yelped Marco. "Ah, Flora, how I've missed you."

The glass girl stood proudly. "You'll notice that my head is four times harder now, so watch what you say."

"Are royals always like this?" Simon looked at Hans.

"Oh yes, delinquent," said Hans. "I have to admit, I was enjoying the quiet that their unfortunate separation had brought."

Simon looked back to Isobel and Marco, where their bickering had grown even louder.

"You don't really care about me, do you?!" screamed Isobel. "So long as you get a nice *cushy* dowry and a nice *cushy* throne, and get to still go out to taverns and pinch plump *cushy* wenches and drink grog—"

"I don't pinch wenches—"

"Without any responsibility! I suppose you think I'll just run the kingdom when we marry—"

"You can have it, I don't want it."

"I wouldn't take it from you if you begged me!"

"I never beg as a rule."

"Unless it's for your life."

Simon tried to interject. "Excuse me."

"What did you call me?!"

"Excuse me," Simon tried again.

"I seem to recall we mutually agreed upon naming our first-born William."

"*Hello!*" Simon shouted as loudly as he could. The prince and princess stopped their bickering, looking to Simon with wide eyes, as though they had forgotten anyone else were around.

Taking a step back, Simon continued. "Wow. This is beautiful, it really is, seeing lovers reunite after all this time. Just warms my little heart. But it seems my mission here is done, and I do hate to be a third wheel. So if you'll excuse me, I'll just go home, and— "

"Stop, thief." Flora slid forward, her fists on her hips. "You're not going anywhere."

"Quite right." Hans joined the glass girl in taking Simon by the arms to hold him still. "You're still under arrest and overdue for your dawn appointment."

"What?" Simon looked to Marco.

"No, Hans, we'll pardon him." Marco shook his head.

"Oh, thank heavens," sighed Hans. "I just abhor executions. All that blood, and grown men crying, and, and blood, and crying—"

"Shut up, Hans."

"Yes, sire."

Flora tightened her grip on Simon's arm. "You got us into this mess, and I don't clean messes that I don't make."

"Well, you clean mine," said Isobel. "But that's beside the point."

"*Way* beside it," said Flora.

Marco shook his head and rubbed his temples. "I don't get it. What even are you, Flora?"

"I'm your betrothed's handmaid. You might have seen me make a bed or two, as well."

"Yes, I know that," Marco's voice raised, but dropped again as he gestured to Flora's glass body. "What I mean is, what *are* you?"

"I'm a glass figurine."

"Why?"

"Oh, trying a new look. Does it work for me?"

Isobel stepped toward Marco. "We've been transformed. If you haven't noticed, I'm a marionette."

Marco smirked at her. "I wasn't going to be rude and point it out, but since you've said it . . . Yes, you are."

Isobel grunted. "What a charmer."

Simon spoke up. "It isn't polite to have a lover's quarrel in front of company."

"We're not lovers!" both Isobel and Marco shouted at once.

"Then at least stop arguing."

Isobel huffed. "Then tell the prince to stop being an ass."

"Tell the princess to stop being a royal brat."

Simon struggled in Flora's and Hans' grip. "I'll tell you both exactly what you can do if you don't unhand me and let me go on my way."

"Not before you return us to where you found us," said Flora.

Simon couldn't help but laugh. "What? You were prisoners of a magician! You ought to be thanking me for getting you out of there. And quite daringly, I'll add."

Isobel shook her head. "I wouldn't be so sure we're away from The Maestroa."

"Do you see any crazed puppeteers?" Simon asked, turning his head each way.

"Does this look like a normal forest to you?" Isobel gestured to the trees. "We're still in their world. Their theatre. Their weird, twisted little tale."

"But I got through the gates!"

"A curtained gate?"

Simon didn't respond. He rolled his eyes and looked down at his feet. Of course it couldn't be so easy. How had he not realized it could never be that easy? He'd fallen into the same half-baked schemes as those of his father, and he cursed himself silently for it.

"Sire," began Hans, and Simon noted that his grip loosened beneath trembling fingers. "Didn't we pass through a curtain to get here?"

Everyone looked to Marco.

"Yes," he said. "Well, technically it was a sheet, but we were only talking to a fortune teller."

Flora cocked an eyebrow. "A fortune teller with purple eyes?"

Hans released Simon's arm and put his hands to his mouth with a gasp. Simon took the opportunity to jerk the other arm free of Flora, and he threw his hands up. "All right then, we're still trapped. So let's penetrate the forest and find our way out."

"I can't get out." Isobel shook her head. "I can't go into the real world and be seen like this."

"Are you serious?" Simon could scream. "I'd think being safe would be more important than how you look."

"You've got me all figured out don't you?" Isobel snapped her eyes to Simon. "Poor little princess, worried about my looks and getting some man to save me. I can't live in the real world, genius, I'm an enchanted marionette!" She waved her strings in Simon's face. "I take one step into my kingdom and zap! Puppet. No soul! No moving, no talking. I need my spell broken."

"All right." Simon sighed. "My apologies. So how do we break the spell?"

Flora puckered her lips. "True love's kiss."

Simon turned to Marco. "Well, be a good man and kiss your betrothed."

"I always admired your housework," Hans said to Flora. "I could channel that and peck you."

"*Men.*" Flora slid away from Hans in disgust.

"Is that it?" asked Marco. "A kiss to break the spell?"

Isobel nodded. "Yes, but it's more than that. It has to be the kiss of true love, none of that copping out with pretending, or It won't work."

Simon noted how Marco's shoulder's tensed at this.

The prince let out a tiny cough and stepped back.

"Ah, I see. Well . . . "

"I got the hint when you didn't come yourself." Isobel rolled her eyes. "We're a by-product of an archaic marriage system. There's another way, but it's a lot riskier."

Marco played with his fingers, lacing them together. "I don't really do risk."

Isobel's fingers pulled into fists. "Yes, I learned that when you sent this bumbler instead of coming yourself." Simon opened his mouth to defend himself, but Isobel continued on. "The Maestroa has my heart. Flora's, too. If we get our hearts back, we can get out of here."

"Oh, is that all?" Simon rolled his eyes.

"I think I know where The Maestroa keeps the hearts," continued Isobel. "They're always wearing a strange amulet. I think they're in there. Like a locket."

Simon guffawed. "So you want me to steal something, not just *from* The Maestroa, but *off* The Maestroa?"

Flora tilted her head. "What, pickpocketing isn't on your vast list of skills?"

"We have to go back to The Maestroa," said Isobel.

"But I just dragged you *away* from The Maestroa," said Simon.

"Well, you didn't give me a chance to explain that!"

Simon swept half of a bow to Marco. "Well, your highness, it seems your work is cut out for you. I've returned the princess to you, and now you can begin stealing hearts, and I can find my way out. Thank you and good day!"

He spun around to make his exit, but Flora cut him off.

"Stop trying to escape." She narrowed her eyes at him. "What do you even want with me?" asked Simon. "I'm useless! And I don't plan on finding true love, so . . . " He caught eyes with Marco and quickly looked away.

Isobel threw her hands up. "Useless? You are Bloody Fingers! Fierce bandit! If anyone can steal those hearts for us, it is you!"

"I-I'm . . . " Simon stammered. He'd nearly forgotten his lie.

"You're Bloody Fingers?" Marco raised an eyebrow. "*You?*"

Simon coughed and lowered his voice. "Yes, I am Bloody Fingers. The most feared villain in the kingdom of Incantus."

"Second most feared," corrected Flora. "And why do you always drop your voice when you say that?"

"Dramatic effect," squeaked Simon. "But really, you don't want me to do that. I'm a terrible thief, and I . . . "

He stopped talking. Everyone was looking at him, and all of them had the same expression that any good person can never deny- the look of hope.

Simon's eyes fell to Marco, and he sensed something in the prince's eyes, some sort of gleam that made his stomach feel light and even hopeful itself. The prince looked impressed.

Simon had never impressed anyone before, and he already felt a bit drunk on the feeling it gave him.

With a sigh, Simon bowed, deeply. "All right. A heart thief. I'm your man."

He hoped they didn't notice him gulp. Hard.

11. ENTER THE VILLAIN

There had been a time, though it was long before now, that The Maestroa genuinely believed in fairy tales. They believed in the happy endings. Their childhood had, as had many childhoods before, as had many childhoods after, been spent poring over the pages of storybooks, their world colored in by magic, wonder, and romance. Handsome princes and witty damsels. Dragons that breathed fire across the page. Of clocks that tolled midnight, maidens running barefoot through the guts of pumpkins. They relished the satisfaction at the end of each tale, before turning the page and entering the dangers of the next.

They wanted all the world to be a fairy tale. A stage for that magic and wonder. They still did.

But when they arrived back at the show grounds, they didn't believe in happy endings anymore. What they believed in was revenge.

The heat of anger burned through them as they tore through the flap of their tent, into their workroom where dreams came true with a drop of paint and a toss of glitter.

They ripped off the headscarf and the necklaces. Not their best disguise, but one clever enough to fool a man. They'd planned to trap him in the forest. What they hadn't planned on was seeing the thief stumbling through their forest with their prized marionette and glass figure wrapped in a bed sheet.

Well, they would just have to start rewriting the story, wouldn't they?

They crossed their workshop, stepping over discarded rose-colored ribbons and lifeless arms of unmade marionettes, to the miniature theater that stood atop a black table. The proscenium, with its ornate frame of sirens and fairies, defined the picture around the purple curtains. They tore them back.

The stage was not how they'd left it.

It was supposed to be the wooden princess, levitating above the stage by her strings, with a handsome prince in her arms, twirling in the moonlight. It was a romantic tableau. An expected one.

Instead, they found their wooden princess and glass handmaid plopped lifelessly on the stage boards, forest scenery draped carelessly behind them, the canvas wrinkled. They were unknowing of how the story was supposed to play out. What could happen next.

This isn't what we agreed upon, Isobel, thought The Maestroa.

They wrinkled their nose at the discarded, lifeless puppets. So uncontrolled. Apathetic, both of them. It would never do.

The Maestroa crossed to their worktable where the shelf of blank, genderless pine heads sat in pigeonholes, gawking out with button eyes at their maker. They plucked a head down, attached it with force to a wooden body.

They went to a small, black trunk, and rummaged through the miniature costumes until they found a shirt and jacket, a pair of trousers. They took it back to the table and dressed the body. A slap of paint on the head to make a timid expression, a splotch of hair, and they'd made the fretting manservant that they'd seen in the fortune teller tent not even an hour before. They tossed him to the stage.

Another head plucked, another lifeless body attached. They fumbled through the jackets until they came upon their favorite costume, one they had been saving since this all began. The one fit for a prince, the brocaded jacket and well-fitting breeches, shiny little boots that reflected The Maestroa's grin. They plucked a little crown from a compartment of the trunk.

It pained them to snap the crown in half, but they couldn't help that the trees had damaged the true prince's crown, and they had to be accurate for it to work. The crown landed in two pieces on the stage, along with the puppet Marco's body. Its head bounced as it landed, the stupid smirk never wavering.

"Now for *you*."

The Maestroa's hands shook as they snatched the final head from its pigeonhole. This one needed extra care. They worked diligently, wrapped their fingers through reddish brown strands of doll hair, until it held the waves they first thought to be charming. Almost scampish. Now, they just wanted to yank those locks from his scalp.

With a small brush dipped in black, they painted the face. The eyebrows slanted with sarcasm and confusion. The infuriating, naive gleam in the eyes. A mouth that constantly looked embarrassed.

The Maestroa altered the little green doublet themselves, attaching the hood to the back.

"M-Maestroa?" the voice of the gruff wooden soldier pulled them from their focus.

"What do you want?!" The Maestroa snapped their gaze back at the soldier, their purple eyes nearly a shade of scarlet.

"The prisoners," he said under his breath. "They've . . . well, they've—"

"Escaped," The Maestroa finished for him. "I already know that."

"Shall we be after them, then?"

The Maestroa turned back to their work. "No."

"No?"

"No!" The Maestroa looked back at the soldier, their grip tight around the puppet Simon's neck. "It can never be as it was! The little fool has ruined my entire story. We will have to begin anew."

The soldier shifted his weight nervously. "It's a bit much. Don't you think? Can we change this kind of story—"

"I can do as I please." The Maestroa grinned, delusion glazing their eyes. "*I'm* The Maestroa. It's *my* world."

They peered over at the twisted puppets piled atop the

stage on scraps of fabric and paint that dotted The Maestroa's usually neat workplace.

"Are you well?" the soldier dared to ask.

"No, you idiot!" The Maestroa shrieked. "He stole my puppets!"

Their hands squeezed tighter, and the puppet Simon's head twisted around with an eerie crunch that made the wooden soldier shudder.

"We shall have a different sort of tale." The Maestroa's voice dropped to nearly a whisper. "This time, forget the giant."

"Loot?" asked the solider. "What has he done?"

The Maestroa stood and raised the puppet Simon high above their head. They said, in the energetic, demented tone of an emcee, "At tonight's performance, the role of the villain will be played be *me*."

They crossed to the miniature theater, and with gentle hands sat the puppet Simon against a painted tree. They lightly touched his head with two fingers and turned it around, enjoying the soft crackle of wood against itself, so that it faced rightly again.

"But I think the little puppet thief will find that this tale has no happy ending, after all."

The soldier trembled as The Maestroa laughed, low at first, but steadily picking up volume, until their cackle bellowed through across the entire show grounds.

In his tent, Loot shook at the sound of the laughter. He laughed with The Maestroa at first, but then grew afraid and hugged his knees to his chest, wishing Isobel would come to comfort him.

Inside another tent, centaurs made of steel neighed

and stomped, shot arrows as their gears wound tight, while in another, upholstered mannequins of beautiful sirens sang and pulled toy ships down into the depths of their swimming hole.

The Maestroa went to their desk, where a large roll of parchment lay dusty and untouched. They unraveled it and pored over the map drawn by their own hand. A wooded stretch of their own world, their park of tales. The forest of wishes. Brushing their hand across trees and cliffs, lakes and fallen logs, The Maestroa grinned as the map began to rearrange itself, and what was born was a completely new path, one that ensured the prisoners were far from the tents. Days from journey's end.

They looked at the little tents near the bottom right corner. Scraping their fingernails over the colored parchment, The Maestroa pushed the tents to the topmost corner, and along the way, the wooden soldier was knocked over by the great quaking within the tent, within all of the tents, as they moved and dragged along the earth, the wind blowing the tent flaps violently.

Once they'd reached their new location, The Maestroa pinched their fingers and twisted the image, pulling and smoothing, as the tents all came together, some growing taller, some shorter, until at last they resembled a castle. A dark, striped castle, waiting for the hero to come and meet his doom.

The Maestroa clapped their hands and the thunder boomed, as all of the lanterns snuffed themselves out.

12. THE REGRETS OF BLOODY FINGERS

That same morning, the bandits prepared their breakfast.

They, along with Simon, lived in an old cabin in the forest of Incantus. The paint had peeled off both the outside and the inside, so that every wall was a somber mix of gray and brown. The shutters were weathered and barely hanging onto their hinges. Of course, that didn't really matter since the bandits had nailed boards across the windows so that no one could see inside.

And so, inside the cabin, in the common room which also served as the kitchen, the bandits sat around the long table, which tilted because one of its legs was shorter than the others, and waited while Humphrey made them eggs. He always made them because he took great joy in pretending the eggs were his victims when he smashed them into the skillet.

Bloody Fingers leaned in his chair with his legs up on the table, as he always did when he was pampered. Above him, The Fop kept busy undoing the two curlers that gave Bloody Fingers the shape of his fine black mustache.

"What a horrible night," Bloody Fingers said. "I hardly slept a wink. Tossing, turning, and not one shriek in the night! I am very, *very* disappointed, men."

The bandits all grumbled, except of course for The Jester, who waved his rattle.

"Here we are, all together in our happy hideaway, the sound of breakfast sizzling, the sun rising high and proud. We ought all to be happy, yet we are not. Do you know why that is, companions?"

"Because *you* are unhappy?" guessed The Vizier.

"Because there's no one to maim?" guessed Humphrey.

"Because we haven't any bacon to pair with our eggs?" hinted The Fop.

"No!" Bloody Fingers pounded his fist on the table. "Because we have no slippers to walk around in and laugh about it. Because we have no slippers to gain a great fortune and catapult me up the ladder of crime!"

"Well, 'the best laid plans', as they say," said The Vizier coldly.

"What does that even mean?" Bloody Fingers asked as The Fop smeared pomade on his mustache so that it would be shiny and slick.

"It's a phrase," explained The Vizier, "which means that plans usually fail if they're too good. Although in this case, it doesn't appear they were very good at all."

"How dare you?!" Bloody Fingers swatted The Fop's hand away and stood. The Vizier, though, remained calm and seated. "Not very good plans?!"

"Calm down," advised The Fop. "Let him explain."

"I'm calm!" protested Bloody Fingers. "I *am* calm! I am as docile as a pussycat! But I'm not going to sit here and take this." Bloody Fingers sat back down and signaled to The Fop to continue styling his mustache. He stared at The Vizier. "Go on."

The Vizier didn't fear Bloody Fingers, because he was his right-handed man, even if that right hand was a hook, and so he looked Bloody Fingers boldly in the eye and said, "Your plan stank."

"To high heavens," agreed The Fop.

"And the stars beyond," said Humphrey.

Rattle rattle.

"But we had a cannon!" protested Bloody Fingers.

"Sure, but you shot the Squirm out of it," The Vizier said.

"We practiced!" Bloody Fingers looked at each of his bandits in turn for assurance. "All of us took turns throwing him at the wall the night before, did we not? We did! We rehearsed and rehearsed."

"Yes, but you didn't say what came afterward," said The Vizier. "How was he supposed to get out of that tower with those slippers? He's the worst bandit out of us all."

"Well, I don't seem to recall any questions from you when I went over the plan."

"I was busy crocheting that bunny rabbit," explained The Vizier. "I didn't have time to think about it. And now my poor creation has probably been tossed away. It was my best work, too."

"You can make another," said Bloody Fingers.

THE PRINCE AND THE PUPPET THIEF

"It's not the same!"

Bloody Fingers leaned over the table toward The Vizier. "Why are you being so hostile? It's not in your character."

The Vizier paused a moment, hesitant. "Well, perhaps I'm a little disappointed in you."

"Me? Why?"

"Well, you abandoned your own son after you shot him out of that cannon! We ought to have rescued him."

"Abandoned my— *abandoned*!" Bloody Fingers laughed, "Of course I didn't abandon Simon! I could never! Speaking of which, where is the little squirm?"

He went over to the ladder, which led to the sleeping area of the cabin. "Simon? Simon! Come here, you squirm!"

"He's not there," said The Vizier.

"I would have noticed if I abandoned my own boy and left him to rot all night," Bloody Fingers chuckled. Then his stomach dropped. "Wouldn't I?"

The bandits snickered, but no one wanted to confirm it to him. The Vizier tapped his hook hands together, his own way of saying *'tsk tsk'*. "Your own ambition has gotten the better of you, Bloody Fingers," he said. "That's why I'm disappointed."

"Oh, don't be." Bloody Fingers angrily went back to his chair and sat. "Foolish, that boy always was. If he's gone, he's gone, and that's all there is to it. Humphrey, bring my breakfast!"

"But we have no bacon—"

"Only winners get bacon!" shouted Bloody Fingers.

"You may have your bacon when I have my treasure. As it is, I will have two eggs, poached."

"They're fried." Humphrey brought the steaming plate of eggs to Bloody Fingers and dropped them in front of him with a thud. "And that'll just have to do."

Bloody Fingers looked at his fellow bandits, none of whom would look him in the eye. Even the Vizier had turned his attention to his own egg, which he had speared on one of his hooks.

"Don't be so cross with me," whined Bloody Fingers. "Don't! Ouch!"

He rubbed the back of his head, where The Jester had just hit him with his rattle.

"What was that for?"

Rattle rattle rattle.

"I was not whining!"

Rattle rattle.

"Oh, shut up!" Bloody Fingers quieted for a moment before he added, "We could retrieve him."

"If the king hasn't had him put to death yet, I imagine we could," The Vizier said, uninterested.

"Oh, come now, Vizy," said Bloody Fingers. "Surely that hasn't happened. He's only a boy."

"More a man than you think," said The Vizier.

"You mother him too much for his own good, you know," said Bloody Fingers said. "What with your crocheting and your coddling . . ."

"I can't take any more of this!" Humphrey stood. "If the only way to make you two stop bickering is to get the boy back, than I say we get the boy back! He might be a squirm, but he's *our* squirm."

"Even if he isn't the most fashionable bandit," agreed The Fop.

Rattle rattle, agreed The Jester.

Bloody Fingers gave his mustache a twirl and stood once more, this time, proudly. "The way you care about my boy more than I do brings a chill to my cold dead heart. Very well. Humphrey, fetch me my sword, and Simon's dagger!"

"You even let him forget his weapon again," chided The Vizier.

"No more!" Bloody Fingers warned him. "Bandits, to the castle!"

"Aye aye!" cheered the bandits, who were always excited for a confrontation.

"But first, breakfast!" Humphrey declared.

The bandits cheered again and retook their seats to eat their eggs.

13. GERONIMO

"How long have we been walking?" Marco asked, fidgeting with the two halves of his crown. "My feet hurt."

"Feels like hours," Flora said. "My own feet would hurt if they weren't, you know, made of porcelain."

"Well excuse me for being human." Marco rolled his eyes. He tossed the pieces of crown to the ground and walked on. "Forget it. I have others."

"Leave Flora alone," Isobel said. "Arguing and egging each other on is just going to make this more tortuous than it already is."

Simon stayed quiet. He couldn't help but feel a bit relieved that he had this time to figure out what he was going to do. He had no idea how to steal hearts from a powerful magician. He couldn't even steal a pair of slippers, and that's how he even got into this entire mess.

I should have brought the book, Simon thought. There was always some sort of moment where the hero figured out how to- *you aren't a hero. Guys like you are never the hero*- defeat the villain, and-

He wondered if his father had even noticed he was missing yet.

"Might I suggest," began Hans, "we stop and rest for a spell?"

Isobel looked wide-eyed at him. "Stop? No! We'll never get out of here if we stop!"

"Isobel, we un-enchanted ones need to rest," Marco complained. "Unless you want us to be tired when battling a witch."

This brought Simon out of his thoughts. "Battling? No one said anything about battle."

"Yes," began Flora, "because the Maestroa will just willingly hand you our hearts. Because they're nice that way. Honestly, what kind of feared bandit are you?"

"I always heard that Bloody Fingers was somewhat of a joke." Marco dared a small look at Simon. "More of a clown than a bandit really."

"He is not—" Simon sucked in a deep breath, "I am not a clown! I just, I make a mistake once in a while."

Try all the time, he thought, *that would be a bit more accurate.*

He shook his head to get the thoughts away and calm his irritation. First of all, no one was allowed to talk about his father that way, except for him. Second of all, he didn't know what anyone expected when they got back to the tents, and he was coming up short for plans with no supplies, one sword, and a pair of royals that insisted on arguing constantly.

He scowled at Marco. "I'm not a joke."

"Woah," Marco put his hands up defensively. "I wasn't trying to be rude, I was just being honest about what I'd heard."

"Well, you heard wrong," said Simon. "Now, *I* could use a rest. And if you want me able to get your hearts back, then I have to, or we're all sunk." When everyone was quiet he added, "Alright?"

"Best idea I've heard all day," Marco said curtly, not looking at Simon.

"As though we have a choice," Flora resigned and patted Isobel's arm. "It'll be alright."

Isobel didn't respond. She was looking at the sky, for the sun.

"Oh, good," Hans smiled. "My feet have been killing me for an hour. I would like very much to wiggle my toes."

Marco stopped walking. "Did anyone hear that?"

Isobel furrowed her wooden eyebrows. She latched onto Flora. "Hear what? What did you hear?"

"Nothing bad, I don't think," Marco peered off into the trees. "I thought . . ."

In the distance, they heard the trotting of a horse.

"Apollo!" Marco said, and ran ahead.

The rest of the party had no choice but to run after him.

"Wait, Marco!" Isobel called. "It might be a trap!"

But when they came through the brush, they all stopped and watched as Apollo lowered his head to drink from a large lake, stretching before them. The water was extraordinarily blue, as though it had been painted or dyed, and just below the surface they could see a few rainbow-colored fish swimming about.

"There you are, old friend," Marco went to Apollo and took him by the bridle, petting his head softly.

"*Old friend*," mumbled Isobel with contempt. "As thought that isn't *my* kingdom's horse."

Hans sucked in a breath of air and smiled. "Ah, how nice the breeze is here. I suppose it is as good a spot to rest as any."

Without hesitation, he took his shoes off and began to wiggle his toes, ignoring the disgusted groans of Flora, who had been standing close to him, and was appalled at the unusual length of his appendages as they curled and twisted.

Hans shrugged. "Suit yourselves," he said and went to a nearby patch of earth, where he sat and stretched his legs out on the grass.

Simon watched Marco, who had reached into a satchel hitched to the horse and produced an apple. He held it to the horse, who slurped it up between his teeth with and chomped it away in seconds. He reached back in and produced two more apples.

"Sorry I was rude," Marco said to Simon. "Catch!"

He tossed one of the apples. Simon thrust his hands out in attempt to catch it, but it landed on the ground and bounced, rolling away closer to the water.

Simon felt his cheeks warm up as he awkwardly chased after the apple like a child catching a runaway ball. "Thanks," he managed to grunt out in his embarrassment.

"I can't catch either," said Marco, "I don't know why I throw."

Simon smiled despite himself. It was getting confusing how Marco could be so infuriating with one sentence, and very good with the next. It was also interesting, and Simon tried not to let himself become *too* interested.

The apple stopped rolling just at the shore of the lake, bobbing in the shallow water. He picked the drenched, dirty fruit up and wiped it on his shirt sleeve before taking a bite.

"How is it?" asked Marco.

"Good, thanks," Simon said with a mouthful of apple, his stomach growling for more.

Marco chuckled. "I meant the water."

"Oh." Simon swallowed. "Fine, I guess."

"Excellent," said Marco as he crossed to the rocks on the shore, discarding his jacket as he went. "Care for a swim?"

"What?" Simon nearly dropped the apple as he watched Marco pulling off his shirt before it too was discarded.

Holy crowns, thought Simon.

"I'm hot," Marco said.

Simon didn't answer because he was trying not to look at the muscles on Marco's back as he climbed a rock, where he pulled off his boots and socks. He fumbled with the belt on his breeches.

"Yeah," was all Simon said.

"What?"

Simon's blinked and forced himself to look out at the water. "Oh. Yeah, it's hot I guess."

"Come on!"

Simon allowed himself a short glance and was relieved to see that Marco had left his breeches on. Relieved, and a twinge disappointed, but Simon forced that feeling away immediately.

"Oh, no," Simon was quick to say. "I'm good. Thank you."

Marco shrugged. "Alright, then. Geronimo!"

He cannon balled into the blue water below. A second later he broke the surface, shaking the water from his drenched hair. He shivered, let out a quick, loud, 'woo!' and swam on his back.

"Seriously, come on," he called to Simon. "This feels amazing!"

"I'm good," Simon focused on his apple.

"Can't swim?"

"I can."

"Then come on!"

"I'm tired."

"This'll wake you up."

"Seriously, I'm good, but thank you," Simon said.

Marco stood up in the water, and Simon tried not to notice the droplets running down his chest. "As His Royal Highness, Prince Marco of Lands Upper, I order you to get in."

"Charming," said Simon.

Prince Marco knitted his eyebrows with exaggeration. "You aren't impressed with my power?"

"Nope."

Marco put on a regal air and said, "That's how you address the crown?"

Simon swept a low, dramatic bow. "This better?"

"Yes," laughed Marco. "You broke into my future father-in-law's castle and tried to steal my betrothed's shoes. Then you threatened to kill me with an invisible dagger. You owe me a swim."

"I think I returned the favor when I found said betrothed."

"Just. Please, come on. I look like an idiot swimming alone."

Across the bank, Flora called out, "You look like an idiot a lot of the time!"

"Thank you, Flora!" Prince Marco didn't even look at her. He dropped his voice back to Simon. "Up to you."

Simon sighed. Truthfully, he did want to swim. He just felt weird swimming with Marco in his underclothes. Out and exposed, where he could be seen shirtless. He could practically hear the bandits making fun of his lack of upper body strength as he slowly took off his doublet and shirt.

He caught Marco's eyes on his body, and he rushed into the water, ignoring the cold and keeping only his head above the surface.

He looked to Marco and felt his stomach drop when he saw his frown. Like Marco was disappointed. "What."

"I don't know," Marco shrugged. "I figured you were deformed or something, the way you went on."

Simon nodded, closing his eyes, "What I lack in muscle, I make up for in brains."

"Yeah, I don't doubt that," Marco tipped into a backstroke. "You're pretty athletic."

"I don't want to talk about my body anymore," Simon spoke quickly. "Let's talk about *your* body. No. That's not what I meant."

"Do you have a name, Bloody Fingers?" Marco asked.

"It's Bloody Fingers."

"No, an actual name, that your parents gave you."

Simon quieted a moment. He wanted to tell Marco the truth. But he had already lied to Isobel, and he couldn't dare ruining it.

"Nicobar. But you can call me Nic."

"Hmm. Nice name," Marco said, in a way that made Simon wonder if he'd have said that no matter what name it was. "Well, *Nic*, my real name is Marco."

"You don't say."

"My full name is His Royal Highness Prince Marcolino Reginald Bartholomew Edward Victor Edwina Of Lands Downer, if you'd rather call me that."

"I would not." Simon smiled. "Edwina?"

"Marco it is," Marco shrugged, smiling back.

After a second too long for eye contact, Simon looked down to the water and pretended to tighten the waist of his trousers.

"Sire," Hans interrupted the silence. Both Simon and Marco jerked their gaze to him, surprised by his silent approach. "Should we head on? The princess is getting, shall we say, antsy."

Isobel came up behind him.

"It'll be dark soon," she said, "We really should be going."

"If it's getting dark, then we should stay put," Marco said. "Who knows what's out there at night?"

"Who knows what's *here* at night," protested Isobel.

"It's better to travel by daylight," Marco argued back. "If we get attacked head on we need to see it coming. And us humans need to sleep at some point."

Isobel looked around the clearing, across the lake. She looked up toward the sun, which was quickly beginning its descent to the horizon. "Then I need privacy."

"What?"

"I want my own bedroom! I want it now!" demanded Princess Isobel.

"Are you kidding me?" Marco jumped in the water, "And where am I to find you a bedroom?"

"Just do it."

"No?"

"Do. It!"

"Why are you being such a spoiled-"

"Stop, both you," said Flora. "Isobel, we'll find a nice quiet area of our own to pass the time. They'll sleep over there somewhere," she gestured to the clearing behind them. "Alright?"

Isobel nodded, her lip quivering. "Alright."

She stomped away.

"What is wrong with her?" Marco asked Flora. "I mean, I thought she was a bit spoiled, but never so . . . "

"Live under a curse, we'll see how unhinged *you* get," Flora said and followed Isobel away.

Marco shook his head and smirked at Simon. "Why'd I ever let you find her?"

"True love?" Simon offered. "Royal duty?"

"Oh, I remember now," Marco grinned. "To save your life."

14. MIDNIGHT

They divided what was left of the food between the three travelers who could eat. Simon noticed Hans stuff his portion of bread in the pocket of his jacket and he wished he'd done the same. He looked out at the expanse of forest left before them. Hopefully, they'd reach The Maestroa before starvation became a problem.

At the same time, he hoped it would take a bit longer, as he wasn't looking forward to fighting the magician.

"I miss eating bread," Flora said with a melancholy sigh as she watched Marco greedily swallow the last of his piece. "The fluffiness. The buttery taste. The way it practically vanishes in your mouth like clouds."

"You're making me sad," said Isobel. "What I wouldn't give for some of cook's strawberry cake."

"Cook can't cook," said Flora. "She always burned the edges."

Isobel shrugged and stood. "It's getting darker, Flora.

Shouldn't we find some place to . . . don't know, pace around until dawn?"

"I miss sleep, too," said Flora. "I used to have funny dreams."

"We'll talk about it later." Isobel nudged Flora on the shoulder with a wooden finger. "We really ought to get out of their way."

"Oh! Right. Yes, let's go."

Simon narrowed his eyes as Flora stood dutifully and followed Isobel through the trees.

"They're being a bit peculiar, don't you think?" He cocked his head to Marco.

Marco was busy wiping the crumbs from his shirt. "They're from Incantus, aren't they?"

Simon snorted. "That's true."

"They're right about one thing, though." Marco stood. "We *should* try to sleep."

Simon patted the hard ground beside him. "Hard as a rock. I shall never book a room in this tavern again."

Marco laughed and headed to the trees, opposite the clearing of Isobel and Flora. "I have a better idea. You coming, Hans?"

"I think I ought to mind the fire, sire," Hans said.

"Well, find some firewood while you're at it."

"F-firewood, sire?" Hans looked to the trees timidly. "You can't mean I fetch it."

"Of course I do."

"I-In the forest, sire? Alone?"

"Well, don't go *way* into the forest. Just get some twigs or something."

"But—"

"That's an order. You can take Apollo with you."

Hans looked fearfully at the horse tethered nearby, and back to Marco. "But what about bugs and worms?"

Marco crossed his arms. "I thought you wanted to go on a quest."

"I do!"

"Well, this is an important part of that."

Hans' lip quivered, but he pushed himself to his feet. He grumbled as he crossed to the trees, "I've stoked fires all my life, and never once had to collect twigs."

"I could have gotten it," offered Simon. "If he was too scared."

"He's fine," Marco said and continued on to his side of the clearing. "It's my little payback for him almost soiling himself on my horse."

"Wait, what?"

"Don't worry about it." Marco walked on and Simon followed. "Would this suit a fierce bandit?"

He gestured to two piles of leaves. A lantern sat on a rock between them, its flame low. One of the piles was much larger than the other. Simon started for the smaller one.

"If it's good enough for His Highness, it's good enough for me."

Marco pointed to the larger pile. "That one's yours."

Simon felt his stomach flip. "Why?"

"I like sleeping lower to the ground." Prince Marco shrugged.

"Oh." Simon went to the larger pile, embarrassed to

even let himself think Marco had been thoughtful for him. But still, he did make him a bed, at any rate. "When did you do this?"

"When you went to grab our clothes from the bank," Marco explained. "And you were trying to ring out your trousers."

Simon plopped down onto his pile, surprised to find that the leaves were soft. "Well, we can't all have fast drying linen breeches," he said. "Perfectly tailored too, I'll bet."

"Oh, they are." Marco pinched a bit of the fabric between his fingers. "Sometimes I think they're *so* tailored, I'm afraid I'll split them if I run too fast."

Simon blushed and felt grateful for the dark. "Oh."

He listened to Marco chuckling as he laid down on his own pile. Simon looked up at the sky through the treetops, the bright stars that sprinkled the purple blue sky. In the distance, night owls hooted while crickets struck up their symphony.

"How can anyone sleep with all this noise?" Marco pushed the leaves together beneath his head like a pillow.

"I'm guessing you've never gone camping before," said Simon.

"Of course not." Marco gave up on the leaves and clasped his hands beneath his head. "Once I got too drunk to find my way back into the tavern and I woke up in the alley next door. Does that count?"

Simon snorted. "I'll allow it."

"So, no offense, but you don't seem old enough to be a big bad bandit." Marco propped himself on his arm and cocked his head to Simon.

Simon tensed, feeling the flush of being caught taking root in his stomach and working its way up into his throat. "Yes, you'd think that. I'm seventeen, but I'm pretty tough for my age."

"Mhm." Marco narrowed his eyes.

"Word of mouth," Simon tried a different route. "My reputation precedes my truth. Are you sleepy? I'm sleepy. Goodnight." Simon turned his head away and closed his eyes tightly, but he felt Marco's eyes staring at the back of his head.

"Don't lie to me," he said.

Simon jerked his head back to Marco. "What?"

"Admit it." Marco leaned in. "You're not sleepy."

∽

In the shadows of the forest, Hans stumbled, reaching out for twigs and loose branches to take to the fire and go to sleep for the night. He held his breath for as long as he could, as though a ghost would crawl inside of him should he breathe in.

Finally, he needed oxygen. He heaved the air in, the sachet of herbs swaying and thudding against his chest.

"Some future king," he muttered. "Can't even get firewood."

He journeyed on, breaking pieces of twig here and there, no longer considering if they were large or dry enough to burn. If they were even worth carrying at all. For all Hans cared, the fire could burn out and they could all freeze to death.

The sachet thumped his chest like a heartbeat as he

walked. Every now and again he caught a whiff of the herbs inside. Strange smells, like bitter candy. Ones that reminded him of shadows and melancholy places like tombs and dungeons. Places he tried to avoid.

"Silly, stupid Hans," the servant grumbled. "What could they ever care for you?"

He thought of the thief, this Bloody Fingers boy, who just appeared out of nowhere and received all of the attention from the prince.

Ill-mannered sod, thought Hans with a curl of his nose.

"I suppose they must be best friends now. Silly, stupid Hans," he muttered. How could he ever believe he might have a friend in this world?

Marco never hid his annoyance with Hans. How could he ever believe he was actually needed or wanted here?

He tripped over the root of a tree and cried out as it wrapped around his ankle. A bough lowered and caught him like the protective arm of a well-meaning guard. The sachet tore against one of the boughs, and the herbs spilled out.

"Oh no!" Hans reached out to clean the mess, the smell of ashes and peppery licorice rising through his nostrils.

He sneezed, coughed at the sudden intrusion into his nose. His eyes watered as his face twitched and twisted.

Everything slowed down around him. His vision clouded and blurred at the edges. All he could see was the dark figure ahead.

"Do not fight it," a dark voice said in a slow, sweet drawl. "Let it fill you up. Breathe deep. Be calm."

Hans whimpered with silent terror as the figure sauntered toward him.

"I really wouldn't taste too good," Hans cried softly. "I'm spoiled. Rotten, I am."

"Breathe in," the voice said. "Let it consume you."

"Oh, I am too young to die! So many places I have never been!"

"Let the darkness consume you. How they mock you. How they use you and roll their eyes whenever you speak."

Hans stared silently at the dark figure. He could see nothing but darkness over them. Just a shadow, fading into the night. He stared straight ahead, feeling those shadows before him and around him, and shadows of his own creeping through his bones, where he felt the anger he'd held down for so long.

"I feel the darkness," he mumbled below his breath, his voice deeper and darker than ever before. "How do I . . . make it . . . Stop . . . ?"

The voice laughed. "You don't."

∼

"What time is it?" Isobel paced the shore of the lake, her wooden feet leaving nervous footprints weaving in the sand. She eyed the moon above, full and white, as it painfully took its time to reach a high point.

"I don't know." Flora went to her, took her arm. "I'm sure it's almost midnight."

"We can't miss it," Isobel whispered. "Now that they're here, we might not get another midnight."

Now that Marco was here, it meant that her life would soon be over.

She held back misty tears that refused to fall. If she were still flesh, she could sob all she wanted. But as a wooden girl, she had no choice but to hold onto sadness that would never let go.

Flora bit her glass lip. "But think of all the midnights after this is over. And all of the dawns and twilights, too. Focus on the positive."

"How can I?" Isobel began. She stopped pacing, looked to Flora. "When I'm going to lose you?"

Her wooden fingers brushed against the cold gleaming porcelain of Flora's hand. Their eyes met in the moonlight.

"Isobel," Flora whispered.

"I want to kiss you," Isobel said. "Now."

"Wait for it." Flora squeezed her eyes tight, enjoying the feeling of her princess close by. Even if she was wooden. Even if Flora couldn't feel the heat of her as their foreheads touched together. This was home.

"Wait."

"Now," giggled Isobel. "I'm tired of waiting."

"Almost time." Flora breathed deep.

∼

"My mother died when I was seven," said Marco, his eyes on the stars. "They say she got sick, but I think she just wanted to get away from my father." He laughed quietly at himself.

"That's not funny." Simon flipped onto his stomach

and looked up from the leaf he'd been inspecting. "You shouldn't joke about that."

"I joke about everything." Marco knitted his eyebrows. "And I've noticed you do, too. Do you have a mother waiting for you? What's her thoughts on you being a bandit?"

"My mother's a pirate captain," Simon answered truthfully. "She and my father met when they pillaged the same village at the same time. She went back out to sea, and later came back with me. She left me in my father's arms and we haven't heard from her since."

Marco sat up, "Your mother is a pirate?! Are you kidding me?!"

"Hey, we don't pick our parents."

"No, you don't understand. I think that's pretty excellent. So, your father?"

"He's around. He's a bandit, too." Simon caught himself giving it away and his voice tightened. He smirked at Marco. "He's nowhere near as good as me."

Marco squinted. "I'd sure hate to see how bad at it your father is, then."

"Why does everyone assume I'm so awful at it?"

"Did you see yourself in the tower?" Marco laughed.

"Why do you have to be such an ass all the time?" Simon sat on his knees, pulling the leaves into tiny flakes and letting them fall like green snow. "Can you ever be just, I don't know, nice?"

Marco's eyes widened with confusion. "I've been nice to you!"

"All right, but do you have to sandwich it between going out of your way to be a donkey's backside?"

The prince's eyes narrowed as he propped himself onto his elbows. "I joke around. I push buttons. It's my thing. And I thought you could handle it, considering how you spoke in the dungeon. It's how I cope and get by." He pushed himself onto his knees and shoved Simon on the shoulder. "And I don't *have* to be nice to you, thief."

Simon felt his cheeks burn and he shoved Marco back. "Arrogant."

"Fool." Marco pushed.

"Braggart." Simon shoved again, harder.

"Criminal." Marco shoved even harder.

"Lazy- entitled-" Simon narrowed his eyes to slits. "Joker."

"I tell jokes." shrugged Marco.

"You're the best joke you've told so far."

"Terrible thief."

"Drunkard."

Marco pushed Simon with both hands. A second later he was over him, trying to strike as Simon fought him back, and they rolled in the grass.

"Peasant!" spat Marco.

"Charlatan!" Simon shouted once he'd run out of really harsh ones.

Marco paused and squinted at Simon. "Charlatan?"

"It's a fun word." Simon chuckled. "*Charlatan.*"

Marco smiled, and their eyes held contact for a second. One, slow second, as their heads grew closer to one another. But just before they realized it, they heard a *crack* from the other side of the clearing.

"What was that?" Marco rolled from Simon.

"*What* is that," Simon said in awe.

Through the trees, a pale green glow beckoned. Marco fumbled for his sword in the dark, and when he at last found it, he stood and ran to the light.

"Isobel!" Marco called out as he went. "Flora!"

Simon pushed himself to his feet and ran after him. He nearly knocked into Marco's back as he reached the bank, for Marco had stopped and stood staring straight ahead, a look of shock unhinging his jaw.

"What is it?" Simon asked.

"Shh." Marco pointed with his sword.

Simon looked over and his own jaw dropped.

There was Isobel and Flora ahead of them. But not Isobel and Flora. Not the way that he knew them. They levitated in the air, three or four feet above the sand. Their arms were wrapped around each other as they levitated, their eyes locked on one another.

But what shocked Simon was that their bodies were no longer wood and glass. Flesh shone brilliant in the sparkling light. Human hair, Flora with golden tresses, Isobel with hair as dark as ebony. Her cheeks were blushed, her lips pink and full of life.

Simon slid his eyes to Marco. But he didn't see shock on his face. The brows were knit too tight. His jaw was set so still and tight that Simon thought it might crack his teeth if he pressed any harder.

Without looking over, Marco lifted his sword beneath Simon's chin to force his still gaping mouth closed. He looked back to the princess and her handmaid.

Simon didn't think he looked surprised or confused.

He looked disgusted.

He felt his stomach curl in disappointment.

After a minute, the light faded and the girls floated back down to the ground.

But now that they stood back in the dark, under mere moonlight, they were back to their enchanted forms, porcelain against pine.

Simon felt almost sorry for them then, though he didn't fully understand.

Flora giggled, which surprised Simon the most. She tightened her grip around Isobel, but the princess wasn't embracing her anymore.

She pushed past Flora's arms, stumbling as she went.

She stared at Marco, and their eyes locked.

Marco's dark and hard, Isobel's wide and fearful.

"Marco," she said. "Wait!" But Marco walked away.

"Oh no." Flora's voice broke when she saw him and Simon. "Oh no!"

"Marco, wait, please!" Isobel called, running after him, her wooden shoulders hitting Simon's as she went.

"Let me talk to you!"

Marco whirled on her.

"What could you possibly have to say?" he shouted.

"What even was that?"

"Let me explain," Isobel pleaded quietly.

"I don't want to talk." Marco shook his head. "Not right now."

Isobel could not, as much as she wanted to, as much as she needed to, cry. And that made her feel angry.

"Fine!" she shouted. "Let's not talk about me, then.

Let's talk about you."

"I meant at all!" Marco stabbed his sword into the ground.

Flora sunk to the shore and buried her face in her hands. Simon went to her, offered his hand to help her up. But just when she did, just when Isobel was about to scream her response to Marco, and just when he was about to storm away, they all stopped.

Somewhere, in the shadows of the forest, Hans shrieked with glee.

15. A PLUCKING PILLAGE

*B*loody Fingers sucked the air through his rather large nostrils and breathed it out again, sending a satisfying breeze through the bristles of his black mustache. He opened his eyes to the castle, crowned with a holy glow from the full moon behind it.

"It's good to be back, ain't it, boys?" he asked of his bandits.

They all grumbled in agreement, with the smirks of cherubs as they took in the sight of their last failure, now enjoying another chance, and all on the same weekend. This time, they all vowed, they would not fail.

The sound of beads shaking grew louder as The Jester returned from his lookout.

"Ah, Jesty!" Bloody Fingers welcomed the little man. "How does it look?"

Rattle.

"No one on the lookout?" Bloody Fingers furrowed his brow. "Not one single guard?"

Rattle.

"None in the watch tower? No one by the moat? The drawbridge, surely those buffoons from before are at the drawbridge?"

Rattle.

"Strange." Bloody Fingers stroked his mustache in deep thought. "If they no longer guard the castle, then there must not be anything worth stealing after all." He sighed and looked to his bandits. "Well, it looks like there is nothing here worth to stealing! I say we go to the tavern, rustle up some grog, and plan our next pillage. I hear the royal art museum has some valuable pieces. Gold frames and such."

The Vizier shook his hooks in dismay. "We aren't here for anything valuable, remember? We're here for your son."

Bloody Fingers widened his eyes. "Oh! I-I knew that, I was just testing your loyalty."

"Of course you were." The Vizier narrowed his eyes.

"I was," insisted Bloody Fingers. "I would never forget my own son, what kind of villain do you take me for?"

"You forgot him last time, remember?" The Vizier raised his voice. "That's why we're here to begin with."

"No," corrected Bloody Fingers. "We were here to steal the slippers to begin with. Again, what kind of villain do you take me for?"

The Vizier wrung his hooks towards Bloody Fingers as though he would strangle him.

"Let us not fight," said The Fop, producing a silk handkerchief with the initials T.F. for 'The Fop" embroidered on the side and dabbed at his eyes. "All we have is each other and without one another, we're just unemployed fools in fancy costumes."

"You think my bandit attire to be a fancy costume?" Bloody Fingers pulled at his satin black trousers. "I'll have you know that all notable bandits have a look. Costumes? Costumes?! Ha! Any criminal who wears a costume is an idiot."

The Jester frowned as he patted his two-pointed hat, but he gave nary a rattle to protest.

"All right, enough," said Humphrey. "I wanna see some necks slit and some vases smashed, and if we have a right good time, why, I might just rip off a fingernail or two."

"Once again," The Vizier sighed, "We aren't here for any of that, we are here for the Squirm."

"If he's even still in there," grumbled Bloody Fingers.

"Oh, you little-"

"What?!" Bloody Fingers shrugged. "They could have executed him by now, and what need I with a corpse for a son?"

"That is so vulgar." The Vizier rolled his eyes.

"What villain is not?" argued Bloody Fingers.

"It might be said," offered Humphrey, "that only a good villain would be."

Bloody Fingers clapped with delight. "Aha! And that is why I am the most feared villain in the land!"

"Second most," Humphrey corrected under his breath.

"Well, let us not dally any further," said Bloody Fingers. He drew his sword and raised it mightily above his head, pointing it toward the moonlit castle. "Bandits, we pillage!"

The bandits cheered.

"And save the Squirm!" added The Vizier.

The bandits cheered a little more quietly.

They ran to the drawbridge, where instantly, they cowered. They'd expected to be shot with arrows or set upon by the king's guards, yet there were none, it appeared, to stop them. It was strange, to have such an easy time of getting so close, for soon after they were not shot, the bandits dared to inch further, half-steps at a time, their eyes wide and searching as they risked it.

Yet soon they were more than halfway across the drawbridge, farther than they had ever gone, and not a single one of them found an arrow or other weapon in their flesh.

"All right, now to break down the door!" whispered Bloody Fingers. "Who has the lock pick?"

"No need," declared The Fop, who held the giant oak door open. "It's unlocked."

"What?" Bloody Fingers was almost disgusted.

"I merely laid my lily-white fingers upon the knob, twisted, and pulled. And now it is opened," The Fop explained curtly.

"Well, that's just no fun!" said Bloody Fingers. "How am I ever to uphold my reputation of being a frightening and ruthless bandit—"

"Who calls you that?" questioned the Vizier.

"—If I don't even need to break down a door? The king is proving to be a rather unworthy opponent," continued Bloody Fingers. "This is easier than taking candy from a baby."

"So much easier," agreed the Fop.

"They bite so viciously when you try to take their candy," said Bloody Fingers, rubbing the scar in the shape of baby teeth on the flesh between his thumb and index finger. It was, after all, how he received the moniker of Bloody Fingers.

"Enough talk," Humphrey growled. "I wanna slit some throats!"

"And you shall have them to slit!" promised Bloody Fingers. "Step aside, Foppy, we shall all plunder and pillage!"

The bandits cheered, with merry rattling from the Jester. They ran through the great oak door, trampling over The Fop as they went, for he hadn't gotten out of the way fast enough.

In the courtyard of the castle, they splashed in the fountain, and took great pleasure in knocking over statues, giggling at the stone arms breaking off of a chiseled woman in a toga.

After a while, though, this became a bit boring for them. For as they romped, not one guard or courtier had appeared to try to stop them, and they hadn't even heard one single scream of fright at their arrival.

They made their way to the throne room, and stopped short at the sight.

A man with a long white beard sat on the throne. His tattered clothing and small stature made clear that he couldn't be King Anders. He giggled as he watched a group of rats stand upon their hindlegs, dancing to the beat he slapped out on his knees.

"That's it, Ignatius!" the old man laughed. "One-and-two-and-one-and-two!"

"Hark!" called Bloody Fingers. "What is this?!"

The old man at first looked surprised to see them, but then he seemed annoyed as he settled more deeply into the throne. "Yer too late," he spat. "I got here first, and this is my chair now, so back it up!"

"Where is the king?" asked Bloody Fingers, holding up his sword. "We demand the king!"

"Gone," answered the old man plainly.

"Gone?"

"S'what I said!" said the old man. "Gone, and took the guards wit' him."

"Where have they gone?" questioned Bloody Fingers. "I'm here to pillage and steal."

"And taunt their lack of fashion sense," added The Fop.

"And slit their throats," added Humphrey.

"And rescue the Squirm," pressured The Vizier.

Rattle rattle, rattled The Jester.

"How dare you!" The old man waved his fist at The Jester. "I don't insult *your* mother, now do I?"

The rats scurried over to the bandits and whipped their tails furiously at their ankles. The bandits all shrieked and hollered as they kicked the rats away from them, Bloody Fingers giving the fattest one called Ignatius a fierce punt so that it flew and landed on the old man's lap with a thud.

"We want to pillage!" insisted Bloody Fingers.

"And get the squirm," implored the Vizier.

"Well, have it!" the old man said. "Just leave me and my rodents out of it."

"On my honor." Bloody Fingers bowed.

"Except I don't think you'll find any squirms, whatever that is," the old man said.

"He's not a worm, and he can be a bit squirrelly," The Vizier explained. "He was arrested yesterday."

"Oh, you mean that plucky thing with the smart mouth?" the old man inquired. "Them wood people done took him."

"Them what?" Bloody Fingers silently judged the man's grammar.

"The prince was down there, y'see, and they asked me not to eavesdrop but I did. And the prince sent him on a quest and soon after, the wood people took him. Then the king, he sent the prince after the plucky thing, and then hours after that, the king got himself in a state and they all went after the prince, who was after the plucky thing."

"And now we must after the king," concluded The Vizier.

"But treasure!" pleaded Bloody Fingers.

"Don't you see," The Vizier shouted, exasperated. "If we go after the king, who is after the prince, who is after the plucky thing, then we will eventually find and be able to rescue the plucky thing!"

"I don't give a pluck about plucky things."

"*The plucky thing is Simon.*"

After a pause, Bloody Fingers narrowed his eye. "Fine. But if we don't get treasure, I shall hold *you* accountable."

16. AFTER MIDNIGHT

"The darkness, the terrible, terrible darkness!"

Hans writhed, his eyelids closed tight, as he shook and struggled on the small bed of leaves. Marco and Simon held him down, each grabbing an arm.

"What is wrong with him?" Isobel asked.

Marco didn't respond, instead holding Hans down even tighter. "You need to calm down," he urged the servant. "Deep breaths. In and out."

"Who are you to order me about?" Hans muttered in a low voice from the depths of his throat. "Who are you to be respected?"

Marco widened his eyes in surprise at Hans' tone.

"What is the matter with you?"

"The darkness," Hans whispered with a hoarse gravel in his voice. "It is all here around me."

"Is he possessed?" asked Simon.

"If my soul went into Hans' body I'd be quick to get back out," muttered Flora.

"Shh," said Isobel.

"Well it's true." Flora couldn't help but smile. "I mean, have you met him?"

Isobel tried not to giggle. "This is serious, Flora. Something is wrong."

Marco snapped his head to stare Isobel and Flora down, "Could you two stop with the tryst for just a moment and help us?"

Isobel put her hands to her hips. "Well I'm so sorry, Doctor Marco, I didn't realize we were obstructing a great physician."

"Stop," Simon said. "Just all of you stop, before he jumps up and kills us all!"

"Do you really think I would kill you?" Hans' eyes had opened and stared into Simon's soul. "It is not I who wishes your demise, puppet thief."

Simon narrowed his eyes at the servant. "What?"

"Some are not born for happy endings." Hans grinned, and for the first time Simon noticed that his eye teeth were pointed. "Some are merely cattle for slaughter, fools approaching doom like a firework racing toward explosions in the sky."

"Stop talking, Hans." Marco pushed Hans by the forehead back to the forest floor. "You're saying crazy things."

Hans winced at the force of the prince's hands and resumed his wincing and writhing. "Something clings in my heart. Something dark. Help me."

Marco lowered his ear to Hans' chest, listened to his heartbeat. As he did, Hans glanced down at the top of Marco's head and back at Simon before he winked at him. Simon felt his cheeks burn up, tried not to show that he actually felt jealous at this. Prince Marco lifted his head again and Hans resumed writhing as though nothing had happened.

He's faking this, Simon thought. *For whatever reason.*

Simon stood and walked toward the shore of the lake. He'd had enough of Hans for now.

When he'd gone a distance, Hans slowly stopped writhing, breathed deep. "I want to rest now. Please leave me. I need to sleep. That is all."

Simon looked back at the servant to see that he was fast, and deeply, asleep.

"Idiot," Flora muttered under her breath.

"Do you think he'll be all right, Marco?" Isobel asked.

Marco didn't respond to her.

"Marco."

He still did not respond.

"Hey!" Isobel tried not to shout so she wouldn't wake the servant. "Oh, fine."

Prince Marco stood and walked away, toward his own bed of leaves. Isobel stepped to follow him and Flora clung to her side. Isobel put out a gentle arm to stop her.

"Let me talk to him," she whispered, and continued over alone.

Simon turned away and continued his path. When he reached the shore he pulled off his shoes and stepped into the water, embracing the cool, tiny waves breaking across his toes.

"Enjoy the show?"

Simon jumped and looked back to see that Flora had followed him.

"What are you talking about?"

"What you saw earlier. You looked wildly entertained."

"That's just my shocked face," Simon replied dumbly.

"I'm sure you'd never seen anything like it."

Flora tightened her lips. She looked down at Simon with a look that dared him to say anything about it. If he looked closely enough, he could see that Flora seemed actually quite vulnerable, waiting for his response, and ready to fight whatever he would say.

Beyond his own, Simon had never seen real shame.

"You're right. I haven't," said Simon. "Magical transformations aren't something you tend to see every day."

He thought he could almost hear the sound of Flora's breath letting go. Relief? Exasperation? He couldn't be too sure. She slid her glass body next to him, and the water lapped against her porcelain shoes.

"We've been in love for years," Flora admitted as she stared at the sky. "Probably since we were about thirteen or fourteen years old. A small handful of years that feel like a lifetime. Years of holding hands, of sharing secrets." She dared a quick glance at Simon before resuming the stargazing. "Of hiding."

"Well, you're found." Simon gave her a friendly smile. "Peek-a-boo."

Flore snorted. "Marco seemed upset, didn't he?"

Simon didn't respond. Marco had seemed angry. Disgusted, even. He wondered what would have happened if Marco had noticed Simon admiring his shirtless muscles earlier. If he leaned too close or looked him in the eye too long. He resisted the shudder that ricocheted up his spine and tried to hide his shame. His sinking heart.

"So," Flora quietly began. "Is there a problem with that?"

"A problem? No." Simon shook his head. "It's not my business."

"No, it isn't." Flora tried to sound tough, but Simon could hear the relief in the back of her voice.

Simon decided it was time to change the subject before it got too personal. "I'm more concerned with what's happened to Hans, to be honest."

"He's a dramatic little snipe whose enjoying attention from his master for a change," Flora explained simply. "All the servants think they're big and bad once one of the royals even so much as talks to them without giving an order. I imagine that being brought along has gone straight to the simpleton's head. He's playing dramatic little games as though that will make him favored for longer."

"I think there's more to it than that," said Simon. "He seemed to echo something of the Maestroa's plan."

"Marco acts like you're his friend. He probably wants to go out drinking grog with you some night to seduce wenches, since I'm sure he won't have the princess anymore," Flora cut him off. "Hans is jealous. I wouldn't worry about it."

Simon wondered how Flora could be so smart, have secrets of her own, and not see his.

∼

"I always wanted to tell you," said Isobel, holding her hinged knees to her chest with her arms. "I've always wanted to tell everyone. I just didn't know how."

"How about with words?" asked Marco. "Here, I'll give you some words to try out. 'Marco, I am in love with my handmaid, and so I can never marry you.' There, it only took me a half second."

"It's not that easy," Isobel was quick to say. "And seeing the way you reacted, now I know I was right to keep it to myself."

"What does that even mean?" Marco propped himself up at his elbows. No use to pretend to be sleeping if he kept arguing back. "How I reacted?"

"You looked grossed out," said Isobel. "And you yelled at me."

"Yeah, because I just saw you transform twice while you were levitating!" Marco tried not to shout. "Because you've kept important things from me. So what, you were just using me to hide behind for the rest of your life?"

Isobel cocked an eyebrow. "Oh, that's funny. Weren't you using *me* for a throne, Prince Charming?"

"That was our fathers' idea, not mine." Marco shook his head. "I'm going to make one lousy husband."

"I'll be just as lousy as a wife," said Isobel. She slid her hand over to Marco's. Pine on flesh. "You're a good man, really. But your love will never break my spell. I'm sorry I didn't tell you."

Marco shook his head again and sighed. "I think you're right."

"Friends instead?"

"Friends instead. I don't understand though, why can't you and Flora just—"

Isobel snorted. "Live 'Happily-Ever-After'? I don't think I've ever seen *The Princess And The Handmaid* in the castle library."

Marco locked eyes with the wooden princess, a challenging smirk appearing on his lips. "So write it."

Isobel shook her head but laughed despite herself. Finally, she shrugged. "Fair point. So, why didn't you just come yourself?"

"I'm lazy." Marco smiled.

"All right, but why him?" Isobel gestured to the other side of the clearing, to the shore, where Simon stood silhouetted against the low hanging moon. "He's a mess."

Marco dropped his face into the leaves and grunted. When he finally looked back up at Isobel, she saw that his cheeks had flushed a sizzling shade of scarlet.

"Because I think messes are kind of cute."

17. SWASHBUCKLER

"Do you think we're getting any closer?" The hinges on Isobel's knees creaked as she spoke. "My legs feel like they'll fall off from overuse."

"Please, we're all tired," Marco said. "The last thing we need is for you to become unhinged. Well, more so than you already are."

Isobel made a fist and burst into giggles. "I will punch you again. I have an incredibly strong fist. I believe it's pine."

Marco laughed in response, to Simon's relief. The two royals had been friendly all day, which was a welcome change from their usual arguing. He didn't know what they'd spoken about the night before, but the conversation had lasted most of the night, and now, today they were joking and playfully jabbing one another like old friends.

Simon suspected a conspiracy between them, but he was at least glad that Marco seemed able to move past what they had seen between Isobel and Flora. He couldn't help but wonder if the prince would be able to move past Simon's own feelings about him, if he knew.

Don't think about it, Simon thought and shook his head.

Why should he care what His Royal Highness thought of him? He needed to think about how he'd break into The Maestroa's lair and retrieve those hearts. Then he could disappear out of their lives and on to better things.

"But really," Isobel said, "I never get tired, and I'm getting tired. These hinges are—" S*queak*. "Ah! Do you hear it?"

"I do and it's horrible," said Marco. "Stop it."

"I can't!" Isobel protested. "They need a rest!"

Marco, who walked alongside Apollo, tugged the reins, forcing the horse to halt. He nudged at Hans, who was bent flat on Apollo's neck, asleep.

"*Mmph..*" Hans grunted. "Please don't make me dance."

"Hans." Marco nudged the servant again. "Wake up."

"I don't want to dance!" wailed Hans.

"Hans!"

"Oh!" Hans cried out, sitting up and looking around with wide, unblinking eyes. "Oh, dear. You mean to tell me this wasn't all a dream?"

"Sorry, but no," said Marco.

"I was just in the castle, where some strange old man wearing a fat rat on his head was trying to make me dance."

"That was a dream," said Marco.

Hans' lip quivered and he shook his head.

"Get off Apollo for a while. It's Princess Isobel's turn."

"But sire," said Hans, rubbing the sachet around his

neck. "She's made of wood and doesn't need to rest. I am made of flesh, and—"

"Down, Hans!"

With a frustrated sigh, Hans thrust his arms out. Marco helped him down, holding him like a child. When there were only a few feet to go, Marco dropped him. Hans cried out, but landed on his feet just the same.

Marco turned, reaching for Isobel's waist. Flora slid forward.

"I will help her, thank you," she said curtly, and lifted Isobel onto the horse.

Simon cursed himself for imagining Marco lifting him like that. Or the other way around.

They resumed walking and went mostly in silence, except for Hans spewing out unintelligible grumbles to himself, and the clopping of Apollo's hooves against the dirt.

But as they walked on, the air became scented with an inviting, cozy smell. Simon sniffed.

"Do any of you smell something?" he asked.

"I don't smell anything," said Flora. "Then again, I *can't* smell anything. Glass, you know."

Marco nodded, and he sniffed as well. "I smell toasted bread."

"Oh, Your Highness!" Hans screeched and ran to the prince, pushing a hand against his forehead. "I fear you are having a stroke! Lie down, I shall nurse you to health."

"No, Hans." Marco shoved the servant away. "I really do smell it."

"So do I," said Simon.

Marco tilted his head back farther, sniffed even deeper. His eyes lit up and he grinned.

"Also . . . I smell . . . grog!"

He moved quickly ahead, following the scent.

Simon looked to Isobel. "He can smell alcohol in the distance?"

Flora rolled her eyes. "Some are like dogs that way."

They followed Marco. As they made their way through the trees, they could see the promise of some sort of structure ahead, and soon it became clear that they'd stumbled upon a tavern, covered in moss and vines, with a large sign for grog above the red door.

"Yes!" Marco cheered. "Oh yes! Just what I prayed for!"

"Marco," began Isobel, "I don't think we should go in there."

"Shh," said Marco, "I'm savoring this moment. How I've longed for a pint!"

"Marco," said Isobel, more pointedly, "do you really think we ought to go into any establishment in The Maestroa's forest?"

Simon nodded, not feeling ready for any fighting. "I agree with Isobel. We should keep moving."

"Either way we need to rest," said Marco. "Come on, Flora! I know you could go for a pint."

Flora grinned. "Oh, you know I could. I would. Except, you know, I'm made of glass and can't drink anything."

Marco's face dropped. "Oh, right. Well, come on, Nic! One should never drink alone!"

The rest of the party groaned, but followed Marco to the door.

"Maybe we have to go here," Simon offered.

"Does anyone *have* to go to a tavern?" asked Isobel.

Simon shrugged. "It could be part of the journey. The story, whatever you call it."

Isobel's expression darkened. "In that case we really do need to be careful. Not everything is as gentle as Loot."

"He was gentle?"

"You didn't cuddle him correctly."

"They aren't letting me in!" Prince Marco pointed at the door. "I've knocked three times."

"Step aside." Simon approached the door. He'd done this enough with his father to know that at some taverns it isn't how polite you can be, it's who you are. He pounded his fist against the red wood.

A window slid open in the center of the door and a pair of black eyes peered out. "Who goes there?" asked the owner of the eyes.

"I am Bloody Fingers," Simon said in his deepest voice. "Open up immediately, I want a pint."

"Why should I?" the man retorted.

"Because if you don't," Simon did his best imitation of his father, "I'll have Humphrey cut out your tongue and string me a new necklace."

The eyes widened. "Oh, yes, sire! Yes, of course!" The door swung open.

Simon looked over his shoulder at Marco and savored the stupid look on the prince's gawking face. "See, it works on *some*."

"That part grossed me out," protested Marco. "It was the blood thing that didn't work."

The one who guarded the door, a burly man wearing a metal cap with horns, stepped aside. "Just, please, don't break or pillage anything."

Simon led the way inside the tavern.

"I still don't think we should go in," said Isobel. She looked to Flora and tugged her arm. "What do you think?"

Flora considered the princess a moment. "It wouldn't be much fun for us. We'll just stay out here."

Isobel looked relieved. Marco opened his mouth to say something, but Simon cut him off. Clearly, the two wanted to be alone.

When Hans reached the threshold, Marco stopped him.

"But sire," Hans said, "I don't want to be out here!"

"Tether Apollo first," Marco said.

"Won't you come with me?"

"Apollo. Now."

And the red door shut in Hans' face.

∼

Apollo gnashed and let out a neigh as Hans finished tethering him to the stake. This made Hans' heart speed up violently and he wailed with fear, throwing his hands in the air.

"Whatever is the matter?!" he cried. "Apollo?!"

The setting sunlight flickered through the trees, as though the sun wasn't even real. It changed colors. Blue, then pink, orange, back to yellow, over and over again, flickering in and out. The forest plunged into total darkness, and now it was a nighttime sky.

Hans quivered and tried to run for it, but he was stopped short by the sight of the figure, drenched in shadow, standing before him.

"Not again," whimpered Hans.

"I have a task for you, dear Hans," said the figure, taking a step closer.

"I don't want your task," said Hans. "Please let me be. I like my friends, and I want them to be well."

The figure laughed. "You think they are your friends? Really, Hans. Could a prince ever be friends with a servant?"

Hans did not respond to this. He feared that anything he said The Maestroa would use against him, and so he decided it better to say nothing at all.

"As I said, my little comrade." The Maestroa inched further. "I have a very important task for you."

Their hand reached out, and in their palm Hans could see the purple lump of a glistening plum.

"Ensure the thief eats this," said The Maestroa.

"What will it do to him?" Hans asked. "Will it...will it kill him?"

The Maestroa grinned. "Would you like it to?"

Hans shook his head fiercely. "No, of course not! Why would you ask me such a thing?"

"I did not mean to offend you."

"I would never wish anyone to be dead."

"Of course you would not."

They can see right into my soul, thought Hans. He secretly wouldn't mind if Simon were dead, though he did not know why that was. Ever since he had breathed in the herbs from the sachet, he had felt such a dark stirring in his belly, as though his soul were turning as black as dirt and all that was bad in the forest filled his lungs and spread all through his insides.

Resigned, he took the plum. It was firm and plump, a perfect piece of fruit. He could hardly resist taking a bite, especially when he took a deep inhale of its ripe, luscious scent.

"Don't do it, Hans," said The Maestroa as though they could read his thoughts.

"But what will it do to him?" Hans asked.

"Do not worry about that." The Maestroa faded away in the dark. "It will not harm him. I promise you that."

~

Something's off about these people, Simon thought as he looked over the tavern from his seat in a darkened corner.

Patrons clad in fur and metal crowded the tables, guzzling pints of grog and ale. A small man with a long beard lay asleep atop a barrel, snoring as grog dripped from his lips. A bartender continued to fill tumblers with golden brown liquids and sling them down the bar at a pair of ruffians that couldn't seem to drink fast enough. Everyone gulped, whistled, and yelled throughout the room.

But Simon couldn't stop looking at their feet, where alcohol pooled deeper the more they drank. As though it had nowhere to go but to the floor.

I've heard some have a wooden leg, but this is ridiculous. Simon shook his head and turned back to Marco.

The prince looked undisturbed by the floor as he sat across from him with that perpetual smirk only growing. He tapped his fingers happily on the tabletop and bobbed his head back and forth as he glanced around the room. He lifted his glass to his lips and swigged another drink.

"All I'm sayin'," he said, his speech beginning to slur, "is that maybe we just need to give The Maestroa a nice stab in the heart, since they're so keen on taking other people's."

"Lower your voice!" Simon whispered. "They could be listening in."

Marco squinted at the taverners. "They're far drunker than I am."

Simon pursed his lips and watched a splash of ale hit the floor as it leaked out of a chugging man across the way. He squinted at the man's arm, and noticed faint wrinkles webbing their way across his flesh. Like wadded paper after it's smoothed out again.

"You haven't had any." Marco looked at Simon's drink. "Don't make me drink alone!"

"Oh." Simon shook his head. "No thanks, I'd rather not blur my head. "

"Chug!" Marco grinned. "Chug! Chug! Chug!"

He beat the table and kept chanting louder and louder. Simon felt his face get hot as the taverners took note of them. He lifted his drink and tilted it to his lips, downing as much as he could. He slammed the drink down and let out a loud hiss as it burned his throat and opened up his sinuses. The taverners cheered, but none as loudly as Marco, who gave a round of applause.

Simon's stomach did a flip when he noticed Marco's grin and looked away instantly. The beer was already messing with his head.

Did he notice me blushing? Simon winced. *Did he care?*

He tightened his grip around his drink.

'What does it matter?' he heard a voice whisper. *'It's not like anything would come of it.'*

Simon froze and lowered his eyes to his beer. His reflection in the drink was talking. He bit down on his lip to ensure his mouth was really closed as the reflection said, *'You realize you're an idiot right?'*

Simon squeezed his eyes closed and shook his head. When he peeled them open again, the reflection had returned to normal, and he blinked back at his unaltered, closed-lipped face.

~

'Is this all you can do?' Marco's reflection asked him. *'Just party on and hope no one notices what a lying sack of nothing you are?'*

Marco picked up his drink and sloshed down another gulp. Who was a tumbler of grog to speak to him that way?

That'll teach you, he thought as it poured down into his stomach where it couldn't talk to him anymore.

'You left your betrothed outside,' it managed to say anyways. *'You realize anything could hurt her, right? But no, you'd rather just pretend like there's nothing important to do and make eyes at the guy*

you can't even have. Drink the problem away for a few hours instead of solving it. You're such a—'

"Shut up," said Marco.

Simon, who had been staring into his drink like it held some dark secret, looked up at him and blinked. "What was that?"

"Not you! Um. I don't know who needs to shut up . . . but . . . someone does."

~

Simon looked back down at his drink, and back to Marco. Were the drinks really to blame?

Grog can't talk.

"Okay?" said Simon. "I really think we should leave. Something's not right."

"Everything's fine," said Marco, shaking his head. "It's all good."

Simon grunted, looking back at the taverners. For a second, the horns on one of their helmets seemed real, like the horns of a monster. He blinked the vision away, and it was a normal, human, man again. He looked to the floor. The pools of grog had become deeper.

"Are *you* all right, Nic?" asked Marco.

That's isn't my name, Simon wanted to say but couldn't.

"I just feel," he began slowly, "that we should get going. The ladies are waiting, and—"

"They aren't my responsibility," Marco spat out. "I never wanted—"

"You might not have wanted, but you—"

"It's not my life!" said Marco. "But here I am, doing it

anyways, so god forbid I stop for just one little break before I marry off my happiness for dear ole daddy."

Simon wasn't sure what to say. Marco took a deep breath, and for a moment Simon thought he looked relieved. Like a weight had slid off his shoulders. They sat in silence for a moment. Simon debated taking another sip to fill the quiet, but decided against it, not wishing to risk it messing with his head any further.

"So don't," he finally dared to say. "You have a crown, power, and money. Do as you please."

Marco laughed at this, shaking his head. "That's not how it works. *You* have no duties or expectations to fulfill, so *you* do as you please."

At this, Simon guffawed. "You think it's that simple? The only reason I'm on this death mission is to even have a *chance* to do just that! I can't just take off."

"Neither can I."

Their eyes locked on each other. Two seconds. Four. After seven or so beats, Simon blinked and glanced at the table. He wondered what they were even talking about.

If we could run away together, we would, but he can't.
That is not *what he said. He's trapped in his life, too.*
That's it.
So . . .
That's it.

"Fine." Marco broke the silence and pulled Simon out of his thoughts. "We've had our fun. Let's leave."

"This was fun?" Simon stood from his chair and turned. He jumped and nearly stumbled back, finding himself face to face with the man who had let them in.

"Not so fast," the man said.

Simon's knees shook under the stature of the large man, almost as large as The Vizier, looming over him with huge fists on his hips.

"Problem?" Simon squeaked.

"Bit of one, yes," the man said. "Were you planning to *pay* for those grogs?"

"Well, yes." Simon sighed and rolled his eyes. "Is that all? Marco . . ."

He glanced back at Marco to see his eyebrows raised.

"Oh. Yes. My manservant has that. He's just outside."

The man grunted. "Likely story."

"No, seriously," said Simon. "Let him go get—"

"That's a nice jacket you have there," the man said to Marco. "I think it'll be worth more than your silly coins. Give it to me."

Marco laughed at this. "I'm not giving you my—"

The man pulled a dagger from his belt and held it beneath Marco's chin. "Let's try this again. Give me that jacket."

"You can't talk to me that way!" Marco's face reddened, and Simon shuddered to hear how his words were slurring under the effect of the grog. "I'm-ther-Prunce-erf—"

"Prince?" A taverner whirled around nearby, eyes gleaming.

"Royal?" Another.

"Hostage!" Another.

They stood, sauntering towards Marco and Simon, knives and clubs drawn. Simon looked over at Marco to see him shivering.

He can't even defend himself.

"Back up!" shouted Simon. He didn't know how he'd keep Marco safe, but something in his gut made him speak. "You heard me, get back!"

"Says who?" a taverner challenged.

Simon puffed his chest out. *Please work.* "Bloody Fingers, the most feared villain in the kingdom!"

"Second most," muttered the sleeping old man on the barrel. He resumed his snoring.

"I don't believe that." The man shook his head. "Who're you really?"

Simon's stomach dropped to the floor. His face grew hot, and somehow chilled at the same time.

He looked across the tavern at all the cutthroats and bullies surrounding them. What would Bloody Fingers do? He noticed the wooden chandelier above them, hanging from a chain.

Not again.

The doorman pushed him back into his seat.

A ruffian, one with a wild beard decorated with beads of silver, had come behind Marco and grabbed him by a fistful of hair. Marco cried out as the man pushed a knife against his throat.

"I wonder how much a vial of royal blood goes for," the ruffian said.

"I saw him first!" The doorman slammed his fist on the table.

"Let me go." Marco tried to pull from the beaded ruffian's grip.

"I'll be," another ruffian, with a hook for a hand, said. "A prince's ransom!"

Simon gulped at the sight of the hook and was

reminded of The Vizier again. How he wished he had an entire band of thieves to back him up now.

The ruffian's shouts raised, as each argued why *they* would take Marco, and how much he must be worth.

"All right! All right!" screamed the doorman and all silenced. "Sit him down!"

The beaded ruffian looked for a moment like he wouldn't comply, but at last lowered his knife and slammed Marco back into his chair.

Do something, Simon screamed silently at himself.

"The fair thing would be to share him," the doorman said. "We'll cut him into even bits, and each may do with their share as they please!"

The ruffians cheered.

Simon squinted at the doorman's wrinkled paper flesh. *They aren't even real.*

"All right, boys." Marco pushed himself up and leaned over the table. "Unhand me and my friend."

"Or what?" A ruffian narrowed his eyes at the prince.

"Or . . . Marco took another gulp of his grog. "Or I shall . . . I shall have to . . . slay you, you dragon!"

The ruffian narrowed his eyes to smaller slits. He folded his arms across his chest. "Boo."

Marco yelped and sat back down as the ruffians burst in laughter.

Get to the chandelier, thought Simon. The grog was hazing his thoughts, and he cringed at the idea of running over to it. Even the thought of standing up from his chair made him dizzy.

But he had to try *something*.

Act really drunk. It hit him.

"Gen'le'men," he said, slurring his words as much as he could and swaying back and forth. "I muz implore ye ter step ay-way."

The ruffian who'd let them in moved his attention to Simon. "And why is that, *Bloody Fingers?*"

"Ber-cause." Simon smiled. "I wanna show you some'fin. Some'fin only Bl-erdy Ferg-ers can do."

The ruffians laughed at this, but then the one with the horns bowed. "By all means, oh feared one."

"Second most," the sleeping man hiccuped.

Simon gripped the edge of the table and pushed himself up. He walked a tilted path to the table at the center of the room and lay face down on it. Slowly, he pushed himself up onto his elbows and stood. His eyes lost focus as he took in the room from higher up. He stared at the ruffians.

"Well, go on, so we can break your neck and steal the prince," the doorman said, and the others snickered their agreement.

Simon gave a slight bow and he gestured to Marco's sword.

"What?" Marco asked him, clutching his tumbler with an iron grip. He'd been sitting and staring ahead, his face red with what seemed to be shame.

Simon eyed his sword again.

"What do you want?" Marco threw up his hands and the grog sloshed.

Simon nudged his head toward the sword again. Finally, Marco understood and pulled the sword from his belt, tossing it to Simon. Simon reached for it, but it landed with a *clang* at his feet. The ruffians all laughed.

"The great Bloody Fingers can't catch?" asked the leader.

Simon grunted and bent over to pick up the sword. He took a deep breath, tried to focus, and then— he jumped, grabbed the chandelier, and pushed himself along until it swung.

Everyone just stared at him, unsure what exactly he was trying to do.

Finally, the chandelier had motion, and he swung above the crowd, back and forth, back and forth. His stomach heaved as the grog splashed along his insides and Simon groaned at the horrible sensation.

But when at last the chandelier had reached its peak, Simon swung from it, back flipping off and landing near the rope that held the chandelier aloft.

"*Ooooh,*" said the ruffians at once.

"Gentlemen." Simon bowed and, relieved that he hadn't vomited. "Come on, Marco!"

The prince stood from his chair and rushed to Simon, narrowly avoiding the sweeping arms of the ruffians.

The ruffians tried to follow, but once they reached the center of the room, Simon slashed the rope with the sword, and the chandelier came crashing down on, crumpling them as it landed.

Simon and Marco both blinked in awe. The ruffians, cutthroats, and thugs were merely torn paper and wire, strewn across the floor.

"I *told* you something wasn't right," said Simon, tossing the sword to Marco.

"You saved me." Marco slid his sword back into his belt. He looked over at Simon, smirking yet again.

"Why?"

Simon shrugged. "I thought you needed to be saved."

"That's a nice change of pace."

"Come on." Simon grabbed the prince's arm and ran for the door. "We need to get the girls and get out of here."

He pulled Marco through the door of the tavern, out into the night.

They slammed against a figure and fell to the ground.

"Oh, god," Marco grunted.

"Seriously?!" Simon's voice broke.

They looked up at the scarlet face of King Anders. "Arrest him!"

18. CHOICE

Marco pushed himself up and jumped in front of Simon as the guards closed in. He put his palms out toward the king, who stared back, red faced with his fists on his hips.

"Just a moment," Marco said.

"I've given you several moments," King Anders said. "Days of moments, to be exact. I'm tired, I'm angry, and my hair needs a nap. Gaspard, tell the guards to arrest the fugitive!"

The gangly servant peeked his head from around King Anders. "Guards, arrest the fugitive."

Two guards took a step further, swords at the ready.

"It's alright," Simon muttered behind Marco. "You tried."

No, I didn't, Marco thought bitterly. This was his fault. If he hadn't have insisted they stop, they would still be well ahead of his future father-in-law and all of this trouble.

Isobel pushed her way through a line of guards, Flora quick on her heels.

"Papa," she protested. "Listen to us. Nic is trying—"

"He's trying my nerves!" King Anders spun on his daughter and took her shoulders gently. "And look at you. My beautiful daughter, a marionette and cavorting with thieves."

"You aren't listening to me."

"No need to thank me. We will make it right. Papa is here now."

King Anders turned from his daughter and made his way to Marco. The prince ground his heels into the dirt and stood up straight. He was the only thing between the thief and an army of guards. He couldn't mess this up.

Behind the king, Flora reached for Isobel's hand and took it.

Isobel pulled away and looked nervously at the guards. Marco narrowed his eyes at her, as Flora wiped at her own knuckles, as though polishing the glass. As though nothing had happened.

That's my future, too.

"Marco, my boy," King Anders said. He slapped the prince hard on the shoulder and Marco fought not to grunt. "I think you've had a bit too much grog."

He took Marco by the scruff and pulled him forward, away from Simon, and the guards stepped in. Marco looked back just as they slapped irons around Simon's wrists.

This is my fault.

"How did you get here?" Marco asked.

King Anders folded his arms. "When you didn't come back, of course we had to come after you. I told you I would. And by luck, we happened upon a gracious fortune teller. I don't much believe in that foolishness, but this one had purple eyes. I thought maybe she knew what she was talking about. And she *was* the real thing, because here you are! I ought to have you arrested, too."

Marco swallowed.

"But," King Anders continued, "you apprehended the fugitive and for that I thank you. Not to mention you found Isobel at last."

He smiled at Isobel, who wouldn't even look at him. He thrust his hand out to Hans, who stood nervously behind a guard, focused more on his fingernails than what was happening.

"Hans," the king said, "give Marco his effects. I believe there's something he'd like to give the princess."

Marco gulped. The jeweled slippers. The thing that bound him and a princess together in a future of loveless marriage and guarding one another's secrets.

Marco absently outstretched his hand as Hans came forward and draped the strap of the satchel over his wrist. Inside, the slippers clinked together. He looked back at Simon, who inspected his irons, like he was desperately searching for some sort of way to break them off.

He wouldn't be here if not for these slippers. If not for Marco's living lie.

He looked at Isobel and they locked eyes for just a moment. What was she thinking right now? Did she hope Marco would keep playing along? Just finish the story laid out for them and never face the truth? Or did she secretly hope he would stop it, here and now?

He wanted to stop it. Simon's words in the tavern were repeating themselves, over and over.

You have a crown . . . do as you please.

With a deep breath, Marco reached into the satchel and hooked two fingers into the heels of the slippers. He pulled them out, letting the satchel fall. The jewels caught the moon and the light from the tavern, lighting the jewels in a rainbow of color.

"Isobel?" King Anders reached an arm to his daughter.

Marco narrowed his eyes at Isobel. She hesitated, just for a moment. Behind her, Flora bit her lip.

Isobel took her father's arm and allowed him to bring her forward to Marco. Like some possession to be handed off. A teapot or a necklace. That's what she was in this whole ordeal.

Marco bit his tongue. Even if he did love her, he couldn't accept someone that way.

"Marco?" King Anders raised an eyebrow. "Remember that I cannot abide ugly grandchildren."

The prince looked to Isobel and back to the slippers. His eyes slid to Simon.

"Marco," whispered Isobel.

"I can't do it."

"What?" The king narrowed his eyes.

"I can't do it," repeated Marco. "*Papa.*"

He thrust the slippers into Simon's hands.

"What are you doing?" Simon's eyes widened.

"They're mine to give," Marco said, pulling his sword. "And they're yours."

Simon only blinked back at him. Marco smirked.

"This is an outrage!" King Anders bellowed. "A scandal! Guards, remove those slippers from that fugitive's grubby hands, or . . . "

Marco grabbed Isobel by the arm and spun her in. He held the sword to her throat.

"Let him go," Marco shouted.

"What are you doing?" Isobel's voice cracked under her breath.

"Trust me," Marco whispered.

Flora ran forward, nearly slipping on her own glass feet. "Don't hurt her!"

"Guards!" King Anders pointed at Marco, and the guards marched forward.

"Let the thief go, Your Majesty!" Marco shouted, and hoped no one would notice the sword trembling in his hand. "Or explain to all of Incantus why Princess Isobel has returned as a pile of sawdust."

King Anders pursed his lips tightly. Marco kept his eyes locked on the king, though he desperately wanted to look over at Simon. The king darted his eyes between Marco and Simon, until a gleam of understanding finally lit up his irises.

"Oh no," the king smiled. "Oh, no, no, no. This can't . . . you . . . Oh, no."

"Let him go," Isobel said. "Now."

The king looked at his daughter as though she had betrayed him. With a sigh, he nodded to the guards who held Simon. Marco breathed out relief as they produced a key and unlocked his irons.

Simon shook his head at Marco, holding up the slippers. "Why?"

"You saved me," Marco said. "I'm returning the favor. Now run."

"Marco—"

"Run!"

Simon hesitated, shaking his head in disbelief. He looked down at the slippers, and pulled them to his chest. He looked back at Marco.

Then he was gone, disappearing through the thicket of trees. Once the sound of his footsteps had died away, Marco lowered his sword and gently pushed Isobel forward, freeing her of the charade.

"Arrest him!" King Anders ordered.

Marco didn't resist as the guards came forward and pushed him to the ground. One took great pleasure in kicking him in the gut. Marco clutched his stomach, willing the grog to stay down.

"No!" Isobel knelt, taking Marco under the arms and helping him to stand again. "Isn't it obvious? He wasn't going to hurt me."

"It does not matter!" The king said. "Just *look* at you, Isobel! How is he ever going to-"

"I wanted to," Marco said, wincing through the pain. "Please know that I wanted to."

"I know," Isobel said. "Now *you* run."

"How will you—"

"It's not our story," Isobel said. She took his hand in hers and squeezed. "But yours just ran into the forest. Go."

Marco gave Isobel a tight, disbelieving stare. Finally, he nodded. She gave him a gentle shove, and he stumbled toward the line of guards that had closed them off from the trees.

"Stand aside," Isobel shouted at the guards.

The guards slid their eyes to the king, who merely rolled his eyes. Slowly, the guards parted.

Flora came forward and picked up the satchel. "Go."

She tossed it to Marco, and he slung it over his shoulder. He looked at Isobel once more.

"It's alright," Isobel said. "Please go!"

Before he could change his mind, Marco ran between the guards and disappeared into the forest, hoping he ran in the direction of the thief.

19. FORBIDDEN FRUIT

Thick fog shrouded the forest, and the moon sliced it into ribbons of light that bounced up the trees in ghoulish shades of pearl and teal. It unnerved Simon, causing him to stop and spin around, trying to find his bearings. But all that surrounded him was forest, for miles it seemed. No sign of The Maestroa's showgrounds.

No shelter. No direction. Just Simon and a pair of jeweled slippers.

"Well," he muttered. "I got the slippers, Father."

Yet, he still didn't know what came next. The empty spot in his doublet seemed much larger than ever, and he desperately wanted his book. Not that it would tell him anything. But when one is lost in the wilderness without any sort of direction, it is often a small familiar thing that makes you better.

Twigs snapped, and he whirled to the sound, raising the slippers to use as a weapon if need be. A figure stumbled through the fog and Simon took three steps back.

"Get back or I'll strike!" He forced out.

The figure raised an arm to protect themselves. "Some thanks for saving your life again."

Simon heaved a sigh and doubled over. "You."

"Me." Marco stepped closer, and the stupid smirk appeared in the dim light. "I thought I'd lost you."

"I thought I'd lost *all* of you," Simon said, righting himself. "Where are the guards, the king—"

"It's just us," Marco said.

Simon shook his head and considered the slippers. "Why did you come after me?"

Marco shrugged, daring another step. "You have my slippers."

"You *gave* them to me."

"Yes, I was there."

Simon could practically feel the heat from Marco's chest, he'd gotten so close. But he didn't step back. He stayed his ground, clutching the slippers tighter. "Why?"

"Why was I there?"

Simon grunted. "Why did you give me these? Why did you help me?"

Marco tilted his head. "I thought it might be getting obvious."

"What?"

The prince's finger slid beneath Simon's chin and lifted his face so that their eyes met.

Marco glanced at his finger. "Does that make you uncomfortable?"

Simon shook his head, and before he could stop himself, he moved his lips forward, until they landed against the prince's. The contact sent sharp tingles through his arms and he nearly sent the slippers to the ground. After a moment, he pulled away.

"Did that make *you* uncomfortable?"

Marco shook his head. "No."

His hand rested against Simon's cheek, and he kissed him back. Simon counted to four in his head before Marco pulled back.

"All right," said Marco. "If we're going to do this, I need you to close your eyes."

"What?"

"You're leaving them open. It's creepy."

Simon's eyes widened and he turned away. "Okay, now I'm embarrassed."

Marco laughed and grabbed Simon's hand, pulling him back and planting a princely kiss on his knuckles.

"Holy crowns, this is a bad idea," said.

"Oh, it's terrible," Marco muttered, kissing Simon's wrist. "Horrible. We'll regret this come sunrise."

He made his way up Simon's arm, kissing the shoulder of his doublet before finding his cheek in the darkness.

Simon willed his heart not to completely explode as the shoes slipped from his fingers. They slid down Marco's back and bounced against the soft earth. But he didn't bother to check on them, instead linking his arms around the prince's neck and resting his forehead against the prince's.

"But for now, there's the moon," whispered Simon.

"Scoundrel," Marco whispered.

"Braggart."

"Thief."

"Charlatan."

∽

"We must be after them at once!" King Anders ordered. "If for no other crime, than for making me anxious."

"Papa." Isobel followed the king to the royal carriage, cringing as the hinge in her knee squeaked. "Just let it go. He didn't love me, he could never break my spell."

"True love's kiss only," muttered Flora.

The king whirled around, so violently that Isobel thought for a moment that he might strike and she stumbled back, her wooden hand knocking against Flora's porcelain skirts.

"Oh, he will break it," the king promised. "He will break it, or I will break *him*."

Isobel rolled her eyes. "This is why no one wants to come to your garden parties."

The king scoffed. "My subjects *love* my garden parties. They have to! It is the law."

"It's a stupid law," said Isobel. "When I'm queen, I shall—"

The king cut her off with a bellowing laugh. "When you're queen, you'll honor your king. I know you don't love each other, I'm not a fool. But it's a marriage. Love has nothing to do with it."

"So you would rather I be heartless!" Isobel's voice raised. "Not even able to feel. Like I'm . . . well, made of wood!"

King Anders winced. "You make it sound so terrible. I don't seem to recall you taking issue with it before."

"You didn't listen before," said Isobel. "You never listened to what I wanted. Why do you I think I even asked The Maestroa to . . . " she stammered. "You're right. It's been an eventful night."

But King Anders had already cocked his head at the princess and leaned in. "What did you just say?"

Flora stepped forward. "She's confused, Your Majesty. Being enchanted does quite a number on the mind, you know."

"Silence, handmaid," the king said, his eyes remaining on Isobel. "What do you mean, asked The Maestroa?"

Isobel twisted a lock of hair around her finger and looked to the ground. "They promised a fairy tale romance. I just wanted to be in love, for real. I just wanted the person I marry to be my hero. They made it sound so simple."

"Simple is for illustrated princesses," Flora muttered. Isobel shot her a look and she pursed her lips.

"So all of this was your choice." King Anders shook his head. "You kidnapped *yourself*."

Isobel crossed her arms and lifted a painted eyebrow at her father. "Well, I had to do *something* before I signed my name away and inevitably died in childbirth."

King Anders took a deep, shaking breath, his expression darkening. He reached behind himself and pulled open the gilded carriage door. "In. Now."

Isobel tilted her head at the king, raising her eyebrow further. "Still not listening."

She jumped as the king took her by the wrist and flung her into the carriage.

"I don't care to listen!" he shouted at her, turning to Flora, who held her hands up in a surrender.

"I'm getting in," Flora said. "Easy now, I'll shatter."

She slid into the carriage, and the king slammed the door.

"I wish I'd given him a splinter." Isobel smiled. But Flora didn't laugh. "We need to talk."

∽

"Seriously." Simon gripped a lock of Marco's hair and gently tugged. "How is your hair always so perfect?"

Marco grinned down at him. "It's not real."

"What?" Simon squeaked, and Marco let out a loud laugh.

"I'm joking!" He shook his head. "I don't know. Just grows this way, I guess."

He kissed Simon's forehead and rolled over onto the earth next to him. Their fingers found each other and laced together as the pair of them looked up at the moon.

"Did you know about me?" Simon asked. "That I might like you?"

"Not exactly," said Marco. "I just kind of hoped."

"When did you first realize? That you wanted to kiss me?"

Marco was quiet for a moment, his lips twisting into a thoughtful expression, before saying, "When you asked if I wanted to see your dagger."

"Really?"

Marco shrugged. "What about you?"

"I don't know. I guess it sort of happened. I didn't want to entertain it too much."

Marco's fingers tightened around Simon's. "Nic."

Simon sighed. Now would be the time. The time to tell

him his real name, his real identity. Things were nice between them, it would be best to get it done now. Simon took a deep breath and sat up. "I need to tell you something."

"One second." Marco pointed. "Do you see that star?"

Simon looked up at the sky. "Can you narrow that down?"

"The sort of blue one." Marco pointed higher. "The smaller one, with the blue ring. You see it?"

Simon scanned the sky until his eyes landed on the tinted star. "Oh. Yes, I see it."

"That's the one that leads to Lands Upper. Where my home is. I'd like to take you there, if you'd like." He propped himself on his elbows and grinned up at Simon. "You can speak to the dwarf council about their questionable business ethics. Canaries shall build a shrine to your activism. Can't lie, I respected you for that."

Simon snorted. "Really?"

"Well, yes. Who cares about canaries?"

"No," said Simon. "I mean, you want to take me to your *home*?"

The smirk again. Simon would have to get over that, or he'd be in trouble for the rest of his life. "I just peeved off a king and possibly sparked a war. I'm going to follow through. On this." Marco slid his hand to Simon's cheek. "On you, Nic."

Simon's heart flipped, and every ounce of courage he'd felt moments before sank to the bottom of his soul. "What were you going to tell me?"

Blinking, Simon shook his head. "Oh. Um. I'm hungry."

Marco laughed. "You're hungry?"

"Well, I haven't eaten in a while." Simon looked away.

The satchel laid discarded a few feet away. Marco rolled over onto his knees and reached for it, digging inside.

"I think we ate it all, but . . . oh. Hold on. There's one thing left."

"Oh, you can have it. I'll find something."

But Marco wasn't listening, staring at the piece of fruit that rested in his palm. A plum. It was the most brilliant purple color that Simon had ever seen, almost glowing beneath the dim light of the moon. He stared at it with longing, his mouth watering insatiably.

Eat me, the plum seemed to whisper in Simon's inner ear. *Just one bite, dear.*

"Want to split it?" asked Marco.

"All right," said Simon, hungrily.

With his thumb, Marco broke the flesh of the plum, a stream of lavender colored juice dripping from its meat. He tore the plum into two fleshy halves and gave the bigger half to Simon.

"I don't remember even packing this," Marco said and he bit into his half.

Simon didn't respond, the first bite on his tongue, oozing juice and flavor like he'd never tasted. He chewed slowly, considering how strange the fruit was as it buzzed and tingled in his mouth. His eyelids drooped, and soon were heavy. "Simon?"

His head dipped down, his forehead suddenly very heavy. He had to lay down. Just for a moment. He fell deep asleep before he could swallow the bite.

20. VISIONS OF SUGARPLUMS

He awakened on a bed of velvet. A crushed, purple velvet, soft and wet with the smell of saltwater. For a fleeting moment, he thought himself to be inside of the plum itself. Inside its dripping flesh, resting upon the pit like a tiny insect, a mere worm, and for a second he feared he would be devoured.

The velvet he lay on hit against something and rocked him violently, forcing him to sit up on his elbows and look around in the haze of fog that kept his mind drunk.

He found himself in a gondola, docking at the garden of a white palace. He saw trees strung with purple lanterns, servants in velvet breeches wearing white masks, dotted with purple teardrops. Curls of purple powdered wigs framed their masked faces.

"Lord Simon," a servant said as he pulled the gondola to the dock. "We have been expecting you."

The servant helped Simon to stand, and as he bent his knees, Simon found that his loose brown trousers had been replaced by fitted white breeches of satin, tucked into shining black riding boots. He felt for his doublet, but it too was gone. In its place, he wore a white jacket, also of satin, brocaded in blue and silver. A cravat threatened to choke him and he instinctively slipped a finger between it and his throat, trying to loosen the fabric and breathe.

He allowed the masked servant to help him onto the dock. For the first time, he saw a string of people in dark purple and silver, making their way up the palace steps, and he turned to see more gondolas arriving. Party goers in dripping gowns and gleaming jackets, masks of cream, black, and violet. Styles of harlequins, rabbits, and horses.

"I don't have an invitation," Simon quietly admitted.

The servant smiled beneath his mask. "So you don't."

He escorted Simon up the steps to the palace entrance. They arrived at the door so quickly. Hadn't they just been on the dock?

"Welcome," a different servant stationed at the purple curtained entryway said. He reached for a long cord.

"I have no mask," Simon heard himself say, though he didn't open his mouth to speak.

"So you don't," the servant said. He tugged the cord and the curtains parted.

Simon stepped through, finding himself at the top of a large, white marble staircase. He felt humiliated and at the same time excited to find hundreds of curious and brightly masked faces smiling up at him from below. Faces powdered white, dotted with faux beauty marks of black and blue.

Women in wide skirts shaped like sofas swirled across the floor. The orchestra played a pas de deux, their heads covered in burlap sacks. They wouldn't know when to stop playing, and the music would go until dawn.

Simon laid his hand on the marble rail of the steps, and slowly made his descent to the ballroom floor as the servant at the entry announced him.

"Lord Simon of Squirm," the servant's voice echoed throughout the ballroom.

The silver chandelier above, with its purple candles flickering flames of green, swayed gently, stirring in a breeze that billowed the long silk curtains that streamed above the dancers.

Simon reached the bottom of the steps and made his way across the floor, past twirling dancers, elbows against elbows, his jacket brushing the fabrics of the others' fine suits and gowns.

His eyes met the others as he passed, but none were familiar. None grabbed or stirred his heart, and now that he'd reached the middle of the floor, he realized that he'd been expecting someone. He felt disappointed they weren't there.

Or were they?

Turning, he caught sight of a figure at the top of another staircase, leaning broodingly against the rail.

Funny, thought Simon. *There hadn't been another staircase a moment ago.*

The young man was dressed in black, unlike the other party goers, his jacket brocaded in gold. His mask, also black, was tight on his face, threatening to betray his features. Simon's dark eyes met the young man's blue.

His feelings betrayed him, and Simon felt himself smile as the young man descended the stairs toward him.

He wore a red cape that rippled in the breeze as he came, like the heroes of his long-gone book.

The young man stood before Simon now, and still Simon could not place his face. He might have been handsome, and he might not have been. Simon didn't care.

The young man's hand wrapped around Simon's back, digging with all the force and gentleness of a first-time lover as he swept Simon into the orchestra's beginning waltz, the music rising and falling like the waves he'd arrived upon.

Simon furrowed his eyebrows, looking deep into the young man's eyes, and felt like he would cry with the familiarity of the feeling he had, like the broken heartedness of a murderer who'd just been found out. The young man knew all of his secrets, Simon felt.

His face neared the young man's, their lips on a path that could only end in collision, a road with no spot to turn about, as the party goers stopped dancing, stopped moving at all. Their masked eyes slide to Simon and the young man. Silent praise.

Their lips were one inch away from one another. Yet Simon found his hand sliding upward, between those lips, blocking their meeting, as his fingers pushed gently at the mask that hid this young man's identity.

It was Marco, Simon knew. It was Marco, and he was about to see him unmasked. He pried the mask from the young man's face and it tumbled to the floor.

Simon gasped and stumbled backwards as the deep blue eyes of the young man flashed purple, and he stared not into the face of Marco, but of The Maestroa.

"You've failed."

Something hot dripped on his hand, and Simon looked down to see purple wax burning his skin. He looked up. Above the rain of wax, the chandelier was melting. He stepped back as it fell, crashing between him and The Maestroa and sank into the floor, through a bubbling puddle of plum juice. He looked at The Maestroa on the other side.

But it was no longer their face. It twisted and changed. A black mustache appeared above their lip as the face became his father. "What a disappointment."

"No!" Simon fell backwards. He caught himself with his wrists against the marble floor.

The face twisted again, and Simon shuddered to see King Anders.

"Arrest him!"

The orchestra players sprang from their chairs, dangling in the air, half lifeless and kicking, hanged faces masked by burlap hoods. Simon screamed.

He ran. He ran as far as he could, as fast as he could, and yet he wasn't moving at all. His mind ran, but his legs stood quaking upon the floor.

The walls of the ballroom crumbled, the silk curtains fluttering away into the black night, the party goers all laughing, crowding around Simon. They screamed laughter in his face, the juice of plums spewing from their mouths and spraying onto Simon's white jacket as he screamed and pushed at them to get away.

They gnashed and sprayed, bit at him. They would rip him apart.

Simon looked through the crowd to The Maestroa,

who now looked like Marco, cackling. They vanished, leaving behind only a white grin.

Somewhere in the crumbling world, a clock struck midnight, the bell slow and hallow, echoing through the ballroom.

Simon pushed free of the crowd and bounded up the crumbling staircase. He ran through the purple curtain, now blazing in lavender flames.

The gardens outside withered, the trees turning to paper and canvas, shredding and ripping with every step that Simon ran.

He skidded to a stop on the dock, nearly toppling over the edge. He glanced back at the palace, now engulfed in purple flames and burning to ash, crumbling in a haze of smoke.

He peered down into the dark wine-colored waves that lapped at him like a taunt. Where was his gondola?

Simon looked around but saw no means to leave. He looked to his feet, and saw that his gondola had transformed into a mushy, rotten plum, buzzing with flies and maggots on the planks.

A hand appeared from thin air, slapped him hard across the face.

"Wake up!"

Simon's eyes jerked open, expecting to see the moonlit sky once more. Instead, grinning down at him, was The Maestroa.

21. PRIDE AND THE LACK THEREOF

Isobel forced a laugh. "I don't understand. Why are you being so cold?"

On the opposite seat of the carriage, Flora set about polishing her skirt, the sound of glass against glass dragging a shrill screech as she rubbed at the spot. The sound made Isobel tense, as much as a wooden girl can tense. When Flora looked back at her, her eyes had reddened from the sting of tears that would never fall. Her painted mouth had drawn itself into a tight bow, and Isobel thought she looked rather like a frustrated duck.

That's her angry face, Isobel noted, and thought it best to remain quiet until Flora broke the silence.

"Oh, I don't know," said Flora. "Woke up on the wrong side of the forest, I suppose."

Isobel rolled her eyes. "We don't have time for this. We need to get out of here."

She gripped the carriage door and pushed. It didn't give. She turned to the opposite door and tried that one, but it too would not open.

"They're locked," said Flora.

Isobel snapped her eyes to Flora. "Yes, I imagine they are. Why hadn't I already thought of that?"

She threw herself back against the plush backrest and threw her hand against her forehead. "Think of something. I can't, I'm in too much distress."

Flora grunted. "That's not going to work on me anymore."

Isobel lifted her hand just enough to look at Flora with one eye. "What's not going to work?"

"The distressed princess act. I've put up with it for long enough." Flora cocked an eyebrow. "It's a bit tired, don't you think?"

Isobel sat up, her pine fingers poking tiny holes in the upholstery of the seat under her grip. "Well, I don't know what else to do."

Flora's eyes slid to the ceiling. "I can think of a few things you could try."

Beyond the window, the guards were gathered around King Anders. He stood making some sort of speech with great passion. *Pretending to give orders as though he knows what he's talking about*, Isobel assumed. Probably some way to get Marco and Simon back in custody and her back in her pink stained nightmare of a bedroom in the castle keep. Probably forevermore.

"We have to get out of here," Isobel said. "If they take us out of this forest without our hearts, it's done. Over. *We* are done."

"You can say that again," Flora grumbled.

"What?"

"I don't know. Perhaps not having a heart would make me feel a lot better."

"What are you even talking about?" Isobel pinched the space between her eyes, but it did little to soothe her wooden head.

Flora leaned forward, the glass of her bodice sliding against the skirt with another screech. "Isobel, the jig is up. Marco stood there, in front of *everyone*, and made it known how he feels about Simon. That was your chance, and you pulled away from me. It made me realize that you are *never* going to be all right with yourself. And I can't go on loving someone who doesn't love me enough to say it."

"I *do* love you!" Isobel fought not to shout, lest they be heard. "I'd do anything for you."

"You'd *say* anything for me, you mean." Flora settled back into her seat and looked to the floor. "Not do."

Isobel's chin trembled. "I love you."

Flora looked at Isobel once more, the red in her eyes even darker. "So why doesn't our spell break when you kiss me at midnight?"

Isobel opened her mouth, but no words came. She stared back at Flora, at the reflection of the guards in her shining cheek, just beyond the carriage. Two worlds across one face. Still, the words didn't appear.

Flora sighed. "And there's my answer."

"I love you," was all Isobel could think to say.

To this, Flora laughed. "So much that you sought the help of a magician to give you a—" she quoted with her fingers, "—*'Fairy tale'* that you decided you're supposed to have, the way you were *told* to. Can you maybe, I don't know, think for yourself?"

"That's not fair."

"You dragged a man you would *never* love into it, you've got a thief on the run for his life, and at any second I could fall for you even more. But here's the thing about me, Isobel!" Flora's voice had raised so loudly that the window treatments vibrated as she leaned across the seat, her hands pushing into Isobel's knees. "If I fall, I break."

Isobel pulled her eyes from Flora and glanced out the window. The noise had caught the attention of King Anders and the guards. They stared back at her, their faces worried and tense.

Opening her mouth, Isobel beat on the window. "Fire! Fire!"

"What *are* you doing?" asked Flora.

"Getting us out of here," said Isobel. "Fire!"

King Anders ran to the carriage. "Open the door! Quickly!"

The driver came around to the door and pulled a golden key from the inner pocket of his coat. He fumbled it into the lock and pulled the door open. Isobel tumbled out, quick to push herself back to her feet.

"Come on!" she called back to Flora, breaking into a run.

"Isobel!" Flora angrily called after her.

King Anders slid in front of Isobel, putting his hand out. "What are you doing? Stop!"

Isobel threw back her arm and returned it with a tight fist, slamming into the king's chin. He went tumbling to the ground, his gray curls bouncing against the earth.

"Did you listen to *that?*" Isobel called back as she jumped over her father and made for the trees.

Behind her, she heard the clinking of Flora's feet against pebbles. Beyond her, the pitter pat of Hans, stumbling behind and calling out for them to wait for him. But no guards came after them, too busy trying to right and fluff up King Anders again.

She darted between the trees, towards the direction that she hoped would lead to Marco and Simon.

They couldn't call it a journey and be done. She needed her heart back. Not just to live, but to know what it wanted, so that she could follow it.

22. THREE LITTLE WORDS

"Hello, puppet thief," The Maestroa cooed.

Simon rolled over and scampered from beneath the magician, quick to push himself to his feet and stumble back. The moon had grown lower in the sky, lighting them from behind. It made them seem even more imposing, more dangerous. The spikes of their skirt seemed to have grown sharper. A collar now sliced the air around their face. Like a poisonous dragon ready to breathe fire. Were their eyes even more purple, glowing in the dark?

Simon coughed, and the pit of the plum shot up through his throat. He spat it out and shuddered, the taste of the dream, the nightmare really, still fresh on his tongue. He didn't remember even biting into the pit.

Simon looked down at Marco, who lay passed out on the ground.

"Marco!" he said. "Wake up!"

The Maestroa laughed. "That isn't going to work, puppet thief."

"What did you do to him?"

Inspecting a long fingernail, The Maestroa shrugged. "Same thing I did to you. I don't think he's finished dreaming yet."

Simon bent down, reaching for Marco's sword. Just as his fist closed around the handle, The Maestroa thrust out their hands and he flew backward. The sword pulled from Marco's belt and tossed itself through the air, stabbing the ground just before The Maestroa.

Just as he was about to slam into the trunk of a tree, the boughs came down and caught him, wrapping around his torso, wrists, and ankles, holding him in place above the ground.

The Maestroa gripped the handle of the sword and used it as a cane as they came toward him. "There is no reason we can't do this the easy way."

Simon struggled against the tree boughs, but they would not release him. He gave up with a frustrated sigh and glared down at The Maestroa.

"What are you going to do?"

The Maestroa chuckled. "I already told you. Gab."

"I'm not big on gossip."

Rolling their purple eyes, The Maestroa looked back to Marco, who still lay perfectly still on the ground. In the dark, he looked almost lifeless, and it sent a chill through Simon.

"Charming, isn't he?" asked The Maestroa, pinching their lips into a puppy dog pout. "And so good, to give up everything for an hour with you. That must have been quite flattering."

"Let's just say I've had worse gestures." Simon narrowed his eyes.

"Tell me." The Maestroa stabbed the sword into the ground and clasped their hands together. "Could you taste his dinner when you, what shall we call it?"

"Kissed?"

"Good idea." The Maestroa grinned. "Keep it clean for the kiddos."

"That's all we—" Simon raised an eyebrow. "I don't kiss and tell."

"Well, that's not plum-juicy, is it? It really is a shame." The Maestroa's voice lowered and dragged, the velvet of their voice scraping across the gravel of their throat.

"When the sun rises, it will all be for nothing, won't it?"

"What do you mean?"

With a singular laugh, The Maestroa stepped closer. "I think it's obvious. There's still the matter of the wooden princess. Out there, all alone, with no one to help her."

"I don't know," said Simon. "She seems pretty tough."

Their tongue slid over their unnervingly white teeth, like a wolf happening upon a chicken. "That's not the spectacle I designed, or the script I was asked to write, now was it?"

A hot wave of fear sloshed through Simon's chest. "It's not your story anymore. This is real life."

"Is it?" The Maestroa reached into their ringleader coat and produced a small leather volume. Simon's heart skipped and he struggled against the boughs as The Maestroa held the book of tales up for him to see. "I found this. Took the liberty of having a glance, I hope you don't mind."

"How did you—"

"I have my ways." The Maestroa flipped through the book, more interested in its pictures than the thief hanging over them. "Aren't you a bit old for it? I can't imagine what's in here for you."

"Give it back."

The Maestroa's eyes snapped to Simon's. "Wait, did you think it's all going to be like this in the end? Oh, you dear little piglet. There's the three little words at the end that you are not going to hear. That *none* of you will hear. Do you know what those three little words are?"

"Don't eat plums?" Simon guessed with as much annoyance as he could work in.

"*Happily ever after.* Could have had it, but then you stole my puppets, stole her prince, and ruined it all."

"Maybe I made it better," shouted Simon.

The Maestroa laughed. "Oh, no, honey. No." They made their way over to Marco, stabbing the sword into the ground with each heavy step. "You think he can just gallop you into his kingdom on the back of a steed? Won't that raise eyebrows? Nary a dwarf could respect *you* as a royal, even by a sham marriage. As we've seen with this one, it doesn't take much to get him going on his easy way out."

"You're wrong."

The Maestroa reached over the sleeping Marco and picked up the jeweled slippers. They made their way back to Simon, waving them around so that the colors bounced in the moonlight and made Simon squint.

"Am I? Go on, then." The Maestroa tossed the slippers to the ground. "Give those back to him. Tell him why. See if he returns them."

"Why are you doing this?" asked Simon. "Why does any of this even matter to you?"

The Maestroa's grin grew even larger as they struck a pose, with one hand on the sword and the other waving high above their head with a bent wrist.

"Because I'm the villain, darling," they said. "I wasn't going to be, but you didn't take my giant seriously enough. I had to do better. And I can't *bear* to see you all make fools of yourselves. Better you learn while you're young."

"You're wrong," Simon repeated under his breath.

The Maestroa produced the book once more. "Let's see . . . 'the prince and the princess' . . . 'the princess and the prince' . . . 'the knight and the maiden' . . . Hmm. I don't see 'the same-sex couple'." They tossed the book to the ground. "We aren't in here, darling."

The Maestroa turned and made their way across the clearing as Simon struggled more violently against the boughs. At last, the tree gave way and he slipped to the ground. He fell on his knees and reached for the book. The Maestroa snapped their fingers over their shoulder and the book burst into purple flames.

"No!" Simon screamed. But when the flames died away, he looked only at a pile of lavender ashes, already scattering in the breeze.

The Maestroa turned around, putting a hand to their lips. "Oh my, did I do that? Why, it's almost like we don't really exist."

"What is wrong with you?" Simon spat out. "I'd think you would *want* to help."

"Why?" The Maestroa challenged. "No one ever did the same for me."

A purple cloud surrounded them, and once the smoke dissipated, they had vanished.

Simon watched the final ashes of his book blow away. The moon dipped behind the trees, and the tissue paper sun rose. Another day in the forest of false enchantment.

Feet away, Marco slept on. Simon had to wake him up. What happened in all those stories he read, about the sleeping princesses?

He crawled over to Marco and kissed him softly. The prince remained still for a moment, and then his eyes fluttered open. Simon sighed in relief as Marco coughed and tilted his head, the bite of plum he had taken rolling from his lips into the grass.

Marco sat up, blinking and rubbing his eyes. His eyes fell on Simon, and he smiled.

"I don't think I like plums very much," he said uncomfortably. "Choking hazard. You already up?"

Simon looked away, over to the discarded slippers. They nearly blinded him, gleaming so bright in the morning.

"I was just having a think."

Marco held an arm out to Simon. "Come here, tell me about it."

Simon thought for a moment to go to him. He could lay down and just pretend like it was all fine. Like The Maestroa didn't just show up and set his book on fire, remind him of everything he feared, though he didn't want to admit it.

He looked at the slippers. Did he really have a right to keep them? It's not like he could wear them. Would Marco really take them back, and if so, where would they go next? To who? The thought hurt too much to think about it. He shook his head and pushed himself to his feet.

"It doesn't really matter," he said. "I'm fine."

Marco smirked at him, but didn't argue. Simon noticed the smirk was tighter than usual. Forced, perhaps.

"Okay," said Marco quietly.

"We should get going. Isobel and Flora need us, and . . ."

"Woah, wait a minute." Marco stood up, brushing off his jacket. "No one said anything about going back. We have to go onward and get out of this forest. It's not our problem anymore."

"And what *is* our problem?" Simon asked before he could stop himself. "Ride into Lands Upper together? You with another man wrapped around your waist? I'm sure your family would just *love* that."

Marco tossed his head, looking up at the sky. "I don't care. That's the whole point of us running together! I thought last night, we—"

"We did. Last night." Simon dug his heel into the ground. "And now it's morning. There's a wicked magician after all of us. Not to mention an angry king and his army. We can't just waltz off into a sunset, it's not that easy."

"Maybe it should be," argued Marco.

"It absolutely should be," agreed Simon. "But it's not."

Marco sighed, dropping his head. His eyes looked fierce as he stared at the grass, deep in thought.

"All right, fine," he said at last. "I guess we can't do this, then."

Simon snorted before he could stop himself. It was the only thing that distracted him from his entire heart falling through his chest and down into his feet. "Wow. That didn't take much to break you."

Marco looked at Simon, his eyes glassy. "I just don't know what you're wanting right now."

Simon took a deep breath. He wanted Marco to fight for him. He wanted him to calm his fears and make him forget every lie that The Maestroa just tried to shove down his throat. But this wasn't some game. It wasn't a half-baked scheme that his father had cooked up, and it certainly wasn't a fabricated show for The Maestroa anymore.

"What I want," he said, picking up the slippers and reaching for the satchel. "Is to go get our friends, be done with The Maestroa, and *then* see what you're thinking. We can't ignore all of the problems and run."

He dropped the slippers into the bag with a definitive *clink*.

Marco gave a slight shrug. "It always suited me just fine."

Simon pursed his lips. "Then I guess that's where we differ."

He pulled the satchel strap over his chest and moved

to leave, but halted when he heard the thud of Marco's boots coming after him.

"Fine," the prince said. "We'll do it the hard way, then!"

Simon looked back at him, and now *he* was the one smirking. "Really?"

"Only because you're distracting me from my usual self." Marco tilted his head and gave Simon an accusatory stare. "Are you always so distracting?"

"Only when I'm around you."

Marco kissed him, and for a moment, the fears were gone. The Maestroa was wrong.

They existed.

"Let's go help a damsel in distress." Marco smiled when he'd pulled away.

Simon opened his mouth to respond, but a cry in the distance stopped him.

"Was that who I think it was?"

"This way." Marco took Simon's hand, and they ran for the trees, towards the direction Isobel had screamed.

23. A ROYAL BLUNDER

The wheels rattled as they dipped into a rut in the forest road, and the entire carriage jolted, forcing King Anders to clap his hand onto his head in order to hold his royal wig on.

"Gaspard, please tell the driver to be careful!" he shouted. "Or I shall lose my hair!"

Gaspard dutifully stuck his head out the window and shouted, "Be wary, driver! Or the king shall lose his hair!"

The driver didn't look back as he responded, "I heard him the first time."

"If I lose my hair, then he shall lose his head!" King Anders shouted even louder, tugging his wig with great force as it threatened to slide off once more.

"If he loses his hair—"

"I heard him!" snapped the driver.

King Anders huffed and resigned to look out the window at the muddy forest. It was no wonder that his castle had gardens to stroll in, so he didn't have to venture into this muck.

"Of all the nerve," he muttered. "Send a prince to do one thing! One thing! Apprehend a criminal. Is that so much to ask? And here we are, going to apprehend *him*. And his little thieving friend, and not to mention my *daughter*! Do you think it made her daft, turning into wood?"

"Young people today." Gaspard dabbed his powdered white face with his handkerchief. "Lazy, arrogant, entitled—"

"And to think that piece of nothing shall marry my only wooden daughter." King Anders sighed. "Oh, if we didn't need diamonds so much, I'd tell that mining kingdom where to shove their canaries."

"They do employ dwarfs, sire," offered Gaspard.

"I'll tell them where to shove their dwarfs, too," said King Anders. "Gaspard, you don't suppose Marco could have been forced to side with the thief for fear of danger, do you?"

"That thief, sire?" Gaspard questioned. "Dangerous?" He couldn't help but snort.

"I don't know, but he's wiry," Kings Anders said. "You can't trust the wiry ones. Less muscle to hold them down."

"Alright then, sire." Gaspard still giggled at the thought of the wiry boy actually able to take down anyone.

The carriage lurched again, and the horses neighed and bucked. It jostled King Anders hard against the sides of the carriage, sending him into Gaspard's lap momentarily, who quickly tried to help and fan him.

"Unhand me, you fool!" King Anders pushed

Gaspard's flimsy hands away and adjusted his hair. "Driver! Did I not warn you!"

A face swung down and peered through the window. Dark hair hung in front the man's face, mostly from the fine black mustache that he sported.

"You did, but he does not care what you think."

King Anders yelped and threw himself into the arms of Gaspard, who shook with fear.

"Driver! Quick! There's a ruffian in my window!"

"I don't believe the driver would wish to help you," said Bloody Fingers with an upside down grin. "He's on our side, you see. And there is quite a difference between a ruffian and a bandit."

A clinking knocked against the window and both passengers turned to see The Vizier waving his hooks at them.

"Driver! Whatever happened to your hands?" wailed Gaspard.

"I'm with him." The Vizier gestured to Blood Fingers.

"And I'm afraid we are commandeering this carriage for our own use," said Bloody Fingers regally. "If you would kindly vacate the premises immediately."

"We shall not!" King Anders protested. "This is my royal carriage, for I am king! Who are you, who frowns so?"

"Frown?" asked Bloody Fingers. "Whatever do you mean?"

"He's upside down," Gaspard whispered to King Anders.

"Oh," said King Anders. "Who are you who smiles so?"

Bloody Fingers back flipped off of the carriage and bowed through the window. "I am Bloody Fingers!"

"No!" The passengers screamed and held each other.

"Most feared villain in the kingdom!"

"Second most," said Gaspard.

"Ahem," Bloody Fingers ignored the offending passenger and continued on, brandishing his sword. "I thank you for making it so easy. You see, when you were distracted and running after a well-made puppet and what appeared to be a waddling teapot, we were all too happy to take over."

"That was no teapot," King Anders said. "That was my daughter's handmaid."

"Intriguing," said Bloody Fingers. "I'd love to hear more, except we are rather busy commandeering your carriage."

"Well, you can't have it!" said King Anders. "I need this carriage to find my daughter, who is after my future son-in-law, who is on the lam with an uncoordinated criminal. Therefore *I* need the carriage!"

Bloody Fingers looked through the window to the Vizier, who was still looking through the opposite window. "Vizier, please have Humphrey forcibly remove these royal shrimps from my carriage."

"Don't you dare!" King Anders cried out.

But Bloody Fingers was laughing, and he turned around to take in his victory. He was met with the head of the King's army, who punched him hard.

Bloody Fingers dropped to the ground and passed out cold.

When Bloody Fingers snapped awake, he found he could hardly move, wiggling against a tree. All around him were his fellow bandits, bound and gagged on the forest floor. The Vizier's hooks had been removed, and he looked at them longingly where they were tucked into the captain of the guard's belt.

"Ah, you're awake," said King Anders as he sipped a cup of tea. "Rise and shine."

"Unhand me, you blackguards!" Bloody Fingers threatened. "Or I shall have Humphrey cut out your tongue and string me a new necklace!"

King Anders chortled, and Gaspard joined in along with the guards. "Oh, don't be silly. You've been apprehended. Now, have you anything to say before my guards hang you and your, um, crew, from that very tree?"

Bloody Fingers sighed. A noble end for a noble career.

"Not one thing, but a request."

"And that is?"

"That 'uncoordinated criminal' you're after is my son. And he's a fool who can't do anything right. So if you're going to hang me, promise me—"

"What? That I will not harm him? That I will let him go free?"

"Kill him fast and painlessly," said Bloody Fingers. "Put him out of his misery."

"Well, he ruined his own beautiful execution that I choreographed," scoffed the King. "So I don't know about that."

"What if," said Humphrey, who could never stand to

hear two imbeciles bicker for long, "we help you find them?"

"Don't be silly," scoffed Gaspard. "We would never trust the likes of you."

"We know woods," said Humphrey. "Better than any of you. We could find them faster than you could ever hope to."

King Anders considered for a moment.

"You're trying to trap us," he said. "You probably have an entire scheme planned out to overtake us."

"Not at all!" said Bloody Fingers. "We are too impulsive and idiotic to ever plan ahead."

The Vizier turned to Bloody Fingers. "Of course, *now* you admit it."

"But the answer is plain." Bloody Fingers ignored the un-hook-handed-man and continued. "If we find the squirm, we find your daughter."

King Anders leaned to his captain of the guard and whispered, "What do you think, Raul?"

"You don't pay me to think," Raul responded without blinking. "You pay me to rough people up and light things on fire."

"All right, well what if I *did* pay you to think?" King Anders rolled his eyes.

"I think you ought to at least give them that chance," Raul responded, stone faced, for he was quite tough. "We'll never get out of these woods otherwise, and my feet are beginning to hurt. We have been marching for days, and even I grow weary now and again."

"Very so, very so," agreed King Anders. "We shall allow you to help us, ruffians—"

"Bandits."

"But any funny business and the guards shall slice you to ribbons. They've only to wait for my word. Do you understand?"

"And what do we get for it?" Bloody Fingers demanded.

"Your necks unbroken," decreed the king.

"Not interested." Bloody Fingers shook his head.

"Oh yes you are!" cried The Fop. "Yes he is, your majesty!"

"Cowards, all of you," Bloody Fingers spat.

The Jester shook his rattle with his bound hands. *Rattle! Rattle! Rattle!*

"Not you, of course," Bloody Fingers said to him.

Rattle.

24. TRUTHS

Simon and Marco ran through the brush, pushing past twigs and vines, to the direction of the screams. The closer they got they could hear beyond Isobel.

"That's Hans," said Marco, noting a particularly high pitched shriek.

When at last they came through the brush, to the next thicket of trees, they looked up to see Isobel and Flora dangling in the boughs. A few yards further, a branch rocked Hans like a baby.

"Not these again." Marco drew his sword.

Simon took the weapon and ran forward. He was getting pretty tired of trees having their way with him.

"Wait!" Marco ran after him. "You could get hurt!" But Simon didn't listen, slashing at the tree's roots. The bark groaned, as the boughs unclenched their thorny fists and dropped their friends.

"No!" screamed Flora as she tumbled down.

Marco stuck out his arms and caught her, but the

weight of her glass skirts brought him to his knees and he dropped her, sending her rolling a few feet into the grass. She lay there, blinking up at the sky, as though unsure if she were still in one piece or not.

"Are you all right?" Simon called out as he helped Isobel to stand.

Flora sat up and looked around herself. She picked up a small, white shard and screamed. "I'm broken!"

Marco rushed forward and helped her to stand up, inspecting her arms and face. She swept her hand over her nose and breathed out a sigh of relief that it was still attached.

"It's from your skirt," said Marco, pointing to a small hole in her petticoat.

"Oh, that's fine," said Flora. "I hate skirts, anyways."

"What are you all doing here?" Simon handed the sword back to Marco.

Isobel smoothed back her hair. "Looking for you! If my father had gotten us out of this forest, the best use I'd be is to keep a fire burning."

A few feet away, Hans had rolled over and pulled himself into the fetal position. "Is the quest over, sire?"

"Afraid not, Hans." Marco pushed his sword into his belt. "Though I wish it were."

Isobel stepped forward. "Look, I'm sorry. I really was all for you two running off together, but considering I don't have all of my vital organs, I need help."

"We understand," said Simon. When Marco guffawed and opened his mouth to protest, he repeated, "We *understand*."

Marco snapped his mouth shut and closed his eyes.

"Fine. Yes, we will get your hearts back. Shall we resume our journey to certain death?"

"That's the spirit." Simon winked at him and turned to head back through the forest.

All right, Simon, he thought, *time to figure this grand plan out.*

But no ideas came. The Maestroa knew they were coming. They knew how to break him, too. They'd already tried and made that quite clear.

Every now and then Marco's fingers would brush against his knuckles as they walked, and each moment of contact made his heart clench even more. If they did somehow succeed, what would afterward even look like? How could they possibly be anything but a secret, like the princess and Flora, who he had noticed kept grunting and rolling her eyes at Isobel whenever the princess looked away?

He'd seen it with that stupid plum. He'd be chased away, always on the run. That's all he was. A fugitive with absolutely nothing to give.

"We should rest a bit," Marco said after a long while.

"My legs are on fire."

"You should run from the law more often," joked Simon. Marco only winced, and this made his heart sink.

Isobel groaned. "You mortal humans and your muscles. Fine. I'll rest my hinges."

She sat upon a boulder and smiled at Flora, patting the space next to her. But Flora slid in the opposite way and lowered herself onto a tuft of grass.

"Perhaps I shall take a nap," said Hans. "I didn't sleep

much last night, but I don't think any monsters lurk in the daytime."

"That's fine." Marco waved his hand, dismissing the servant. Hans disappeared through the trees, and without him the tension only grew between the two couples.

In the satchel, the slippers felt heavy. Simon laid his hand on the soft fabric, feeling the spikes of the heels pushing against his palms.

The voice of The Maestroa kept ringing in his ears, daring him to give them back.

Finally, he took a breath and whispered to Marco, "Can I talk to you a moment?"

Marco furrowed his eyebrows, but nodded, and Simon led the way through a bit of brush to the other side of a large oak.

"What is it?" Marco asked when Simon didn't begin.

Simon pulled open the flap of the satchel and reached in for the slippers. "I wanted to give you these."

He dared to look at Marco, and blushed to see that smirk, his brows slanted in a confused expression. "Oh?"

"They aren't really my style. And I have a feeling they're too small."

Marco laughed at this. "I didn't expect you to wear them."

"I just . . . " Simon looked to the ground. "I just know that we're about to get hurt. And I thought you would want them back."

Now the prince *really* laughed. "Don't decide we'll get hurt. If you decide that things will end up bad, then they will. Don't choose that."

"I can't really help it," said Simon. *Tell him your name.*

"Okay, can you not involve an innocent party, then?" Marco put his hand on his heart. He was still smiling, trying to joke, but Simon could see that he was being serious.

"What did you dream about last night?"

Marco stiffened. "I don't remember. Why?"

"Never mind."

Simon turned away, but Marco grabbed his wrist gently, the side of his hand brushed against the slipper's heel. "I gave those to the person I *want*. If you don't want me, that's all right, just say so."

"It's not that. I just, I realized that you don't actually know me."

"What?" Marco laughed again. "Of course I do, Nic, you're—"

Simon sucked air in, loudly, causing Marco to snap his mouth shut.

Here goes, thought Simon. *It was nice, knowing you liked me, for a minute.*

"I need to tell you something."

Marco's expression darkened. "Yes?"

"I'm—"

"Come on!" Isobel came running through the trees. Simon dropped the slippers back into the satchel and wiped an eye with the heel of his palm. "Come see!"

"What?" Marco rubbed his temples.

"Come look!" Isobel grabbed Simon's hand and pulled him along before he could protest. "Where is Hans?"

"Napping," said Marco. "What is it?"

Simon tugged on Isobel's hand. "I need to say something."

"Not now." Isobel pulled Simon further through the trees. "Come look."

She pulled him along, Marco and Flora following. They came to a dip in the ground, and Simon found himself looking out over the cliff, across the forest. In the distance, he saw towers, striped in purple and blue. An entire striped castle looming, all too close.

"Oh no," said Simon.

"Oh yes!" Isobel jumped up and down. "We're nearly there! I can almost hear my heart beating."

Simon's beat so loudly, he worried it would fall through his feet and into the ground beneath him.

"And my first pint of grog in far too long," said Flora.

Marco slapped his palm against hers. "Atta girl!"

The skin on Simon's face felt so tight he could hardly turn his head to look at them all. He stood frozen, just waiting for it all to fall in on his head.

"All right." Isobel clapped at him. "What's the plan? How do we get in?"

Simon stared ahead.

"Hell-*o*." Isobel snapped her fingers at him, two sticks clicking. "Bloody Fingers. Bandit extraordinaire."

"I thought I'd figure it out," Simon mumbled.

Flora's glass skirts clinked as her fists went to her hips. "What?"

Simon dared to look at Marco, who was looking at him curiously, confused. "I was trying to tell you."

"Nic?"

"That's not my name."

Everyone stared at him. He wanted them to react. To

yell at him or push him off the cliff. *Something*. But they only just stared at him.

"As in, I'm not Bloody Fingers."

Isobel blinked, "But you said—"

"Bloody Fingers," Simon took a deep breath, "is my father. My name is Simon. The Squirm."

"No," Isobel protested. "You're just trying to get out of the deal. You're—"

"Somehow," said Flora, "I find 'squirm' a lot easier to believe."

Simon hung his head and looked to the ground. From the corner of his eye, he saw Marco pace.

"You lied to us?" Isobel raised her voice.

"I needed you to come with me," said Simon, his voice small. "I thought you'd be more willing if you thought I was some big bad bandit, and not some idiot forced into this."

"I don't understand," Marco spoke finally, and the confusion in his voice made Simon's heart sink even further. "Where's the man I met?"

Simon forced himself to look at the prince. "The man you met?"

"Where's that funny, devil-may-care man that flew through the tower window?" asked Marco. "The one who back flipped off a chandelier?"

"That man," began Simon, tears burning the back of his eyes, "was just a boy who was stuffed inside a cannon by his father and left to figure it out. That was me, just trying to survive. I gave myself a title, but I've been myself this entire time."

"But why lie?" Marco looked angry now. "Why not be honest?"

Simon almost couldn't respond. But then the words forced into his throat and tumbled from his mouth. "You just looked so-so *impressed* with me. Maybe I wanted you to like me."

"I might be shallow." Marco folded his arms. "But I'm not *that* shallow."

Isobel had drawn up her strings and stood clutching her cross, her grip threatening to break it in half at any second. "So you can't get our hearts?"

Simon really was about to cry now. "I couldn't even get your slippers."

Marco snatched the satchel from Simon's shoulder. "Yet you did."

Isobel looked at Flora. "I wish so badly that I could cry right now."

Flora tilted her head at Simon. "I ought to—"

She came towards him, headfirst, her glass form threatening to push Simon from the cliff. He raised his arms in defense, but Marco caught Flora and held her back.

"Leave him," said Marco.

"Marco, I—"

Marco's eyes narrowed. "Sorry. I don't want liars using my first name."

Simon's lip quivered as Marco turned with Flora and headed into the forest.

"Come on, Isobel," said Marco. "Let's find Hans and get out of here."

"But—"

"We'll have to find our own way."

The party walked to the trees. Simon stumbled after them.

"Wait! Please, I didn't mean to—"

Marco whirled on Simon, his eyes dark. Simon shrank away as Marco came upon him.

"You should have just been honest," he said. "You acted like everything would be all right. You said you could do more than you really can and you've been leading us into danger without any idea what you're doing. We trusted you."

"You didn't really give me a choice. But let me help and—"

"You're a two-faced, helpless liar."

Simon felt the blood in his face flare. "And *you* are lazy and entitled."

Marco smirked. But then he shook his head and turned away to rejoin the group.

Simon stood on the cliff, alone, as the travelers left him in the forest.

25. THE OTHER PATH

~~~~~

Hans hadn't fallen asleep. He couldn't even consider doing so, as his mind was stuffed with guilt. The Maestroa had made him do it, he knew this. But still, what if the plum had harmed His Highness? Hans had to stop giving in and fight against it.

His hand went to the sachet around his neck. That's what had begun the whole trouble in the first place. He would just take it off and then he would feel himself again. He wouldn't have to obey The Maestroa, and all would be well! Yes, he'd just take it off and—

"I wouldn't do that if I were you," a voice said all around him.

Hans' knees wobbled as he attempted to stand, shaken by The Maestroa.

"Please no more," he said. "I don't want to be a bad person. I wish to help my friends."

"They are not your friends." Hans could practically hear The Maestroa roll their eyes. "How many times do I have to make that clear? They are using you. You ought to use them right back."

Hans didn't want to think about what The Maestroa could have planned next. "H-how?"

A tree limb lowered and Hans jumped out of its way. It nearly crushed him, its leaves and twigs rumbling to the forest floor. The twigs parted like a curtain, revealing a path that had not been there before. Hans blinked and wiped his eyes, adjusted his vision to the new view.

Beyond the path, he saw the looming, striped towers of The Maestroa's tented castle beckoning.

"I know of a shortcut through the forest," The Maestroa said. "Lead them this way, and I will ensure that no harm comes to you."

"But what of them?" Hans' voice shook. "What will become of them?"

"Do not worry, my little minion," The Maestroa laughed. "Just do as you are told."

"I don't want to."

A clap of thunder boomed just above Hans' head, and he cowered on the forest floor.

"Please don't make me." Hans quivered, burying his face in his arms.

"Hans?"

"I don't want to—"

"Hans! Wake up!" A firm hand clapped him on the back.

Hans looked up to see Marco standing over him. The prince looked upset, his face stony without a hint at whatever the trouble was.

Trying to still his shaking hands, Hans let out a sigh. "Oh, hello."

"You looked like you were having a nightmare."

"Oh." Hans took a deep breath, and his nostrils were filled with the wickedly tempting licorice smell again. "Yes. I must have been dreaming. Thank you for waking me."

"We need to move on." Isobel paced. "We can't give up."

"Where is the thief?" asked Hans.

Marco snorted. "Who?"

"Get up." Flora nudged Hans. "You heard the princess, we need to move on."

Hans stood slowly and gestured toward the path.

"I . . . I think this is the way."

Flora looked over her shoulder. "But wasn't the castle just . . ."

"Great work, Hans," Marco said, stepping beneath the tree limb, setting his foot on the path. "Thank you."

Hans looked to the ground. "Do not thank me. Really."

∽

It was up to Marco now. He'd have to find a way to get Isobel and Flora's hearts and defeat a wicked magician that he'd only met when they were disguised as a fortune teller. He didn't know what was waiting or the power they had. He had no idea how he could possibly be of help.

This is what we were avoiding, thought Marco. *We could have just skipped straight to this part if you had manned up and gone after Isobel yourself, but no. You just had to get involved with* him.

Simon The Squirm. Simon. The Squirm. Marco rolled the name in his head over and over. How could he not have seen it? Clearly Simon wasn't who he said he was. He'd bumbled his way through stealing the slippers, and he clearly only lucked out at the tavern. How could Marco have been so stupid?

Because you wanted to believe it, Marco thought. *Because you liked him and you'd have believed anything.*

Marco cringed to himself. If that's where love got him, lied to, then forget it all. He could live happily on his own with flowing grog.

He sighed. He wanted more than that, of course. He didn't want to hide behind partying and joking his way through everything. He wanted to prove he was more than that.

And here was his chance. The time was now. He'd have to rescue the princess, the exact same story he didn't want to live in the first place.

But at least Isobel knew he could never love her. And he knew she could never love him.

Yet, they were still stuck playing out the same old story.

"So what shall we do?" Isobel walked next to him, lowering her voice to a whisper.

Marco looked over his shoulder. Behind them, Hans and Flora stumbled over roots and vines.

"I have to be honest," replied Marco. "I have no idea."

"Me either," Isobel sighed. "We just need to get that amulet."

"We'll have to kill The Maestroa in order to get that."

Marco slid his eyes to Isobel.

"Right."

Marco grunted. "This definitely isn't the life I'd imagined for myself."

"And you think it's mine?"

"All right." Marco waved his hand. "Let's not argue. We're a man down, and still no more prepared to do this than we were just days ago."

"We might have saved time if you'd just—"

"Come myself. I know that."

Isobel went quiet, and they walked a long stretch in silence. The castle seemed to never get any closer, yet they must be getting close by now.

Finally, Isobel broke the silence again. "Do you think we'll ever see him again?"

"Simon?"

"Yes."

"I don't know."

"I feel kind of bad for leaving him now. Alone. What if something happens to him?"

Marco's heart tightened. He hadn't thought about that. Simon alone out in enchanted woods with no weapons, no supplies. Nothing.

Not even a friend.

"I'll find him," Marco vowed. "Once we're through here, I'll find him."

I just hope I'm not too late.

Ahead, a twig snapped and Marco halted, putting his hand out to hold Isobel back.

"Did you hear that?"

"It was just a twig—"

"Shh."

Marco looked back and motioned for Hans to stop. Hans sighed and obeyed, looking sorry for something Marco couldn't fathom. He looked back to the path ahead. Beyond the trees, twigs were snapping in quick succession, the sound louder and louder.

"Run!" Marco spun Isobel around and pushed her ahead, drawing his sword as the wooden soldiers came running from the trees.

Isobel took Flora's arm and pulled her along, but stopped. More soldiers were appearing from the opposite direction.

They were completely surrounded.

"Marco," Isobel said cautiously. "Lower your sword." Marco shook his head, keeping it raised.

"Lower it," Isobel insisted. "Before they hurt us."

A wooden soldier came forward, and in a gruff voice said, "You heard the princess. Sword down."

Marco slowly obliged him, his face red with embarrassment at backing down.

Good fighting, great job, he thought.

Isobel dared a step forward and looked at the soldier who had spoken. "You don't have to do this, Lefty," she said. "You can pretend you never saw us."

Lefty sighed. "I am sorry, princess, but it is you or us."

He nodded to the others, and they all came forward, surrounding the travelers so that they couldn't escape.

Lefty took Isobel by the arm and Marco bounded forward.

"Unhand her!"

With a short, stiff movement, the soldier swung his

arm out and struck Marco across the face. He fell to the ground and sucked in a mouthful dirt.

"Gentle," a voice said. "Do not hurt my latest acquisition."

Marco looked up, cupping his jaw, to see The Maestroa standing above him, surrounded by a dissipating cloud of purple smoke.

"So you're the evil witch," he spat.

The Maestroa smiled, putting a hand to their heart. "Thank you." They turned to Hans. "And thank *you* for your help."

"You?!" Isobel, Marco, and Flora said at once, looking to Hans, who stood fretting, keeping his eyes on the ground.

"I am so sorry," he said feebly.

"How could you?" shouted Marco. Could he trust no one?

"I'm so terribly sorry," said Hans.

"Soldiers." The Maestroa snapped their fingers. Chains pulled up from the ground like snakes and wrapped around Marco's arms and feet. He looked frantically around to find Isobel and Flora fighting against their own shackles. "Carry my lovelies home and do be careful."

"Witch!" Marco yelled at the Maestroa, as angrily as he could.

The Maestroa rolled their eyes. "Flattery will get you everywhere."

They disappeared in purple smoke once more.

"I'm so sorry," Hans cried. "I'm terribly, terribly sorry."

26. TRY

"You have to stop doing that." Flora slid in front of Marco, forcing him to stop pacing. "You're making a trench in the floor."

Marco looked to his feet and saw that, indeed, the earth floor of the cavern was getting lower beneath his foot prints. He had been pacing since The Maestroa had them tossed in here, though he still couldn't wrap his head around how they weren't able to get out when there was no door, only darkness.

He looked around at the great cavern, a mere room of rock with stalagmites glistening around them. All boulders and piles of sand. He supposed it was the closest thing to a dungeon that this tented castle could have.

"Not like there's much else to do," he grumbled, and went to a nearby boulder to sit. He rested his elbows on his knees and buried his face in his hands. "Just wait."

Isobel, who had been braiding and re-braiding her hair, looked up. "What we need to do is find a way out of here."

"Do you have any ideas?" Marco snapped his head up and stared at Isobel. When she sighed, he couldn't help but smirk. "Exactly."

"There is a way in." Flora pointed to the dark corners of the room. "Therefore, there is a way out."

"We tried leaving," said Marco. "The darkness just pushed us back, remember? The old witch has enchanted it."

"Do you suppose," when Isobel began, she spoke quietly, as though weighing her words before saying them, "if we hadn't left Bloody F—Simon . . . that we might have, I don't know, that we—"

"Would have been victorious in the face of evil?" laughed Marco. "Not likely, with Hans betraying us the entire time. When I get my hands on him, I'll—"

"Vows won't do us any good," said Isobel. "Really, I just wish we had Simon here."

"Why, so he could keep lying to us?" asked Marco.

Isobel shrugged. "All I know is that he'd have gotten us through unscathed. He did get Flora and I to the forest. And you out of that tree. And—"

"I get it." Marco waved her off and threw his face back into his hands.

The truth was, Marco wished Simon were there, too. He missed having someone to joke and talk with. He missed Simon's smile, always flashing beneath his unsure eyes. Like he was never certain if Marco liked him or not. He wanted to tell him how he felt again. And again.

Simon. Nic. Bloody Fingers. Whoever he was, Marco missed him. Maybe someday he'd show Simon the mines and the canaries.

"It's no use," Marco whispered to himself.

"Don't say that!" shouted Isobel.

"I wasn't speaking to you—"

"If we give up now, it's all lost." When Marco looked up, Isobel's wooden lip quivered. "That might be fine for you. You never really cared about any of this. But I'm going to be a marionette forever. And Flora...Flora!"

Isobel ran to Flora and threw her arms around the glass girl. For a moment it seemed like Isobel was crying, but Marco saw no tears. His heart hurt a bit for Isobel. Not being able to truly show her emotions. To be with the person you love, but to be kept apart by a curse, waiting around for one minute every midnight to just be themselves.

Marco shook his head and stood.

"I'm sorry, Flora," said Isobel. "I was so afraid."

Flora patted her back. "I know. I'm working on forgiveness."

"One day I'll kiss you and—"

"Stop, or I'll get angry again," said Flora, in a gentle tone.

Isobel sobbed with unfortunately dry eyes. "We're going to be like this forever."

"I won't let that happen." Marco stood. "And I do care."

"Sure," said Isobel, her face buried against Flora's porcelain shoulder. "What changed?"

Marco shrugged. "I think we all know what."

He needed to move so that he could think. He walked deeper into the cavern. There had to be a way out of the cavern, and he had to find that way before they got into any more danger than they already were.

He couldn't completely focus. His mind also kept going to where Simon might be and what he might be doing. Was he all right? Or did The Maestroa send some unknown horror his way to fight alone?

Marco grunted. He never should have left him, and he should have been more reasonable when he learned the truth. He knew it all along, deep down. There was no way that Simon could be Bloody Fingers. It just didn't make sense. Of course he didn't really know what he was doing. And really, it was Marco's fault for pushing Simon into it. Of course Simon had to lie.

How could Marco have been so pigheaded not to just deal with it then and there and move on?

He thought about the strange dream that the plum had given him.

He'd arrived at his own palace, in his own kingdom, in a carriage. It was the strangest carriage he had ever ridden in, as it was actually a large plum atop wheels. He saw the purple lanterns in the trees, the party goers drifting inside.

When he entered the ballroom, though, it felt different from his palace. It looked just like it and yet it had felt so cold. Empty, despite the mass of dancers swirling over the ballroom.

He'd been so happy to find Simon, the one familiar face in his cold new home. They'd dance, as any couple would. As his brother and his wife would do. As his parents had done.

He felt normal. He *was* normal.

But Simon's face changed, and he was The Maestroa. Then he was his own father, decrying his love for Simon. And then he was King Anders threatening him. On and on, back and forth, changing as quickly as he recognized them.

He was swept away from Simon, the crowd between them.

Simon managed to get away, running up the steps.

But when Marco finally broke free of the crowd and ran after him, he halted halfway down the steps. Simon was long gone, yet there was his shoe— a shining gentleman's dancing shoe.

Marco lifted Simon's shoe and held it to the light of the stars. It burst, melting away into a steaming stream of plum juice. It oozed between his fingers and dripped to the dock. He blinked, and the juice changed to blood.

Marco shuddered.

He kicked a pebble as hard as he could. It swung up off the ground and dove through the air, into the shadows of the far end of the cavern.

Marco listened for it to land, but the sound never came.

Drawing his eyebrows together, Marco paced closer to the shadows. He lifted another pebble and threw it as well, but that one didn't land either.

Just as Marco was about to try it for a third time, the first pebble came back, flying through the air and landing at Marco's feet.

He picked it up, tossed it into the shadows.

The pebble flew back.

Deep in the shadow, a soft rumble began.

"Isobel?" Marco widened his eyes and called back to the princess. "Flora?"

In the shadows, the rumbling grew louder, forming into a single, gruff word.

"*Loot.*"

Marco stumbled backwards. "Guys!"

"*Looty-Loot!*" the voice came closer, louder.

Marco turned to run and slammed into Isobel as she ran forward. Marco grabbed his shoulder and rubbed it.

"Good god!" he said. "Easy on the flesh and bone, please."

"Shh." Isobel waved him away, her eyes on the shadow. "Loot! It's me!"

Marco steadied himself as the ground quaked, the thunderous footsteps coming forward. He screamed out as the form of the wooden giant was revealed, the giant grinning and clapping as he stared at Isobel.

"Get back!" Marco pulled at Isobel's arm. "It could kill you!"

Isobel laughed and shoved Marco off. "He wouldn't hurt a maggot even if The Maestroa told him to. Isn't that right, Loot?"

The giant giggled and knelt, lowering his head to the princess. She laughed and kissed him on the cheek.

Marco jumped as Flora whispered to him. He hadn't realized she'd come behind him. "I won't lie, that makes me feel a bit jealous."

Marco shook his head, taking in the sight of the princess kissing the wooden giant.

"You know this thing?" he asked.

"He's not a *thing*," Isobel protested as Loot muttered something unintelligible, his huge hands pulling into fists. "He is a giant, just as cursed as I am. The Maestroa wanted to make him a villain, but we know better, don't we?"

Isobel scratched the giant's ear and he erupted in giggles, the bass of his voice vibrating in Marco's chest. "*Looty-looty-loot-loot.*"

"I assumed you weren't in here," Isobel said to Loot. "I was afraid The Maestroa had locked you someplace else."

Her eyes lit up. "Loot, do you remember Simon?"

"*Loot?*" asked the giant, and Marco thought it sounded as though he were asking '*Who?*'

"You know, the boy on the rope? The one who upset you?"

"*Loot!*"

Marco felt confused, but kept quiet, listening to Isobel.

"He's in the forest somewhere. Do you think you could find him? And-and tell him that we're sorry and that we could really use his help right about now!"

The giant grinned and nodded like a happy dog. But then his wooden face drooped and he squeezed his eyes shut.

"*Looty-loot,*" said the giant, disappointedly. To Marco, this must have meant '*If only we weren't trapped.*'

Marco paced again, pulling his arm from Flora's reach when she tried to stop him. He had to figure something out. He'd been useless for most of this mess, and after all, he was the reason that Simon was even involved in the first place. Now was the time to give something. To try.

Across the cavern, they heard the sound of a key turn

and a door open. Marco squinted through the shadows, wondering how a tent even had a door.

Through the shadows stumbled Hans, carrying a tray with half a loaf of old bread and a glass of water.

"You!" Isobel scowled.

"No! No!" whimpered Hans. "I've come with food!"

"I don't want your food," Marco spat.

Flora slid towards Hans. "I'll hold him down, and you kick him in the shins."

Hans dropped the tray and cowered. "Oh, please! I-I didn't have a choice! The Maestroa made me. They kept enchanting me and forcing me. I never would— I wouldn't ever— oh, sire!" He threw himself at Marco's feet, and kissed his boots. "Please forgive me! Oh, say you forgive me."

Marco surveyed the servant, trying to think of something.

Time to save a canary, he thought and knelt, patting Hans on the small of his back. "There, there. It's all right."

Hans looked up, and Marco put his hands behind his back, like a diplomat.

"Really, sire?" asked Hans.

Marco nodded, and stuck his fingers out behind him, wiggling the key he had just swiped from Hans' belt loop. He slid his eyes to Flora. She nodded her understanding.

"I have one condition," said Marco.

"Anything, sire! Anything!"

"You will take me to The Maestroa at once."

Isobel gasped. "No! Marco, you can't. They'll do something wicked to you—"

"I know." Marco waited for Flora to come around behind him. When he felt her slip the key from his fingers, he held his arms out toward Hans. A surrender. "I wish to see them immediately."

Hans stood, and with shaking hands produced a set of chains that he wrapped around Marco's wrists.

"Don't do it," said Isobel. "Loot, sick the pathetic little man!"

Loot growled at Hans, who quivered and cried out.

"No, Isobel," said Marco. "This is the only way."

He stepped to the shadows, feeling Hans close on his heels, whimpering and quivering at the sight of the giant.

"Marco!" Isobel called. "You don't know what you're doing!"

Let's both hope that you're wrong, thought Marco, the shadows enveloping him completely.

27. HEARTLESS

Marco walked alongside Hans through The Maestroa's castle, a collage of circus tents smashed together and twisted about in such a way that he could hardly tell one way from the next.

They walked in silence, and the clinking of Marco's chains were the only sound that kept it from being unnervingly quiet. Marco kept a lookout for anything that might help later. A broken window, a pole to use as a weapon, some other magical creature like the giant.

But the entire castle seemed, and felt, empty.

Marco glanced over at Hans and thought how similar this was to when they first spoke, when Hans escorted him to King Anders' chambers. He didn't know the man then. Now he was an enemy.

"Why did you do it, Hans?" Marco finally broke the silence.

Hans looked fretfully at Marco, shaking his head. "I told you sire, The Maestroa forced me."

Marco's eyes went to the sachet around Hans' neck. "Take that off."

"What?"

"The necklace. Take it off before The Maestroa makes it worse—"

"I will not!" Hans clutched the sachet. "It has been more honest to me and treated me better than you or any royal ever did."

"I'm sorry," said Marco. "Really, I am. I'll be nicer. Just please take it off."

"Absolutely not." Hans halted outside of an oak door, and Marco stopped behind him. "Now mind your manners and no funny business."

He reached for the large brass knob and twisted it, opening the door slowly. A cold gust of air escaped, and Marco squinted through the cold to see a large, dim room beyond the doorway.

Hans grabbed Marco's elbow and shoved him through, and once inside Marco could see that it was no ordinary room. It was a theater.

Rows of red velvet seats filled the space, with ornately decorated boxes that ascended the walls. Marco looked at the ceiling to see a purple chandelier hanging just beneath a high catwalk.

The stage was closed off behind a purple curtain. Lights of green, blue, and pink in patterns of leaves and stars flickered in and out against the velvet.

"No!" a voice boomed, and Marco immediately recognized the voice of The Maestroa, somewhere in the dark theater. "That is not correct! Did you even look at my lighting design?"

The lights flickered off and back on, this time it appearing in the shape of letters spelling out 'ACT ONE'.

"Much better," said The Maestroa.

"Y-your wickedness?" asked Hans said, softly.

"Where is the orchestra?" The Maestroa boomed. "Bring me my orchestra!"

"They can't hear you," Marco whispered. Turning his head to the ceiling, he shouted, "Hey-yo, witch!"

There was a clatter from above, and Marco looked up to see a pair of purple eyes peering over the rail of a higher box.

"What is he doing here?" The Maestroa spat through a strangled voice. "It is not time!"

"I asked to see you." Marco put on his most charming smirk. "Demanded, actually."

"Put him back in the dungeon." The Maestroa leaned away and disappeared into the box. "And leave him there this time."

The Maestroa grumbled something as Hans tried to pull Marco away.

"I only wished to meet the great and powerful Maestroa that I've heard so much about," he said. "I thought surely they couldn't be so beautiful as they say."

Silence. Then, the eyes peered over the edge of the box once more.

"What kind of foolish trick is that?" The Maestroa asked. "Either you are very stupid, or very hopeless."

"Let's go with both!"

The Maestroa rolled their eyes and snapped their fingers. Marco's ears popped and he squeezed his eyes shut as the breeze around him picked up. When he opened his eyes again, he found himself sitting in the box next to The Maestroa, on a purple chair, looking down at the curtained stage far below them.

"You prince's are all alike." The Maestroa scoffed next to him. "The minute you hear of someone's beauty, off you go running with the hope of rescuing a damsel and a happily ever after."

Marco swallowed hard, being so close to the person who could rip his heart out and turn him into a frog at any second. He forced himself not to lean away.

"I just—"

"Well let me tell you something, prince." The Maestroa's voice hardened. "I am no damsel. And I no longer believe in happily ever afters."

"You know, me neither," said Marco, and his eyes fell to the large, purple stone that hung around The Maestroa's neck. If he could get that, then they could defeat them. He would have to be sneaky. "And to be perfectly honest, uh . . . your wickedness, I've found that I don't much go for damsels."

The Maestroa shook their head impatiently. "I know that. So what do you want? To kill me? Toss a bucket of water and see if I melt? Ha! I'm not a witch, you foolish boy."

"I don't want to harm you," Marco said as kindly and evenly as he could manage.

"Then what *do* you want?"

To distract you, thought Marco. He'd almost expected for Loot to escape before he even made it to The Maestroa.

Flora had the key to get out, so what was taking them

so long? Had he grabbed the wrong one? Was the door jammed? Marco had to keep the conversation going.

"I just wanted to know," he said, feeling his stomach tie into knots as he realized this would probably get him sent back to the dungeon immediately, "about you. You're a villain—"

"By choice."

"So you must have a pretty great reason." Marco smirked. "Princes may be alike but so are villains, don't you think?"

"Ah, so you read." The Maestroa narrowed their eyes at Marco.

"Absolutely not. But it is just a fairy tale, isn't it?"

The Maestroa lifted a hand and he winced, expecting to be harmed or transformed. But when nothing happened, he opened his eyes to see that The Maestroa had covered their mouth, stifling a laugh.

"Oh, come on." Marco tossed his head casually. "I know you love to tell stories. Tell me one."

The Maestroa slowly nodded and waved their arm out over the edge of the box. Marco glanced to the stage curtain, where the lights changed, and silhouettes drifted across the velvet.

He saw a little girl with a crown, running.

"Once upon a time." The Maestroa looked back at Marco. "Don't you just love that opener?"

"It's the best opener," said Marco. "I don't think you could ever top it."

"Once upon a time," The Maestroa repeated and turned back to the curtain. "There was a young princess who had everything she could ever hope for. She had mountains of toys, the brightest and fastest ponies. She even had a fairy godperson who would watch over her, and see to it that all of her dreams came true."

Another silhouette flew across the curtain. A person with wings and waving a wand soared over the little princess, and candy showered from the sky. The little princess clapped.

"For a long time, the little princess loved and wished all the time for her fairy godperson. Just little things. A toy, a fluffy bed, a piece of strawberry cake. To get over a cold, or have the perfect hairstyle at the latest ball. But it was not meant to last.

"For as the princess grew, she came to know that she was not like other princesses."

The silhouette of the princess grew, and Marco recognized the shape of Isobel, walking alone through her castle. She came to another figure, a servant girl. She reached for the girl's hand.

"For she wasn't the kind of princess waiting for a prince to find her," The Maestroa said. "She was more interested in her handmaid. Their love could never see the light of day, they knew, for girls like them don't get fairy tale endings."

The silhouette of the fairy appeared again, growing larger as they took center stage and the princess and the servant disappeared.

"The fairy godperson wished to help. They wanted their little princess to have the fairy tale that she so deserved. And so, when the princess asked, the fairy godperson stole her away."

The princess appeared again, this time in a bird cage.

The fairy godperson flicked their wand, and the strings sprung from the princess' hands, her movements became stiff, and she struggled and fought against those strings until at last she became an enchanted marionette.

"So you're Isobel's fairy godmother?" Marco cocked an eyebrow.

"Godperson," The Maestroa corrected him. "As you can see, I've had the best intentions. I want everyone to have the story they deserve. But then you ruined it all."

The purple of The Maestroa's eyes soured, a frown scoring their face.

"Me?" Marco's voice broke. "How did I ruin it?"

"When you sent the thief instead of coming yourself." The Maestroa sat down next to him. "You've ruined my whole story. I wasn't supposed to be the villain! The giant was! Not I!"

The Maestroa's voice continued to raise, until they were shouting right in Marco's ear.

"I'm not really a villain! I am not wicked!"

"Maybe you didn't start that way," Marco said. "but clearly . . . "

Marco stopped talking, his face flushed. Just outside of the theater, a deafening yell rumbled. Marco felt the vibrations of the sound run through his chair. The Maestroa snapped their gaze to the ceiling.

"What is that?" The Maestroa shouted. "What is happening?!"

Marco eyed the Maestroa's amulet, dangling as they leaned over the box. He would have to be fast and he'd have to be accurate. He slowly lifted his chain-bound hands.

"It's the giant!" a wooden soldier called below. "He has escaped!"

"After him, you fools!" The Maestroa shrieked. "Get him back!"

Marco reached for the amulet. Almost there, just one more inch and . . .

The Maestroa spun around, their eyes burning like violet fire as they wrung their bony hands towards the prince.

"I ought to have known."

"But you didn't," Marco pointed out, and he pushed himself forward, knocking into the Maestroa. They slammed against the rail of the box.

Marco threw himself over them, grabbing at the amulet. His hands squeezed it and he tried to yank it from The Maestroa's neck. They bolted up, slamming a fist hard into Marco's jaw.

"Ow!" Marco yelled. "Why does everyone go for the face?"

He knocked his forehead into The Maestroa's shoulder in retaliation, but they stood their ground this time. Wrapping a hand around his throat, they lifted him from the ground. The toes of his boots dragged the floor.

Marco choked and coughed as they held him, his feet kicking against The Maestroa's legs.

"You want so badly to be a bigger part of this story?" The Maestroa grinned at him. "You want one of your own? Fine, then. Once upon a time . . ."

Marco screamed out what air he could from his lungs as The Maestroa squeezed his throat, and another hand reached for his chest, ripping his jacket open.

Marco reached his hands forward. He only needed to get the amulet.

His fingertips brushed the purple stone.

The Maestroa's fingers plunged into Marco's chest and he cried out again, their hand wrapping around his heart, pulling. His heartbeat amplified, ringing in his ears, the sound pouring out of his chest and into the theater.

The Maestroa dropped Marco and he landed on the floor, clutching his chest. But he didn't feel any pain. Or fear.

He felt nothing.

He looked up to see The Maestroa smiling down at him, his heart still alive and beating in their palm.

Marco pushed himself to his knees and reached for it. Purple smoke surrounded his vision, blinding him, as his ears filled with the sound of wood, snapping into place over his skin.

28. DARING RESCUE

~~~~

Simon had stayed on the cliffside for as long as he could, letting the tears of frustration make their way out of him. Finally, he'd had enough of that. Whining would get him nowhere, after all. He had to find the group and explain himself. He had to help.

He had to defeat The Maestroa. It was the only way to redeem himself and have any chance that Marco would like or trust him again.

He walked quickly onward, trying to remember the direction of the tented castle. It had seemed so far away. He wasn't sure if he would catch up with them in time.

But he had to try. He had to prove that he could be the hero of his story. Not just some squirm that everyone rolled their eyes at or crammed inside of cannons.

He walked. And he walked. And he walked.

There was no sense of direction in the forest. It was all identical trees and lines of shrubs. A great curve of earth that just seemed to go on and on without ever reaching a destination.

Finally Simon stopped walking and tried to make sense of it. Ahead stood a tree.

Of course it's a tree, idiot, Simon thought. *You're in a forest.*

But still, there was something familiar about that tree. He approached it, sucking in his breath when he saw something golden shining at its roots.

Simon let out a loud groan. The gold was a shard of crown. This was the same tree he'd cut Marco down from. The very one he'd come to right after dragging Isobel and Flora from The Maestroa's compound. He'd walked in a great circle.

Simon screamed in frustration, and backed away from the tree before it fought at him again.

It's no use. Simon stomped the earth.

"Simon!"

A voice rang out, and he froze. He turned around, not believing his ears for a moment.

"Sim*on*!"

It can't be. Simon half-chuckled and kept walking. For a second he had thought the voice sounded like his father. *No way. He's not going to be out looking for me.*

He jumped, for through the trees ran a figure, straight towards him. Simon felt for his dagger, only to realize yet again that he had forgotten it that morning, when all this mess even started. He held his hands out in defense.

"At last, I've found the squirm!"

Bloody Fingers came at him and pulled Simon into a tight hug, lifting him off the ground in a display of affection like Simon had never seen.

"Father?" Simon choked the words out. Bloody

Fingers held him so tightly that he could barely breathe. "What are you doing here?"

"Why, looking for you, my boy," said Bloody Fingers. "You don't think I'd have forgotten you?"

"Yes." Simon sucked in oxygen as Bloody Fingers put him down. "I did."

"He did." It was The Vizier who spoke, coming through the trees. Simon noticed that he didn't have his hooks. "And don't you let him think otherwise."

Rattle. The Jester came behind The Vizier.

"Tattle tales," Bloody Fingers scoffed at his bandits, smoothing his mustache with his fingers. "To think I'd leave my poor dear boy to die."

"You did," said Simon.

"Oh, I am so happy to see you!" Bloody Fingers patted his hands on Simon's shoulders. "I could just kiss you."

"Please don't," said Simon. "How did you even get here?"

"It was the strangest thing." Humphrey came forward now. "There we were, running through the forest, when we came upon a great purple curtain."

"Purple is the most fashionable of colors." The Fop straightened his hat and wiggled its feather. "By far the most expensive. I simply had to get a feel of it."

"And when he did," said Bloody Fingers, "it opened to reveal this forest. And now here we are, and here you are. But where is the treasure?"

"What treasure?" asked Simon.

"You know," said Bloody Fingers. "The very legendary lost treasure? That talks? And wears slippers that I very much would like to try on?"

Simon felt his heart sink again. "Oh, the princess."

"Yes."

"She's gone."

Bloody Fingers choked on his own breath. "Gone? She's . . . gone?! That wasn't part of the plan!" He looked to The Vizier for back up.

"You didn't tell Simon the plan,"Tthe Vizier said. "He wasn't there. Remember?"

Bloody Fingers stamped his foot and turned to Simon. "Can't you do anything right?! You were supposed to have the princess ready to give to His Majesty!"

"How do you know that?" Simon raised an eyebrow at his father.

"I had it in strictest confidence," said Bloody Fingers. "By an old man and his rats. You came here to rescue the princess. But I see now you've merely been frolicking."

"I do not frolic!"

"Whatever shall we do?" Bloody Fingers swept the back of his hand to his forehead. "The plan is ruined!"

He fell backwards, pretending to faint. But no one stood near enough to catch him, and so he tumbled o the ground. He yelped with pain and grabbed at his back.

"Where is she?" The Vizier asked Simon.

"Gone," Simon repeated. "Her and Prince Marco set off alone with the servant and the handmaid and left me here."

Because I'm a big liar and a dope. Simon kept this part to himself.

"Wrong answer," said a voice behind Simon.

He whirled around to see King Anders, arms folded.

His hair was immaculately curled, and a servant behind him stood, admiring the king's hair proudly.

And over the king's shoulder . . . a line of soldiers ready to draw their swords at any second.

"Y-your majesty." Simon bowed.

"So you did not rescue my daughter?" asked the king, his tone cold and hard.

"I-I found her," Simon stammered. "They left me. But we can find them!"

"All you bandits say the same thing," said the king. "We'll find them! We'll get them! We'll deliver them wrapped in a bow! Well, enough! It was silly enough for my future son-in-law to trust you, and it is even sillier for *me* to trust you."

"Your Majesty," began Simon, "I might not have them here this instant, but I know exactly where they're going.

We can—"

"Silence!" The king clapped his hands and Simon gulped. "As it is, I am feeling generous today." Simon dared glance up at the king.

"Oh, so generous a king," said Bloody Fingers said. "And how much, pray tell, are you willing to pay?"

Simon heard the Jester smack Bloody Fingers on the shoulder with his rattle.

"So generous," the king said. "That I shall allow you to choose which tree I hang you from."

Simon's heart dropped, and Bloody Fingers came forward then, shoving Simon out of the way.

"You can't do that!"

"What? Kill your child?" asked the king.

"Let him pick," Bloody Fingers said. "He's not great with decisions. I'll choose."

Simon shoved his father in return and pointed at the fighting tree. "That one."

King Anders glanced at the tree. "That was a fast selection. What kind of trick is this?"

"Not a trick," said Simon. "I just like it's green leaves."

King Anders glanced at all the other trees with their leaves of green but shrugged. "Very well. Guards—" he gestured to the captain, who held a long rope "—that tree, if you please."

The captain of the guard went to the tree as the others came forward with chains to bind Simon and the bandits. Simon focused on the tree ahead, watching the captain get closer to it.

The captain tossed the rope at the tree's boughs, and . . . *Schwack.*

The branches came down, slamming the captain to the ground.

The soldiers all gasped, running to the captain. The trees boughs lowered again, crashing each soldier down in turn. It's roots curled up, wrapping the soldiers, taking them all hostage.

"Witchcraft!" cried the king.

"Come on!" Simon called to the bandits. "Before they've escaped!"

"But I wanna watch the tree torture them!" said Humphrey. "Just listen to their glorious screams!"

"I order you to stay put!" shouted King Anders. "And wait patiently until they have freed themselves so that we can dispose of you."

The soldiers struggled against the tree as it waved them through the air.

"Come on," said Simon again.

Bloody Fingers shook his head. "I will wait until the tree shakes all of the spare change from their pockets. There must be twenty or so shillings to be had."

"But there is so much more treasure in the *castle*," Simon tried.

Bloody Fingers slid his eyes to Simon. "There is a castle?"

Simon nodded. "With gold, and treasure, and magic."

"Are there any slippers to try on?"

Simon rolled his eyes. "Sure."

"Bandits." Bloody Fingers raised his hand. "Let us run, while they struggle!"

"A fabulous idea," said The Fop.

Rattle.

"You're too late!" shouted King Anders.

Simon and the bandits spun to see that the guards had freed themselves of the tree, surrounded now by lifeless, dismembered branches.

"It looks like *I* shall choose the tree for you," King Anders said as the guards lifted their swords to the bandits. "Let's see."

The king turned to survey the forest and Simon began

to think even more desperately how he would get out of this and closer to the castle.

But his thoughts were soon shaken by the sound of thunder in the distance, coming closer and closer.

The guards screamed and leapt out of the way as a large, wooden foot came down over them.

THE PRINCE AND THE PUPPET THIEF

"Loot!" shouted Simon, and he grinned up at the giant.

Loot bent over and scooped him up in his hand.

"I never thought I would be glad to see you," said Simon.

"*Looty-looty-loot-loot-loot,*" giggled the giant.

"Monster!" screamed the king. "Raul, remove the monster's pinky toe at once!"

But the captain of the guard shook too violently to make any use of his sword.

Below, the bandits had run forward in the chaos and Bloody Fingers came at the giant with his sword. He stabbed Loot in the foot.

"Take that, you scoundrel!" screamed Bloody Fingers. "Unhand my son!"

"*Loot-loot-loot-loot!*" wailed the giant.

Simon held onto the giant's thumb as he swayed back and forth.

"It's all right, buddy!" Simon tried to soothe him. "Father, stop that!"

Once all had quieted down and Loot had been coddled sufficiently, Simon spoke again.

"This is Loot," he called down. "He's a friend of the princess. He can lead us there!"

King Anders considered quietly, and finally said, "If you mean what you say, that you can save my daughter... If you truly mean what I've come to know, then I will give you one last chance."

"Thank you, Your Majesty." Simon clapped his hand against Loot's big thumb in a victory gesture.

The king lifted a finger regally. "But if you don't, and I

mean it, boy, I will have you killed without *any* pomp or circumstance because you won't deserve any."

"Deal," said Simon. "Only one thing. Loot, you're a giant but you aren't tall enough to get me in the towers, are you?"

Loot's grin faltered, and he shook his head. "*Loot.*"

"I just have to think of a way to get into the castle once we get there." Simon looked down at Bloody Fingers, who for once had been quiet for a while. He smiled at his father. "Surely you can think of it. A way to get me in the castle? A way to get to the tower? A very, very *high* tower?"

Finally, Bloody Fingers' eyes lit up and he understood. He turned to the captain of the guard, and said, grinning,

"Captain, I shall require use of your cannon."

29. CURTAIN UP

Simon landed softly just beyond the window of the highest tower of The Maestroa's tented castle. Below, outside, the bandits and royals watched from around Loot's ankles, the cannon still emitting the cloud of smoke that had shot Simon into the sky. He didn't know if Marco would even *want* him to save them. If he'd ever speak to him again. But he had to try.

I'm in my own fairy tale, he thought. *It's mine. I get to decide how it ends.*

He crept along the floor of the tower, finding himself to be on a sort of catwalk that went above the tent below. And what he saw half surprised him. A large theater, with a stage covered by a purple velvet curtain. Below him, an assortment of magical creatures made entirely from paper, gears, and wood. There were the wolves, the centaurs, mermaids in paper pools of blue confetti, dragons breathing false fire. A world of canvas and paint.

None of it is real, he reminded himself. *They can't really hurt me.*

An orchestra warmed up in the pit. But where were the ones he came for? Where was Hans, and Isobel and Flora? Where was Marco?

Where was The Maestroa?

The chandelier dimmed, and all was plunged into darkness as the orchestra swelled. He gripped the rails of the catwalk to hold his balance. His father's sword glinted in the dim light and he pushed it down closer to his hip to keep the bouncing silvery light from giving him away. He crouched in the dark, knelt and peered over the edge of the catwalk as a spotlight magically illuminated the curtain. It parted, and The Maestroa emerged.

The creatures clapped their paper hands and paws, hooted and called with great praise at the magician as they swept a low bow.

"Ladies and gentlemen," The Maestroa began, "boys and girls, welcome at last to the show! A tale of magic and adventure, a story so beautiful, it lights your heart ablaze."

They snapped their fingers, and a dash of purple fire ignited between them. The audience cheered. Clay griffins roared with delight.

Then, when all fell quiet, they began. "Once upon a time . . ."

Lifting their arms to the sky, The Maestroa's hands gave a flourish and the curtain rose to reveal the set. An array of canvas trees, a castle painted on a large backdrop behind them. A moat, made of two lines of cut wood, moved back and forth to simulate waves. Simon squinted in the dark. From behind the trees, a platform emerged, upon which Marco was propped.

Simon leaned further. This Marco was different,

THE PRINCE AND THE PUPPET THIEF

changed. He tried not to gasp as the light illuminated the prince, revealing an absence of human flesh.

This Marco was just like Isobel, made entirely of wood and held on strings that ascended up above the stage, beyond the proscenium. He was a marionette now.

That meant he had no heart, and the mere thought of that made Simon's want to break.

The Maestroa snapped their fingers and Marco lifted his head slowly, looked out into the cheering audience.

"There was a prince," The Maestroa said. "A most handsome and charming prince. He had everything any boy could want. But alas, he wanted none of it. For riches and power held nothing for him. And so he wandered lost through the world, without a purpose. Or a friend."

The audience awed and whimpered, mocking Marco. The Maestroa laughed.

In the darkness, Simon jumped from the catwalk to the balcony below, landing with a soft thud behind a row of gnomes made of cloth and stuffing, giggling with delight at the puppet show, sending a stream of roasted chestnuts spilling from a snack bag.

He had to get to the stage unseen. Behind the gnomes, he took the rickety stairs that led to the lower seats. He went as quietly as he could, sword drawn.

If anything tried to attack him, he'd cut it to bits. It was just paper and stuffing, after all. Childhood toys. Storybook illustrations.

None of it is real, he reminded himself as he stole into a boxed seat.

Across the theater, he spotted Isobel, Hans, and Flora,

who were held hostage by wooden soldiers in a box opposite the theater.

Marco looked out into the audience, solemn and unfeeling. Seeing him in this way was jarring and so sad that Simon balked for just a moment.

He had to save him.

The Maestroa had their back to Simon as they spoke, becoming so passionate in their tale of a sad-eyed prince that they didn't notice Simon creeping from his box toward the stage.

But as he neared the apron, Marco caught sight of him. He blinked, and Simon's heart did a back flip as he saw that familiar smirk, carved of wood and painted, and Simon felt a rush of relief. But how to save him?

The Maestroa moved their arms wildly as they spoke, so taken with it all, their own world, their own creation, and the amulet around their neck swayed.

Marco cocked his head at The Maestroa. *Get them!* His eyes seemed to be thinking.

Simon crept up behind The Maestroa. He could impale them on his sword, he was getting so close. He needed to get that amulet. Just needed to slide that sword through the string that held it and then he'd have it. Quickly, silently.

But when he stepped closer, the spotlight revealed him. The audience noticed. They booed and shrieked.

The Maestroa whirled and put their hand out before he could run, and in a smack of invisible hands, he was pushed back. He slammed to the stage.

"And then a hero came." The Maestroa giggled, sizing him up.

The creatures stomped wildly.

"Let him go!" Marco cried out.

"Oh, but then he'd miss the finale!"

The Maestroa waved their hands and purple flame lit below Marco. "When the prince feels so many desires that he could burst into flames!" Isobel, Flora, and Hans screamed.

"Stop it!" Simon shouted.

"Enough out of you," The Maestroa jeered as they lifted Simon by the collar.

Somewhere in the dark, beyond the lowest rows of seats, the voice of Bloody Fingers boomed, "Unhand my boy!"

And he emerged with his bandits, sword held high, backed by the royal army.

30. THE BATTLE

The Maestroa looked to the back of the theater where the army had arrived to fight theirs.

"Creatures, soldiers!" They raised their fists with fury. "Attack!"

With The Maestroa distracted, Simon bounced to his feet and jumped, slicing his sword in the air, cutting the strings that held Marco. The prince fell, narrowly missing the purple bonfire as it extinguished itself. He tucked and rolled, pouncing back to his feet like an agile cat.

"You came," said Marco. "You seriously came, you found a way."

"I couldn't leave you in this," said Simon. "I had to make sure you were safe."

"Even though I—"

"Everything you said is true," said Simon. "all of it."

Marco leaned close to Simon. "I thought I'd never see you again."

"Me too."

But soon they were surrounded by the wooden soldiers

THE PRINCE AND THE PUPPET THIEF

and creatures, erupting into battle. Simon saw Isobel whipping her strings at a soldier. Flora head-butted a golem with her hard porcelain forehead. They had to fight.

The Maestroa laughed, disappearing in a cloud of purple smoke. Where could they be now? What strings were they pulling to ensure this story would go their way?

The wooden soldiers that surrounded them had drawn their swords and Marco had drawn his. Simon held his high.

They stood back-to-back, leaning against one another as they brandished their weapons.

"For what it's worth," said Marco, "I at least thought you to be a decent swordsman."

"You've never actually seen my sword skills," laughed Simon. "Shall we find out?"

"I thought you'd never ask," said Marco.

And they raised their swords as the soldiers rushed towards them. Steel clanked against steel. They fought, turning as they went, knocking the soldiers back left and right, one on one.

"You were right, too," Marco said has he knocked his sword against a soldier that stood between them now. He glanced at Simon as he disarmed the soldier. "I'm lazy, arrogant, and entitled."

Simon said, "I know," and elbowed backwards as a soldier came up behind him. It doubled over, its nose chipped by the force of his elbow knocking into him.

Simon felt such a rush of excitement. Finally, he felt that he was doing something right. Something good. The liberation that he felt extended his energy, fueled his inner fire and strength as he fought. Simon felt his stomach flip and his cheeks flush as he watched Marco slash through a paper dragon with his sword.

Simon raised an eyebrow. "That was pretty attractive."

Marco winked back at him. "I try."

But soon there were too many things surrounding them. They'd have to run, get off the stage that was presenting them both as perfect targets. He ran to Marco, put his arm around his back.

"What are you doing?" asked Marco.

"Just hold on." Simon tugged a nearby rope that held a sandbag to keep a tree aloft.

The rope moved and they ascended the air above the stage, riding the rope upwards to the ceiling of the theater.

"That was amazing!" Marco said to Simon as they landed on the catwalk. Simon ignored the tightness this caused in his body. Right now they had to fight.

I'll kiss him later, Simon thought, *when we're alive and he's human again.*

"How amazing," said a familiar smoky voice in the darkness. The Maestroa emerged. "Such a clever hero."

Marco raised his sword to fight, but The Maestroa waved, sending the sword out of Marco's hand and over the railing of the catwalk. They snapped their fingers, and Isobel, Flora, and Hans all appeared with them.

"What are you doing?" Isobel gasped, realizing how high they all were now.

"I want to make sure you see the ending of the tale," The Maestroa said as they stalked towards Simon. "How the thief finally meets his doom."

Marco charged towards them, but The Maestroa

thrust their hands out again, and pushed all of them but Simon down with unseen force. They went to him at last, where he was held down by their magic, on his back against the catwalk floor.

Below them, fifty or sixty feet, the battle raged on, bandit against creature, human soldier against wooden, holding back The Maestroa's minions.

"It would be quite a fall," The Maestroa began, "with no strings to catch you."

"Let him go!" Marco pleaded. "Take me instead!"

"That's not the ending I've written," The Maestroa said simply as they neared Simon.

"You're right," said Simon. "It's not. The ending is that you are gone."

The Maestroa stopped and blinked. "Excuse me?"

"If I'm the hero, then it's my story."

"No, that's not—"

"And if it's my story, then I have a happy ending, we all do. But not you, because you are the villain, and therefore, you will fall."

"Be quiet!" The Maestroa warned.

"You created this world, but I've figured out how it works. And you've set yourself up for your own demise."

The Maestroa teetered on the edge of the catwalk, and for the first time, Simon thought he might be able to see fear in their eyes, the purple changing, growing darker, as though all their menacing joy was extinguishing. Their eyes glazed over, as though they were painted, no longer real.

"You're the villain," Simon repeated. "Villains must go."

"Clever, clever boy." A painted tear slid down the Maestroa's now glass cheek. All watched aghast at the slow transformation overtaking them.

Below, all the creatures and the wooden soldiers slowed down as their magic deflated.

"But how will you break your curse without me around?"

"What curse?"

The Maestroa thrust their hand out once last time toward Simon, and purple fog spouted from their finger tips. Simon coughed as it filled his lungs. He felt his arms changing, his flesh growing tighter until it wasn't even skin at all. He could see the beginning of wood appearing.

"No!" Marco screamed and thrust himself forward, grabbing onto The Maestroa, who was now entirely glass. They were laughing maniacally, then suddenly they stopped and let out a tiny, stiff sob.

"I knew, the ;moment I became the villain," they said quietly. "That it would end this way for me."

"It doesn't have to be like this," said Marco. "You could be what you were before. You could—"

The Maestroa fell from the catwalk, taking Marco with them.

"NO!" Screamed Simon, reaching out, but it was too late.

He and Isobel, Flora and Hans all peered over the rail, screaming, protesting, as The Maestroa and Marco grew smaller and smaller below.

31. HAPPILY

*A*s the Maestroa hit the floor of the theater, they seemed to smash into a million pieces, like a teacup meeting its unfortunate end. The pieces scattered in the air, bringing down the stage, the scenery. The tents.

As their amulet hit the floor, it smashed, and a thousand tiny, silver paper hearts blew into the wind, fluttering through the air to the wooden soldiers, the paper creatures, to Isobel and Flora, each little heart finding its owner.

All of their spells were broken.

The purple fog lightened in color, turning a pale pink, until at last it became white, and faded away completely, with only the rubble of The Maestroa's world left behind in evidence that it ever existed.

Simon fell through the air, along with Isobel, Flora, and Hans, landing softly on the earth. They looked around, at the striped fabric of the tents billowing in the breeze. The wooden soldiers broke free of their pines bodies to reveal people of flesh and blood.

A flash of light, bright against the rising, real sun, ignited and they were human again. Each and every one of them. Loot ran fingers through his red hair and giggled delightedly.

"*Loot!*" he sang out.

The wooden soldiers laughed and linked arms as they jigged.

All had transformed.

Except, for Isobel and Flora.

"Why haven't we changed?" asked Isobel, inspecting her arms. "We're-we're stuck, Flora! We're trapped."

Flora slid to Isobel, taking her hands. "It will be alright. Hey, it's alright."

Isobel buried her face against Flora's shoulder and heaved dry sobs with no tears.

Simon glanced at his arm, still encased in wood. He looked ahead and saw that someone else also had not transformed.

He ran to Marco, laying in a wooden heap on the forest floor. A lifeless puppet, draped in strings.

"We-we're human!" Lefty said, looking at the flesh of his hands, pale from years of no sunlight.

Simon ignored him, falling to his knees before Marco.

"Marco?" Simon shook Marco's unmoving arm. "Wake up."

He felt someone come behind him. Then a hand on his back. He turned and looked up to see Bloody Fingers peering down at him under his black mustache.

"Had I known," he said quietly. "I'm sorry, son."

Simon looked back to Marco. "Like it even matters now."

THE PRINCE AND THE PUPPET THIEF

He heard a great cry and looked over to see King Anders running to Isobel.

"My daughter!" he said, "My little girl! It's alright! We'll screw your head back on correctly, and—"

Isobel and Flora were whispering to each other, comforting each other. Simon noted the look of understanding cross the king's face.

"Oh," he sighed. "Oh, I see. I see now. Oh my."

"We can't ever leave," Flora said to Isobel. "We can't ever be human."

"It isn't fair," Isobel said. "I love you. I want to be with *you*."

Flora smiled. "So be with me."

Isobel took in a deep breath and nodded. "Yes. I'll still love you. No matter what."

"No matter how," Flora smiled.

With a smile, Isobel kissed her proudly and ignored the gasp from King Anders.

Simon squinted as pale light, the color of the moon, surrounded the girls and they levitated from the ground in each other's embrace. Sparks whizzed from their wooden and glass bodies, smoke encasing them.

Simon shook his head in disbelief as the smoke faded away.

Isobel jumped back, and Flora yelped. They looked at each other, both made of flesh. With real hair and sparkling human eyes. Flora took in her hands, no longer glass. Isobel felt her face, where there was no trace of pine. They laughed and squealed, squeezed their hands together.

"We're *aren't* stuck," Isobel began to cry, and tear after tear flowed down her cheeks.

Simon shook his head, "How did—"

"We accepted each other completely," Flora nuzzled her head against Isobel's shoulder. "Finally. And we didn't hide."

King Anders shook his head. "I need to process this."

Simon looked at Marco. He would've accepted him as a wooden prince, too.

"It's too late," said Simon, his voice small.

A tear pushed from his eye.

"Son—"

"He deserves a happy ever after," Simon managed to say.

Isobel and Flora came over and placed comforting hands on Simon's shoulders. Hans stumbled forward, rubbing his hands together fretfully.

"I'm really terribly sorry," he said to the lifeless Marco. "I didn't want to cause any harm."

Simon lowered his head, pressing his forehead into Marco's chest.

"You can't go," he wept. "You have to come back." Then, bravely, whispering, he dared to say, in front of all, "I love you."

Everyone silently bowed their heads.

Then, softly, Simon heard the one voice that could calm him in this moment.

"You have to kiss me," the lifeless Marco whispered.

Simon snapped his head up. "Excuse me?"

"It's the way it goes," Marco muttered out of the

corner of his mouth, his eyes still closed. "You have to kiss me to wake me up. Don't you know that?"

Simon smacked Marco's chest, "You ass!"

"Get him!" Isobel shrieked, "Get him good!"

But Marco was grinning, eyes still closed. At last, Simon laughed, and lowered his lips to Marco's, kissing him long and hard. He didn't care that his father was watching. He didn't care who thought what, or if this was the way the story was supposed to end.

Pops and whizzes filled Simon's ears as he kissed Marco. He felt the ground leave them for a long moment, and when at least the grass and dirt returned to them, he opened his eyes to find Marco, completely human, smirking.

"I thought you'd never figure it out." Marco gently opened his eyes. His hand slid over Simon's arm, which was made of flesh once more. "And you're the one who reads *books* and *knows* things."

"You're so- so- ugh."

Marco laughed and pulled Simon close to him.

"I'm so confused," said King Anders. "When I told you to apprehend the fugitive, I didn't mean to *apprehend* the fugitive."

Marco looked at the king with hard eyes, and quickly, Kings Anders softened. "Well. So long everyone is happy."

"At last, there will be laughter in the castle!" Hans mused. "Oh, it will be so good to crack a joke once more."

"You have jokes?" Flora squinted her eyes at him. "Funny, I always thought you *were* one."

Hans winced, but Flora laughed and clapped him on the back. "I'm *kidding*. I'll be nice now."

"I guess we shall have to pardon you all," King Anders said to the bandits. "I feel like my daughter would be upset with me if I carried out justice on the thief's family."

"And the thief," Marco added, planting a quick kiss on Simon's forehead.

Across the way, they heard a loud grunt and looked over to see The Maestroa, crawling along the trees, their hair wild and their clothes covered in glass shards.

"Guards!" King Anders shouted, "Arrest that bedraggled villain!"

"No." Marco put his hand up. "Let them go."

Flora raised an eyebrow and slid her eyes to The Maestroa, who looked at them all with wide, fearful eyes. Eyes of plain brown.

"Marco," Flora began, "they kidnapped us and turned us all into bric-a-brac. They tried to set you on fire!"

"They tweaked my nose once," one of the former wooden soldiers said.

Isobel shook her head. "I agree with Marco." When all gasped, she added, "The two of us have a history. They just wanted to help."

Marco looked over at The Maestroa, who was quickly crawling backwards into the forest. "They just wanted us all to have a great story to tell. And they clearly aren't what they used to be."

The King sighed. "Very well."

Simon smiled at Marco.

"What?" Marco said to him, "I might be lazy, arrogant, and entitled, but I'm also benevolent."

"*So* benevolent," Simon said and kissed him again.

"All has come to a happy end!" mused Gaspard.

All cheered, but Simon kept quiet and kissed Marco instead, and it was no use to try to get their attention. They were in their own world, no longer in The Maestroa's, where they could begin to live happily ever after.

32. EVER AFTER

Dancers swirled across the ballroom floor, wearing masks of white and black, emerald and gold. The silk streamers billowed above them, their colors of green and pink bouncing the light of the chandeliers.

The band, Bloody Fingers And The Bandits, newly formed, provided the music. They solaced their lack of crime with the swiped treat here and there from passing servants carrying trays of hors d'oeuvres, no longer criminals, as the king had made sure they were aware, if they wanted to keep out of the dungeon, or worse.

Hans danced with a woman twice his size and height. Across the room, a strange old man pranced around a circle of rats, paired off and waltzing.

"That's it!" the old man said. "One-and-two-and-one-and-two."

Isobel and Flora, in their black and white masks, held each other's wrists as they swirled, turning happily, laughing at some private joke or other.

Marco smirked at them from a distance for a moment, then moved along. He still had not seen the one guest he'd been waiting for.

"Enjoying yourself, son?" King Piero, Marco's father, had broken from a conversation with King Anders and approached him, clapping him on the back.

"I would be if the one I'd invited showed up," said Marco.

King Piero winced at this, and Marco fought hard to ignore him. But finally, his inner irritability won over, and he asked, "What?"

"Nothing," said King Piero. "I just didn't know you were still invested in the boy."

He said *boy* like it was a dirty word. Like he didn't want to use it in the same sentence as his son. But Marco knew he was trying, and he did come all this way to meet Simon, after all, so he decided not to press the matter.

"Yes, father, I am," said Marco. "I just need to find him."

Simon Holt, which Marco had taken to calling him in his head to erase all memory of fake Bloody Fingers from his mind, had been gone since they defeated The Maestroa. All had been happy and well, an ending fit for a fairy tale.

But when they reached the edge of the kingdom, when they could see the rooftops of the village and the towers of the castle beyond, Simon did not go with Marco.

"I have to find my own way," he'd said. "You can't ever know who I am, if I don't know that, myself."

He'd kissed Marco on his cheek, softly, before he walked away into the crowd of villagers, pulling up the hood on his doublet. Marco merely watched, stunned, and a bit heartbroken, as he grew smaller in the distance, eventually vanishing.

King Piero brought the prince back into the present by saying, "If you want him, then, you'll have to go get him."

"What?"

"You're a prince, son," said King Piero. "Time to assert yourself. Go get what you want. Drag him back in irons if need be. I shall send out some guards."

Marco laughed. "I only want him if he wants *me*."

"I guess you had better find out."

Marco's eyes fell to Bloody Fingers, who waved his conductor's baton with a fury, not even in time with the bandits' music. He beelined to him, nearly knocking into a pair of party goers as he went.

"Hey," he said. "Have you seen Simon?"

"Maybe I have, and maybe I haven't," Bloody Fingers said from the side of his mouth, focused on conducting.

"Where is he?" Marco was quickly growing impatient.

"I'm not supposed to say," Bloody Fingers said. "Something about self-discovery and being more than a squirm. Nonsense if you ask me, he could have played the triangle in the band! Does he not know that playing in a band is a sure way to impress attractive people?"

Marco took Bloody Fingers by the collar and swung him around. "Where. Is. He."

"Unhand me, blackguard!"

"Listen, I'm in love with your son. As in, you might be my father-in-law someday. I am a handsome, charming, *rich* prince of a mining kingdom. I repeat. A kingdom with a *diamond mine.* So tell me where he is, and increase your chances of partaking in that."

Bloody Fingers gaped at Marco, but as understanding crept over his features, he grinned. "A man after my own heart."

"Now then. Where is he?"

⁂

Simon closed the leather-bound book and slid it back on the shelf. He took another from the table and began to clean it with the rag that had become covered in book dust over the course of the afternoon. Once that volume had been dusted and replaced on the shelf, he took his apron off and made for the broomstick in the corner.

Behind him, the door to the shop opened.

"We've closed for the night," said Simon. "But if you know what you're looking for already, I can help you."

"I've known what I've been looking for for a while now," said the customer.

The blood left Simon's face as he turned to face Marco, leaning in the doorway with that smirk he had been dreaming about for weeks.

"Ah, I see," said Simon, his throat tight. He pointed. "The tavern is down the street."

Marco half-snorted. "What are you doing here?"

"What are *you* doing here?"

"I asked you first."

"I work here."

"You're a bookseller?" Marco squinted. "This is your

big self-discovering adventure? Hawking fables to people who don't even read and only want to look intellectual?"

"My customers read," Simon defended himself.

"Reading is a myth, perpetuated by rival kingdoms." Marco folded his arms defiantly.

"Yes, all right." Simon rolled his eyes. "What are you doing here?"

Marco stood straight, came into the shop, the door swinging shut behind him. "You know what I'm doing here. I've missed you. I had hoped you'd come to the ball."

Simon tensed. "Masked balls aren't really my thing."

"No worries, they won't serve you any plums," joked Marco. "Did you get the invitation?"

Simon sighed. "Yes."

"Then you know my father even came all this way to meet you."

"I didn't think I'd be entirely welcome." Simon shrugged. "I didn't know if he'd be ready to see you dancing with a thief."

"Well, everyone is fine with the princess dancing with her handmaid," Marco began but stopped short. "Wait. So you want to *dance* with me?"

Simon rolled his eyes. "You're incorrigible."

"I'm just confused," said Marco. He had come close to Simon now, and his knuckles brushed gently against Simon's, who was gripping the table as though letting go would mean crumbling. He wasn't ready to see Marco again. He'd wanted to be near him so badly, and now that he was he felt scared. "I thought, I mean, I thought we'd, you know, be together."

"I want to be together," said Simon. "But I wanted to be my own person for just a minute. I thought if I was something on my own, I don't know, I thought . . ."

"What?"

"That you'd want me more."

Marco was silent, his eyes getting bigger. "I don't think I could want you any more than I already do!"

"I was afraid that now everything is settled, and we're away from enchanted puppets and magic forests, that you'd find me boring. I thought maybe I should become something, anything, even if it's just some bookseller's assistant in a normal, boring shop. It's something that's my own. You're a prince. You deserve a somebody."

Marco pursed his lips. Simon could feel his heart racing as he felt truths swimming up his stomach into his chest. Things he'd wanted to say, imagined saying, all this time.

"I don't want just somebody," Marco said. "I want the man that flew into the tower and woke me up from an excellent nap. And then tried to kill me with an invisible knife." Simon laughed. "I want the man that tried to play cool and act like some big, treacherous bandit, and instead swung from the chandelier in the most anticlimactic way I had ever seen. I want the man I risked title and future to get him freed from the guards. The man I ate the poisoned plum with and fell asleep, so he had to kiss me awake."

When Simon didn't respond, Marco added, "I want Simon. I love you."

Simon shut his eyes and smiled. "Say that again."

"I love you."

"No," Simon shook his head, trying hard to hide his grin and failing miserably. "The other part, with my name."

Marco returned the grin and pointed at Simon's chest. "Simon."

Simon slid his hand beneath Marco's, took in how the fingers looked entwined with each other. "Marco."

Pecking him on the cheek, Marco took the crown off his head and slid it over Simon's, laughing when it was too big and slid down his forehead to cover his eyes. Simon laughed, lifting the crown a bit to look out at Marco.

"You're giving me your crown?"

"I have others," Marco shrugged. "Oh, and another thing."

He reached inside of his coat, and Simon heard a faint *clink* as he produced the jeweled slippers. "Shall we?"

"You're an idiot," Simon said but didn't protest as Marco knelt. He took one of the slippers and pretended to put it on Simon's foot. It knocked against his plain leather boot.

With a smirk, Marco sat the slipper on top of Simon's foot and smirked up at him. "Perfect fit, right?"

Simon bit his cheek. "I can't stand you."

"I love you, too," Marco whispered. "Can we dance together now?"

"If we're compatible. Are you a leader or a follower?"

"I think I could do both, from time to time," said Marco. "You?"

"Same. Shall we take turns leading?"

"Always."

They walked hand in hand out of the shop, towards

the castle. After a moment of comfortable silence, Marco turned to Simon. "Just don't swing on the chandelier this time. It costs a lot, I'm sure."

Simon tried to think of a smart response, but he felt too happy to think of anything to say. Instead, he playfully punched Marco's arm. The prince responded to this by putting Simon in a headlock.

"Braggart," said Simon.

"Criminal," said Marco.

"Charlatan."

Marco laughed and released Simon.

"Charlatan," he agreed, and kissed Simon again. "So. Shall we go live happily ever after now?"

Simon pursed his lips and turned to Marco, wrapping his arms around the prince's waist. "Meh. I think I've had enough of those guidelines."

Marco dipped his eyebrows together in conspiracy. "So, what shall we do then?"

Simon kissed him on the forehead. "How about we just live?"

And so they did.

ACKNOWLEDGMENTS

Thank you for reading *The Prince & The Puppet Thief*! I hope you had as much fun reading it as I did while writing it. This book would not exist right now were it not for several amazing and beautiful people.

Sarah Spradlin, my high school art teacher, who found my satirical essays and short stories featuring our faculty and student body. Instead of detention, she gave me praise and encouragement, not to mention an arrow for the rest of my life. I'm forever grateful and think about this often.

Ricki Rose and Sally Thorne at Rose & Thorne Pub, who allowed me to sit for hours in their establishment and enjoy the wi-fi while rewriting this book, and for recognizing when a cold beer was needed (and boy, was it!). Also, a huge shout out to Erin Aiken who spent several nights writing her own manifesto across from me, and gladly gorged on chips and queso with me when the writing got too crazy (or just because it was a day of the week ending in Y. That's a good reason, too!).

Rachel Nipper, who hired me for my first professional writing gig. If not for the several stage adaptations of fairy tales over the years, not to mention the sitcom-worthy antics of theatrical people, I never would have written this particular book at all, because the compost for it simply wouldn't exist. The Dumbledore to my Harry, the Moira to my David Rose, the Ron Swanson to my Leslie Knope- I thank you.

And lastly but not least-ly, Elle Beaumont of Midnight Tide Publishing. This book definitely wouldn't be here otherwise, nor the beautiful found community that exists within my fellow authors and colleagues.

ABOUT THE AUTHOR

Justin Arnold is a self-described genre hopper, with a love of fairy tales, horror, supernatural, contemporary, humor, and LGBT (Even better if they're all mixed together!). He is also the director of Red Hen Theatre Company, based in Paris, KY. When he isn't writing novels, he is a playwright with works available through Heuer Publishing at hitplays.com. When not writing, he's teasing his friends, giving his opinion, and debating whether or not to order pizza (the answer is always yes!)

justinarnoldwrites.com

facebook.com/justinarnoldwrites
instagram.com/justinarnoldauthor

MORE BOOKS YOU'LL LOVE

If you enjoyed this story, please consider leaving a review! Then check out more books from Midnight Tide Publishing!

***Villainous* by Lou Wilham**

After the war, Mythikos was divided into three classes Seelie, Unseelie, and human.

For Jericho, a werewolf apart of the Hero Alliance, the world has always been black and white. Heroes and villains. Seelie and Unseelie. Those who protect the humans and those who hurt them. Jericho has always known what side they're on.

But when the villain they've been hunting for the last six months turns out to be their childhood friend, everything Jericho knew is turned upside down. Dusk storms into Jericho's life to show them just how wrong their assumptions are, and that the world is made up of more than just good and evil.

Faced with a world that seems increasingly more grey, Jericho must decide to return to their old life, or trust their friend turned villain.

Available Now

***Magic Mutant Nightmare Girl* by Erin Grammar**

Holly Roads uses Harajuku fashion to distract herself from tragedy. Her magical girl aesthetic makes her feel beautiful-and it keeps the world at arm's length. She's an island of one, until advice from an amateur psychic expands her universe. A midnight detour ends with her vs. exploding mutants in the heart of San Francisco.

Brush with destiny? Check. Waking up with blue blood, emotions gone haywire, and terrifying strength that starts ripping her wardrobe to shreds? Totally not cute. Hunting monsters with a hot new partner and his unlikely family of mad scientists?

Way more than she bargained for.

Available Now

Stokes Brown Public Library
3SB00036151

CPSIA information can be obtained
at www.ICGtesting.com
Printed in the USA
LVHW111546150921
697880LV00013B/224

9 781953 238399